D1125570

wolves in

Chic Clothing

Also by Carrie Karasyov and Jill Kargman

The Right Address

wolves in

Chic Clothing

A NOVEL

Carrie Karasyov and Jill Kargman

Broadway Books / New York

PRINTED IN THE UNITED STATES OF AMERICA

BROADWAY BOOKS and its logo, a letter B bisected on the diagonal,
are trademarks of Random House, Inc.

Visit our website at www.broadwaybooks.com

Book design by Donna Sinisgalli

The Library of Congress cataloged the original hardcover edition
as follows:
Karasyov, Carrie, 1972–
Wolves in chic clothing : a novel / Carrie Karasyov and Jill Kargman.
p. cm.
ISBN 0-7679-1780-4
1. Inheritance and succession—Fiction. 2. Impostors and imposture—
Fiction. 3. Women sales personnel—Fiction. 4. Department stores—
Fiction. 5. New York (N.Y.)—Fiction. 6. Socialites—Fiction.
I. Kargman, Jill, 1974– II. Title.
PS3611.A7775W65 2004
813'.6—dc22
2004057927

ISBN 0-7679-2127-5

1 3 5 7 9 10 8 6 4 2

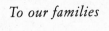

To our families

Manhattan was in a tailspin. Literally. The Westminster Kennel Club Dog Show was in town, and if that didn't clog up midtown's grid of streets enough, it was also Fashion Week. There were bitches everywhere.

The sales floor at Pelham's, the venerable hundred-year-old jewelry store, was packed, and the grand revolving doors were glutted with browsing tourists. Lovers were making last-minute Valentine's Day purchases, and stylists were running in to borrow or return glittering gems for models on the various flashbulb-lined runways of Bryant Park.

A Pelham's trademark little sage-colored box was being nimbly tied with a chocolate brown signature satin ribbon, when the expert fingers were interrupted.

"Julia—we need you." Gisele Beauvoir, Pelham's director of public relations, had unexpectedly materialized, her tone laced with the pulse-pounding gravity of a Defcon One code red alert. "It's an emergency."

Julia's sassy associate (and roommate) Douglas took over the wrapping of an engagement ring for a nervous fiancé-to-be. "I got this, honey—don't worry."

Julia shot him a look that was part *thank you* and part

what do you think this could be about? In response, he smiled and shrugged.

"Girl, you look fierce in that skirt," he whispered as she smoothed her pleats to head up to Corporate. "Baby got back in that. And it works."

"Baby got back*yard*," she sighed, nervously.

"Please. You're the most stylish, knockout girl in this whole damn town."

"Thanks, dude. See you later." She straightened her blouse and went to the staff staircase. *What the hell was this all about?* Was she about to be fired? Was it because of that man who returned the necklace after she'd convinced him it was perfect for his wife? It wasn't her fault, the guy really liked it, or so he said. It was his wife who said it emphasized the elephant-sized lines on her neck. Or was it because she was unable to understand the Russian tourists? What had she done? She needed this job, dammit. Just as things were starting to come together. . . . Well, what could she do? Julia took a deep breath and continued up the stairs.

On the sixth floor, Julia pushed through the carved mahogany double doors leading into the PR conference room, where seven people were pacing in a state of sheer panic. Fourteen sharp Manolo Blahnik stiletto heels were grinding into the beige Stark carpet. The tension was palpable. Suddenly the room went quiet and the crowd parted to make way for Gisele, who was cradling a small velvet box in her perfectly manicured hands and walking toward Julia.

"Julia—here it is. Move over Queen Lizzie's crown jewels—this is one of the largest gems in the Pelham's archives: an antique seventy-carat diamond and emerald necklace from our Van Braques salon," pronounced Gisele. "You must leave immediately. You'll be accompanied by four armed guards."

"To . . . where?"

"Hello? Lell Pelham's bridal suite! At the Waldorf."

"It's only the wedding of the millennium," chirped another PR lackey.

"Oh. Okay. Should I go now?"

"Yes! We have to rush it over this second!" snapped Gisele. "*Vogue*'s photographer is already there setting up lighting, and Ms. Pelham's assistant just called to say she changed her mind and wants to wear this piece instead of the Schlumstein deco necklace. Naturally we had to have it cleaned to perfection, so we've been in an absolute tizzy. This is very late." Gisele looked Julia straight in the eye. It was clear to Julia that her future with Pelham's—if not more—was riding on her skills as a courier.

The next thing she knew, Julia was being handcuffed to a chrome briefcase—apparently the velvet box had been placed inside. A man who could have been a Mr. Smith clone from *The Matrix*, complete with black suit and dark sunglasses, escorted her out of the conference room. On their way out, Julia noticed that he had one of those curly ear wires straight out of a Secret Service detail. They exited through a back door on Fifty-eighth Street. A few passing pedestrians gawked and pointed as they entered a limousine, which quickly pulled away.

Julia could only marvel as the limo cruised through the most fashionable part of town. What a mission! She was certainly a long way from the vineyard in Napa Valley where she had grown up and worked since college. Had it really been almost a year since she'd traded the secure familiarity of home for the excitement and opportunities of the Big Apple? But where else could she advance a career in her dream occupation: jewelry design.

At first she didn't think a sales position at Pelham's would be much of a career stepping-stone, but she needed an income and she got the job after one interview. (She was told that she looked the part—"a spitting image of Carolyn Bessette Kennedy," said her human resources interviewer.) And until she found something better, swiping platinum cards and tying up those little sage boxes at least paid the rent on the tiny two-bedroom she shared with Douglas in the East Village.

And now she was on her way to meet the princess of New York high society—Pelham's creative-director-to-be, the head of every junior committee, the party-picture darling who was a celebutante even Julia's pals back home knew about. It was a little weird that her boss's boss's boss's boss was about her age, maybe a couple years older—but Julia knew how the family business game was played. She figured she'd be dining out on the tale of her critical wedding day delivery for weeks to come.

It was only after she stepped out of the limo that she wondered, Why me? There were several other more senior girls who could have been chosen to bring Lell her jewels. And heck, Julia wasn't even in the PR department. Why had they chosen a salesgirl from the engagement ring section for such an important task?

Gene Pelham studied his stunning daughter as the makeup artist caressed the final dollop of blush onto her cherry cheeks. He was as emotional as he'd ever been. Which was not very.

"The bottom line is this, sweetie. 'To whom much has been given, much will be expected.' That's what Rose Kennedy used to say to her kids all the time, and let me tell you, it's good to remember. Teddy used to tell me constantly. God, Teddy and I had some fun times back in the day—you'll see him tonight. The Schlossbergs can't make it, but they want to take you to dinner as soon as you're back from your honeymoon. They were really apologetic. Did I tell you about the time Teddy, Frank Sinatra, and I are were all on the boat in the Riviera? That Angie Dickinson! Yeah, well, I probably shouldn't tell you that, seeing as you're my daughter. And don't believe what you hear about me and Teddy on the Vineyard—"

"Father," Lell said, rolling her eyes, "I've heard these stories a million times. Could you give them a rest? It is my wedding day."

"You're right, you're right, sweetie. Of course. Anyway, what I wanted to say is that now that you're getting married you have a responsibility to properly represent the Pelham family. You're a crucial part of the business, and that's why I made you creative director. Let's face it, the future of the company's going to be up to you, kiddo. Your brothers are useless."

Lell's brother Augustus, twenty-three, was completing his fifth year at the University of Colorado at Boulder, with a major in Women's Studies, AKA studying women (up close). His minor was Botany. (Translation: pot smoking.) Twenty-year-old Duke, a sophomore who was keg-standing his way through Lake Forest, had expressed little interest in the family biz. Lell's father had been the same way at their age. Once quite dashing and known as a wild playboy who threw famous parties with celebrities and beautiful people at exotic locales, he had only ever planned on living off of the fruits of the business that his Russian great-grandfather, Eugene Pelham (né Evgeny Perhelman), had built up from a small counter in the diamond district to a world-famous New York institution. Until fate intervened. His older brother Martin, the heir apparent with a head for business, who was in fact all business, was killed in a plane crash on his way to the opening of a Pelham's in Dubai. Gene had no choice but to settle down and take the reins at Pelham's.

Twenty-eight-year-old Eleanor (Lell) Pelham was the oldest child of Gene and his wife, Emily Wainguard Pelham, a Philadelphia Main Line WASP who was dropped from the Social Register when she married jet-setting Gene. Though her parents nearly had coronaries when their daughter become engaged, she didn't care; Emily was drawn to Gene's blush-inducing, loud, animated stories and his suave confidence. But that was then, in her youth.

Now she had regressed toward a temperament more approaching her mother's icy reserve. While Gene loved the limelight and the glitzy aspects that his job as CEO of Pelham's allowed him, Emily had become his polar opposite. Taciturn, uptight, and disapproving, she refused almost all social engagements, and spent most of her time gardening at their mansion in Washington, Connecticut. The result was that Lell possessed a combination of her mother's aloofness and reserve as well as her father's insatiable appetite for mixing with glamorous folk. It made for an interesting dichotomy.

"Gene, Lell has to get ready," said Emily, entering the dressing room of Lell's suite and shooting Gene an annoyed look.

"I know, I know. We're just having a little father-daughter chat, before I give my baby away to that rascal."

"Dad," said Lell reprovingly.

"Just kidding, just kidding, hon. You know we love Willoughby."

"He's perfect for you," said her mother, then added, "and us." She gave Lell a sideways look as she straightened a small silk bow on the bottom of her daughter's custom-made Carolina Herrera gown.

"He is the best." Lell's feelings for her mother vacillated between hero worship and hatred, but she was consistently elated to have made a match with a suitor that her mother approved of so heartily—and vocally.

"He better be is what I'm saying, 'cause I just moved fifty million into his hedge fund," Gene teased.

"Must we discuss money now?" Emily's tone was full of irritation.

"Well, I want Lell to know about money and these things. Look, you're protected by the pre-nup. I had a serious talk with Willoughby last week and let him know there will be no nonsense. It's ironclad. The money is in your name, and it's a premarital asset. Of course he'll have access to it now. I figured you kids needed more money to get started."

"Thanks, Daddy."

"And I want you to close on an apartment as soon as you get back. Now that you'll be Mrs. Willoughby Banks, you need to live at a serious address. Park Avenue."

"You're preaching to the choir. It's totally claustro. But Dad, can we talk about this later? I need to get ready."

"Certainly, sweetie."

"Gene, why don't you go find Gus and Duke?" said Emily. "Make sure they're dressed and don't let them be late."

"Right-o."

When Lell's father left, the bride stood up to take a look at herself in the mirror. She took a deep breath with a slow, paced exhale. So this was it. She was a striking young woman, five-foot-seven, with long dark hair and crystal blue eyes. Her skin was that creamy color that looks wonderful with a tan, and Lell and her four bridesmaids had just spent a week lying by the pool at her house in Jamaica in order to look perfectly bronzed for the big day. She would have been smashing walking down the aisle in just the ivory slip that she was wearing, or even a burlap sack for that matter. But she'd look spectacular in the gown that a dozen seamstresses had spent hours on. Carolina herself was scheduled to make the final adjustments before Lell sported it down the aisle.

"You will be a beautiful bride, Eleanor."

"Thanks, Mom."

"Willoughby is a catch."

"I know."

The women shared a contented smile before Emily went to check in with the event planners.

Part of Lell's attraction to Will had been her mother's early enthusiasm for the match. While she was more like her father in her status as a social butterfly, she always coveted her mother's approval, since it was so much harder to attain. All of Lell's previous suitors had been greeted with disdain, but her mother had brightened at the mere sight of Will when Lell had him come to a dinner with her parents at Elio's two years ago. At first she loved to rebel by parading her suitors— disheveled artists in dire need of good haircuts or Brooklyn-based musicians with ear piercings—before her horrified mother. It had been great to see her squirm. She'd gone so far as to taunt her mother by mentioning marriage or out-of-wedlock babies and a life in the East Village. But deep down beneath the mother-daughter catfight, Lell wanted her mother to worship her choice. She wanted to choose the kind of man Emily would wish she had chosen instead of her scene-loving husband.

That was Will to a T. When Lell met him on a sunny day in August on a friend's yacht in the Vineyard, she was immediately impressed by the ease with which he carried himself and the way everyone in their crowd gravitated toward him. She had looked with disdain at her current squeeze, a greasy-haired bassist from Williamsburg, whose pasty butt she had dragged kicking and screaming out of the city, and decided that life didn't have to be so difficult. Why should she suffer through moody artistes who would only end up living off of her money? Will was a much better option.

The unanimous word used to describe Will was *charming*. He was also very socially comfortable; Lell could chuck him in any crowd and he'd swim. That was a relief compared to all the babysitting that so many of her previous beaux had required. And best of all, Will knew at once how to endear himself to Mrs. Pelham, and that was to be the slightest bit snobby and to treat Mr. Pelham with the smallest hint of patronization and derision. Mrs. Pelham thus felt that he was her brethren. The fact that the Banks family was very similar to the Wainguards was just the icing on the cake. Sometimes Lell felt that it was her mother who should be marrying Will. Too bad.

"Here comes the bride!" boomed Polly Mecox, Lell's matron-of-honor, as she burst into the room in her port-wine Vera Wang dress. She was followed by the other bridemaids, Hope Matthews, Meredith Knight, and Lell's formerly fat cousin Samantha Wainguard.

"Are you so psyched?" asked Hope.

"Hell yeah," said Lell with confidence. "I gave my very last blow job last night."

"Lell!" gasped Hope, laughing.

"What?" said Polly. "No one polishes the helmet after the ring's on the finger."

"And your men go for this?" asked Hope.

"I give Henny a hummer exactly once a year. On his birthday," said Polly sternly.

"One too many times a year for me," laughed Meredith.

"This is gross," said formerly fat Samantha with disgust.

Polly, who hated being around the ghosts of obesity past, threw Lell a look that said, Why is your fugly cousin a part of this? Lell shrugged and changed the topic.

"Now I have all my girls around me!" Lell reached out to take her admiring friends' hands. "I'm all ready for this. In fact, I can't wait. Bring it on."

"Um, Lell," said a nervous assistant who appeared on the threshold. "Excuse me, but the photographer's all set, and the girl with the necklace has arrived. She's downstairs."

"Oh, good. Send her up."

chapter 3

The gushing gaggle of bridesmaids cooed over Lell's gown and flowers, pouring lavish compliments over every sparkling detail. Polly was no exception, but she was also thinking about her own down-the-aisle image—she'd dieted to a size 2 for the occasion. Hell, it may be the bride's day but she was walking down the aisle in front of nine-hundred-and-something guests, too. And you know even though it's the "bride's day," everyone checks out the bridesmaids.

"Oh my God, Lellie, your shoes are stunning," sighed Hope, with awe at the one-of-a-kind bejeweled stilettos from London.

Polly nodded but felt a twinge of I'd-love-to-be-in-her-Choos jealousy. Polly Mecox had been the first of the gang to wed, five years earlier, to Henderson "Henny" Mecox IV. Her nuptials at age twenty-three had sculpted her identity. She'd been the first in their set with the glittering rock on her hand, she was the first Mrs.; it made her feel mature, special. But now everyone was getting married. Hope already had two children (although she never worried about sweet, harmless Hope), and it wasn't so unique to be a Mrs. anymore; the novelty and sparkle of having The Ring had worn off. And now it was Lell's turn. How could Polly possibly compete with all the fanfare and photographs? Even though she privately thought all the press Lell was getting for the wedding was frankly tacky, at the same time she frequently felt Kermit-green with pangs of envy.

When the Pelham's heiress announced her engagement at Le Cirque, Polly knew she had to get pregnant to stay ahead of her, so she and Henny pulled the goalie that night. Nine months to the day later, she bore a son, Henderson Mecox V, whom she called Quint. He was only three months old now, but looking at Polly's South Beach diet bod, you'd never have known she'd borne fruit. Little Quint was originally going to be her next project, but most of the duties—the tedium of diapers and nocturnal cries—were left to Daria, her full-time live-in nanny, and Daria's day-off substitute, Lima. She just didn't know what to do with Quint, and was even a little scared to be in charge of such a fragile little thing. And with the nannies being so much better equipped to handle him, she felt it was better to leave him in their perpetual care. Besides, how could she show up at La Goulue with spit-up on her Lora Piana cashmere sweater sets?

As Polly flattened the skirt of her gown, she was starting

to think she needed a new project. Something different, something that hadn't been done before. A baby shower for her friend Lily Adams? Maybe she could host a trunk show? No, retail was too subservient. What kind of project could it be, she wondered. Then, amid the frenzied excitement of Lell stepping into her dress, the new project walked right in through the arched doorway.

The Pelham delivery girl, Polly saw immediately, could have easily been a model. A tall, stunning blonde, she had every ounce of style of a glossy magazine regular, and a cool, edgy confidence that made her magnetic. Attractive blondes were a dime a dozen in their social set, but there was some sort of aura that hung over this girl that made you look at her carefully. Polly found herself flicking through the Rolodex of her brain trying to place this obviously special person. But of course, she was a nobody.

"Hi—so sorry to . . . interrupt," said Julia, feeling as if she needed a visa to enter. Fortunately her passport happened to be locked to her arm. "I have your necklace, Ms. Pelham—"

Lell looked up and smiled. "Please, call me Lell."

"Lell soon-to-be Banks," smiled Polly, curiously looking over the gem-transporter. "And you are . . . ?"

"Hi, I'm—"

"Julia Pearce," said Lell, facing her makeup artists for a powder touch-up. "I've seen you around."

"Oh," said Julia, looking amazed to have caught her boss's boss's boss's boss's eye at all. Weirdski. "Yes. Nice to meet you. And best wishes, you look gorgeous."

"Thanks," said Lell, knowing it.

"Hello," said Emily, walking in after a hairspray. "Are you the one with the necklace?"

"Yes." The guard unlocked the cuffs and then the briefcase, removing the velvet box. When he opened it, the eight eyes of Lell's four bridesmaids popped. Even they were sufficiently dazzled.

"Oh. My. God," said Hope.

"That is stunning, Lell," said Meredith.

"It is really quite something," said Emily with evident pride.

Polly checked out the rocks but looked back at Julia, who in her own downtown-chic way was even more bling-bling than the velvet-packed ice. Her style wasn't polished but it was eclectically chic. Her clothes could have come from a flea market and her granny's closet, but somehow it all looked great. She had a way. A look. Something that Lell, with all her consultants and unlimited funds, could never pull off. Money couldn't buy Julia's kind of fashion savvy.

Julia studied the necklace, which was the most spectacular thing she had ever seen. She watched Lell remove it from its case, and motion for her mother to clasp it.

"So what's your deal, you work at Pelham's?" Polly asked Julia.

"I'm the heavily guarded messenger," she replied. "I felt like I was in charge of the Lost Ark."

"Thank you, that will be all," said Emily dismissively.

"Okay, sure—"

"No, no—" said Lell, shooting her mother a look. "Please, Julia, stay. Have something to eat."

Lell blithely gestured at the smorgasbord spread of towering brioche tea sandwiches, salads, caviar, toast points, champagne-filled flutes, and chocolate-dipped strawberries, all untouched.

Julia was obviously pleased with the offer but apprehensive. She didn't want to piss off the boss's wife. "Oh, thank you . . . I'd love to, but I should probably get back to the store—"

"I *am* the store. Stay and hang out."

Julia glanced at Lell's mother, who had already moved on to pruning the bridal bouquet, and acquiesced.

"All right . . . thanks."

"I asked Gisele to send you over instead of one of those creepy PR flacks. They all try to harvest details of my life, and I know for certain there have been leaks from the press department to Page Six. I wanted someone out of the loop."

"Don't worry," said Julia, "I don't have Richard Johnson on speed dial or anything."

"Have a seat," said Polly, making room for the newcomer. "I'm Polly Mecox. This is Hope Matthews and Meredith Knight. And this is Lell's cousin Samantha—"

"Hi, nice to meet you all. You all look fierce."

"Aw, thanks," said Hope.

"Thanks," said Polly, taking her pashmina from her shoulders. "I just feel a little naked with this strapless gown."

Lell pretended not to hear the comment. She had bought all the girls couture bridesmaid dresses and had thought of giving them each a floating diamond necklace as well, but her mother dissuaded her. She presented them instead with sterling silver jewelry boxes.

"Well maybe you could wear a fun chain or necklace from our—I mean Pelham's—Waterbury Collection, or something," Julia offered.

"We'd thought about it," said Lell, looking at Polly's bare collarbone, "but we thought it looked so long and distracted from the neckline."

"Maybe," said Julia, thinking about it. "Or you could double it up and have one layer a tad longer. That would look so fierce."

Lell considered this. She was right, that could look very chic.

"Hmm. I am liking that. I'm kind of liking that idea. Let's see them in the flesh. Can you call and have someone bring over five right now?"

"Sure, no prob," said Julia, whipping out a cell phone.

Emily sneered. Why were her daughter and her friends allowing this random, slightly unkempt outsider into their most sacred day? She exited to get a lip-gloss retouch.

"So where are you from?" asked Polly, looking over Julia's hip ensemble of vintage (yet sophisticated) threads and tooled leather boots.

"Northern California originally. I've been living here, well, downtown, for about a year this spring. I love it."

"Cool." Polly was a striking mix of her mom's Swedish good looks and her rogue dad's Italian charms. Her dark hair and catlike eyes lent her good looks a mystique that coupled nicely with the cool confidence she'd developed as a lifetime head-turner. But she worked on her looks. Plenty. With weekly blowouts, manicures, and makeup applications galore, she pumped plenty of cash into her appearance. And before her was this Urban Outfitters–esque Julia chick who clearly just threw herself together in two seconds with a sexy 1940s blouse, fishnets, black boots, and a tad too-short skirt. And it worked.

"Okay, Miss Pelham, we're ready," said the photographer, who, with his three assistants, had been tinkering with the extensive lighting equipment for over two hours. And now the portrait moment had finally arrived. The girls were positioned around Lell, who sat erect in an upholstered settee. Hair and makeup artists swarmed to comb errant hairs and pat cheeks with a last-second puff, while Julia looked on from the side, beside an arched-browed Emily.

"Oh, there's a little fold in your veil," observed Julia, who rushed over to Lell to tend to the unsightly crinkle in the tulle. "There we go."

"Thanks," said Lell. "You're sweet."

Gene walked in, snapping his cell shut. "Hey, look at this bevy of beauties. If I only were twenty years younger!"

He caught sight of Julia, as did every man who came within a block-long radius. "Hiya, Gene Pelham—"

"Hello, Mr. Pelham. Julia Pearce. I actually work for you. At the store—"

"Well we've definitely never met because I would not forget you, my dear."

"Daddy, Julia brought me my necklace—look!" she pointed at the blinding collier eclipsing her delicate clavicle.

"That's my girl. I'm so proud of you, Lellie sweetheart. That necklace is going to be in every magazine."

A few minutes later, a sweat-covered assistant from the Pelham's PR department arrived with the bridemaids' necklaces, an old Pelham's standard involving cultured pearls and clusters of diamonds set in platinum.

"Oh, God," said Lell, "I'm thinking no . . ."

The PR girl looked as though she felt personally responsible for Lell's displeasure. "I, uh, I . . ." she said, faltering.

"We could freshen them up a bit," said Julia. "With your permission . . ." She looked to Lell for the okay.

Lell was intrigued. "Be my guest."

Julia took out her trusty toolkit and began to work magic, rehooking the clasps, fashioning an almost new necklace for each girl, checking each from the front before putting on the finishing touch. Lell looked on in amazement as Julia practically reinvented the old Pelham's standby, breathing a new freshness into it with the new length and better closure.

"It's really sexy now, more modern," Julia observed. "Love it."

"It looks really great," Lell agreed. "Thanks."

Polly and Hope admired themselves in the mirror.

"This looks so much better!" Polly squealed. "Love."

"Okay, ladies, we're ready to go," the photographer signaled. "Please take your seats."

The shutter of the camera clicked for seven rolls of film as the girls tilted their coiffed heads and straightened their necks like glitter-dipped swans for the readers of *Vogue*. Their high cheekbones blushed to perfection: they were the pinnacle of breeding, class, and sophistication. And of course, the one uniting bond that tends to tie the elite establishment together: money, honey.

chapter 4

Money was actually exactly what was on Hope's mind as she stood with her frozen smile clasping her bouquet ever tighter as the photographer snapped away. She and her husband, Charlie, had just found out this morning that their bid on a classic seven on East Sixty-ninth Street had been rejected. And as happy as she was for her friend Lell, she was having trouble masking her disappointment. The real estate agent had told her that they had low-balled by two hundred grand, but there was no way they could afford to go any higher. And unlike Lell, Polly, and Meredith, Hope didn't have the endless trust fund to dip into whenever she wanted.

Although Hope and her husband had both grown up with affluent parents and gone to the "right" schools and belonged to the "right" clubs, their friends definitely had much bigger vaults of dead presidents in their family trees. This greenback gap seemed to lead perpetually to situations where Hope felt the impossibility of keeping up with the Joneses— when the "Joneses" were really the likes of Mecox, Knight, and Pelham. The irony was that out of all of her friends, Hope was not in the least bit a social climber. Although she was smart, she was not a snob and never tried to vault upward and forge merger friendships, or what Charlie called "agenting" friendships—where someone profited 10 percent from the relationship. She truly never wanted anything from anyone. She genuinely liked her "posse" as they dubbed themselves. She'd known Polly since they were roommates at Groton, and when she went to stay in the city with Polly on weekends (Hope grew up in Westport, Connecticut), she'd met Lell and Meredith, who had been friends of Polly's since kindergarten at Brearley. But as the rest of her posse acquired ten-room apartments on Fifth Avenue or Park, Hope was biding her time in a rental in the East Seventies, trying her best to make do in the cramped apartment with Charlie and her two small boys, Gavin and Chip. She needed a break.

"Okay, ladies, thank you very much. I want Miss Pelham alone now," commanded the photographer.

"Thank God, I need a total reapplication. My makeup has melted away," Polly said with a groan.

"You look great," said Hope.

"I'm shiny! You could fry an egg on my T-zone. Where's the chick with the powder puff?"

"I'll go get her," said Meredith, on her way out the door. "I want to get my hair redone anyway."

"Good, let's sit down now, you and me," said Polly, pulling Hope onto the couch. She looked both ways, eyeballs darting for eavesdroppers, then whispered, "Meredith is totally bugging."

"I think we're all just nervous. I mean, I never had to walk anywhere with so many eyes on me. And there are going to be celebs and even world leaders there! Nausea."

"No, forget 'nerves.' Meredith is being a total bitch. Did you notice how she pushed her way so she was next to Lell? It's like, what the heck? We're all going to be in the picture, sweetie, so you may as well put your fat ass in the corner."

"Polly!"

"She's totally gained weight, and even you cannot deny it. Probably why she's being such a jerk. Meanwhile Lell's obese cousin Samantha is now Karen Carpenter! Remember what a lard-ass she was at Cotillion? But you still see the ghost of the fatty within. It's like, she's a stick next to Meredith right now! It's so weird, 'cause like, Merde knew this wedding was coming up, and she still hoovered down all those Christmas cookies. It's totally because Andrew hasn't proposed yet."

Whenever Polly was in a fight with one of her friends—which was often, as it was a serious hobby for her—she loved to flaunt whatever she held over them. With Meredith, a frequent target for Polly, it was the fact that she was still unwed and that she usually carried around an extra five pounds that were noticeable only to Polly.

Hope didn't want to get into Meredith bashing with Polly. It was Lell's day. It wasn't right to be squabbling bridesmaids. She looked around the room and noticed the girl who had brought the necklace leaning against the wall in the corner watching the photo shoot intently. Hope caught her eye and motioned her over.

"Hey, I'm so sorry, tell me your name again?" asked Hope gently.

"Julia."

"Sorry, I'm like, retarded with names. Please, come sit with us. Polly, smush over."

"Thanks," said Julia as she sat down.

Polly studied Julia carefully. She liked that the girl didn't seem at all intimidated to be there.

"So, Julia, do you like New York?" asked Polly.

"Yes, I'm having a great time."

"And where do you hang out?"

"Mostly downtown. I live in the East Village."

"Interesting." Polly was about to continue her third degree when Mr. Pelham approached.

"You ladies look just gorgeous," he said, staring straight at Julia.

"Thanks, Mr. P."

"Julia," said Mr. Pelham, staring even more intently. "Why don't you come join us later for dancing and dessert?"

"Oh, well, I—"

"No, you should," said Polly, eager to study her specimen more closely. "It'll be a blast."

"I don't, well . . ." Julia was unsure what to do. She really actually was dying to see how the whole affair would go down, but it would be strange to be there not only as an outsider but as an employee. Fuck, Douglas would freak out to see this scene.

"You can go home, get all dolled up as you ladies do, and even grab a date if you can get one at such late notice. Through I am sure that will not be a problem for a knockout like you."

Julia blushed. "Dancing will start around ten," said Mr. Pelham, more as an order rather than a request.

"Okay, thanks, but is it okay with Lell?"

"I'm sure it is. The entire B list is invited just for dancing and champs, so like, two hundred other people will be rolling in as well," said Polly.

"You should come," said Hope, nodding.

Julia hesitated.

"Lell, can Julia come for dancing?" yelled Polly over to her friend.

"Great idea! Come," said Lell, distracted by a small rose petal that was wilting in her bouquet.

"We need some new blood around here. It's always same old same old buncha stiffs. Snooze," said Polly.

"There's about a thousand people out there!" laughed Julia.

"Yeah, but we know them all, and their stories. We need a fresh face," said Polly in all seriousness. And this Julia Pearce person could be it.

Emily Pelham reentered the room. "Ladies, Lell, darling," she said, clearly excited, "the cars are waiting. It's time to get to the church."

chapter 5

"Eagle is moving." A serious-looking woman in all black, wearing a headset à la Susan from Time/Life standing by to take your order, spoke in curt tones. "Repeat: Eagle in motion."

"Roger that," nodded another sprockety clone. "All units on alert. Repeat: all units on alert, stand by for Diamond Horseshoe. Eagle is moving."

The Eagle was Gene Pelham, father of the bride. The bride herself was Diamond Horseshoe, with a bevy of over thirty headset-wearing facilitators broadcasting her every action on the CIA-level state-of-the-art mini-mouthpieces.

"T minus two minutes. Repeat: two minutes and counting."

Emily straightened her husband's bow tie as they awaited
Lell's move down the aisle.

"Our little girl. Can you believe this?" Gene smiled at his
wife and squeezed her hand. He leaned in to give her a kiss
on the cheek. She retreated, staring straight ahead, watching
everyone assemble.

"This is not the time, dear. Thank goodness my niece is in
one of her thin phases. I was quite worried she would be
rolling down the aisle on a dolly."

"Honey, everything's perfect. Everything will be picture
perfect."

Emily looked around. She saw the girl from the store
standing off to the side at the end, and she motioned for her
to come at once.

"You—" Emily gestured desperately to Julia, who had
been carrying Lell's train with one of the four stylists. "Come
here."

Julia obediently went to Emily's side. "Yes, Mrs. Pelham."

"Listen, I need you in the wings to stand by in case Lell
needs her train adjusted at the altar. It keeps getting tangled
when she walks."

"Um . . . okay." Shit. She didn't know how to adjust a
gown! Okay, she could just follow her instincts. She always
knew what looked good.

"I don't want any wrinkles along these back pleats. So if
you see any folds after her walk, just quietly come around and
smooth out the creases. You look more put together than the
girl who did it in rehearsal."

"Oh, okay. Sure." Surreal, surreal, surreal.

The wedding planner came up and tapped Emily on the shoulder, and she immediately tucked her small hands onto her sons' arms and put on a small, tight smile.

"Iron Maiden has left the launchpad with the junior Eagles," crackled the voice over the headset, as Lell's mother was escorted down the aisle by her sons.

Lell was led to her father's arm in preparation.

"Diamond Horseshoe moving! Repeat: Diamond Horseshoe in motion. Places, everyone. Repeat: places!"

Lell and her father stepped around the corner into the holding pen where her bridesmaids and ten headset people were gathered. Now Lell had her veil down, the ethereal wash of tulle making her stunning face appear even more delicate and radiant.

"And we have a 'go' for the maids. Repeat: that is a green light for the maids. Eagle and Diamond Horsehoe are in position."

The girls obediently lined up, hearts pounding, and as directed, one by one, began their metered walk into the light.

Julia, meanwhile, slipped up the side of the church to hide in the shadows of the apse, on the lookout for errant folds.

The music of Pachelbel's *Canon* rang out from the strings and winds of the New York Philharmonic, which was there to perform music for their shining benefactor. Le Tout New York had turned out in their couture finery. And as befit social ass-kissers, everyone was wearing their best Pelham's jewels.

———

Willoughby Banks took a deep breath and smiled at his groomsmen lined behind him in their white ties and tails. Those guys, he thought, what a friggin' riot—the toasts last night were hi-fucking-larious. Except Skip Milstead making that crack that Will would never have to go to an ATM again, that was crass. The guy was wasted though.

But hey, there was some truth to Skip's remarks—Will, though of Mayflower ancestry, didn't have any real dough. The Banks family was so properly Brahmin you could slash their wrists and the proverbially cobalt blood would ooze out. But their once-great fortune had been frittered away over time, and now the refined, gorgeous Willoughby was the definition of Counts Without Accounts—fancy descent without a cent.

But not anymore. He bagged his equity sales job when he got engaged, and Gene Pelham funneled fifty mill to his soon-to-be son-in-law so he could manage Lell's money. And now Will was free. Well, sort of. Financially free. In a way.

He remembered the advice his late grandfather had bestowed on him after a few scotches one summer night in Newport. "Willo, take it from me! You marry a rich girl, ya kiss one ass. Marry a poor girl, ya kiss a million."

Marriage seemed so far away back then, the crazy nights of getting baked on the beach and hooking up with different girls every night by the bonfire. Now he was standing in front of a thousand fucking people making it official with Lell. Here we go, he thought. The Plunge.

The New York Philharmonic paused after the parade of bridesmaids, each poised and graceful, but quivering ever so slightly beneath the heated gaze of the boldfaced-named guests. The music commenced again, this time Beethoven's *Ode to Joy*, as Gene Pelham, smile shining, stood at the back with his daughter, the new Ambassador of Pelham's and the toast of Junior society, on his arm. The crowd rose and strained to see Lell as if in their sea of velvets and satins and pearls they were desperately thirsting to drink in drops of her angelic radiance.

The bride walked in measured steps, a small, delicate half smile formed by her pink glossed lips (the one she had practiced in front of the mirror for weeks). Will looked on as Lell and her dad walked closer and closer until she was so close he could touch her. Gene lifted her veil, kissed her cheek, and presented his daughter to her groom, who suavely kissed her hand, put his fingers at the small of her back, and gently guided her to the altar. As she stepped up and turned to him, the train of her gown folded a tiny bit, and Julia, dreamy-eyed in the wings, caught sight of Emily Pelham shooting her a vitriolic look of death.

Shocked into action after her peony and violin–laced reveries, Julia snapped back to the moment, knowing the haughty eye-squint was a summons into train-smoothing action. She gently tiptoed into view, though at knee-level, while every eye was on the stunning Lell. Julia knelt down and quickly smoothed out the pleats and lace, then crept back into the wings to watch the astonishingly exquisite ceremony and inhale the intoxicating fragrance of a hundred thousand flowers. She exhaled in relief as she stepped back into the safety of the shadows to drink it all in.

Except something was different. The darkness of Julia's little corner perch didn't have the same anonymity as it had before. Of the two thousand eyes that had just beheld her quick mouselike dart to tend to the bride, two were still lingering upon her. And Willoughby Banks could not look away.

chapter 6

"A dollop of heaven."

"The best party of the year."

Joan Coddington and Wendy Marshall, two of society's biggest gossips, were nestled quite snugly into their corner booth at Orsay sipping piping hot lattes while the snow fell softly outside. A week had passed, but they were still so overcome with the grandiose, Mount Olympus scale of Lell Pelham's wedding, that its dissection was now entering week two. Plus, it was February, so there wasn't much else going on.

"The individual wedding cakes!" said Joan dramatically.

"Nine hundred of them! Three tiers! Interlocking white chocolate L's and W's! Can you even imagine the cost?" asked Wendy, who had already tried to tally it up on three separate occasions.

"The sterling silver picture frames with that darling Patrick Demarchelier portrait of Lell and Willoughby—"

"At every place setting. Not to mention the gift bags—"

"I wore the Hermès scarf yesterday. So thoughtful."

"It was the wedding of the year," nodded Wendy.

"It was better than the Goodyears'," pronounced Joan.

And with that, she silenced her dining companion. There could be no greater compliment than to have outdone the lavish extravaganza that Nigel and Sandra Goodyear had recently hosted in Antigua for their beauty-challenged daughter Kitty.

"You're right," concurred Wendy. "It kicked that tropical paradise crap in spades. Sunshine can be so tacky sometimes."

"The worst! Mmmm. New York. Winter white. To die for."

Across the room, Polly Mecox was lunching with Hope Matthews when Franny Corcoran stopped by their table to say hello.

"Was that fantastic or what?" boomed Franny, the rotund paper clip heiress who was also the leader of the thirty-five–ish social clique, just above Polly's gang.

"It's just such a letdown that it's over!" moaned Polly. "It was like, the only thing I was looking forward to for a year, and now it's finished!"

"You did also have a child this year," said Hope, smiling.

"You know what I mean," said Polly.

"Will Banks was the most handsome groom! And he's such a flirt, that Lell better watch out for him," said Franny with a mischievous glimmer.

"I think she can handle him," said Polly. As if a fatso like you has a chance, she wanted to add. In her dreams.

"Welllll, I'm off to the Carlyle. Are you going to Nina's trunk show? She has the cutest monogrammed linens, totally hand-stitched and imported. Dreamy. Perfect wedding or birthday presents," said Franny.

"We'll be there later," said Polly.

"Bye-bye, then."

After Franny had moved on to another table (and then another, each time talking loudly enough that the entire restaurant knew where she was going next and what she thought about Nina's linens), Hope motioned to the waiter to ask for the check.

"Already?" whined Polly.

"I can't go to the trunk show, I have to take Chip to Diller-Quayle."

"Can't you let the nanny?"

"No I can't let the nanny! He loves it! It's our thing."

"Whatever. It's like, you and all of Trinidad."

Hope pretended not to hear this. "Why don't you bring Quint over later and we can have a playdate with Chip?"

"Yeah, I don't think so. It's snowing and he has his schedule." Polly didn't quite know what her son's schedule was, but since her nanny took care of it, she didn't really pay much attention.

"So, Lelly and Will are back a week from Friday. I can't wait to hear the deets on the honeymoon," said Hope.

"Yes. But why Bali? I have zero desire to go to Asia, it seems so . . . dirty. The heat and the pollution, imagine the stench? Like New York in August. And aren't there, like, bombs going off hourly?"

"I think it seems exotic. I'd love to go someday."

"Well, I'm just psyched for Willoughby's birthday party.

Everything is so boring lately, it will be fun to have something to do."

"I can't believe that Lell's throwing such a huge party right after her wedding. The poor thing must be exhausted."

"There's nothing else to do. Plus, let's face it, you know she's inviting *W* and *Vogue*'s photographers to cover it, she's fully vying for that 'Girl of the Moment' page."

Hope was sometimes scared of Polly. Polly was supposed to be Lell's best friend on earth, but she always slashed her Lady Macbeth–style, and was extremely hard on her at every opportunity. Hope hated to play these games. She knew that Polly was insecure, that if Freud were to analyze her he'd blame everything on her missing father who basically split early in Polly's life, and her mother, who couldn't've cared less about her. It was really sad, and probably the reason that Polly was unable to bond with her own child. But regardless, she did wonder from time to time if she was Polly's personal voodoo doll when she wasn't around to share salads. Why would she be spared when so many others were eviscerated so swiftly? Hope's only solution was to never respond to Polly's comments. Instead, she just signed the credit card bill, swallowing hard and wondering how two Cobbs and two glasses of wine somehow got to $94.

Polly looked out at the downy falling flakes and sighed. "I swear, Hope, I need a new project. I totally have those midwinter blahs."

"Why don't you get a job?"

"Yeah, right." *As if.* Well, she could pull a Susie Kincaid and start a jewelry line or handbag company. Or not. Why be hawking your own shit when you can buy other people's? Plus staging some trunk show in a hotel suite was not for her—she knew she was not suited to any kind of service business. Then she remembered the project she'd toyed with at the wedding.

Polly smiled at Hope. "Well, I do have some idea of what I want to do. I think I'll do something dramatic this time."

"Okay, Miss Cryptic."

"You'll see. It's time to shake things up a bit."

"Drama, huh? Taking acting lessons?"

Polly shook her head slyly. No, she wouldn't be fretting her hour upon the stage, full of sound and fury. She preferred to be quietly holding the marionette strings high above, the one who watched overhead, enjoying a lofty view of those toiling below. And little did her dear posse know, they were about to be players in her perfect mid-winter game.

chapter 7

"I swear, girl, that Arab sheik will be whacking it to your chic ass tonight."

"Douglas!" Julia squealed while turning a shade of hot pink. "Ew, you are so gross."

"What? The guy like stripped you down with his eyes!"

"Nasty."

He started singing. "Julia and Sheik Abdul Mohammed Al-Tariq, sittin' in a tree—"

"Stop!"

"B-o-f-f-i-n-g."

"I need to go loofah my whole body after that grodissimo image. You are dirrrrty. Like Christina Aguilera."

"Haguilera's more like it."

Julia was both disgusted and amused. She had just racked up a $9,000 commission, thanks to a horde of robed Middle Easterners with Amex cards as black as their bulletproof Mercedes caravan outside. The leader of the pack was flirting heavily, and she had to make nice. Such was life in the service biz.

"You are so Goldie Hawn in *Protocol*!" Douglas teased. "Blondie under the burka with the blue eyes coming through the slit! Genius."

"Enough!"

Julia realized she had responded too loudly. Heather, the manager, shot her a dirty look from across the rows of glass cases, and Julia lowered her head guiltily. Julia and Douglas had often been reprimanded for their cacophonous banter.

"You know you'd be like royalty over there as that dude's wife," whispered Douglas.

"Please. What privileges are accorded to wife number forty-seven?"

"Hey, speaking of royalty, when is her majesty Lell Pelham coming back?"

"I don't know. Jeez, that really was some wedding. Such a wacko dream, I'm still not over it—"

"It's so fucking crazoo that we were there. Like, not as bartenders but as guests! I totally thought we were going to be shoved in as coat check whores at any second. The whole night was wild," Douglas recalled, almost in a trance. "I almost shat when you came home and told me to suit up. Lewis was so obsessed. He literally made me tell him every detail! He was all, 'Xerox the room with your eyes!' "

"It was amazing. Lell actually was so nice, too. I had heard she was kind of . . ." Julia looked both ways on the grand floor of the store to make sure no one was listening. "I heard she was very aloof and kind of . . . not the warmest."

"Uh, you mean, like her bi-atch ice queen madre? That woman makes Wollman Rink look like a bubbling lava pit."

The enormous Roman numeral pewter clock struck six, to Douglas's relief.

"Okay, sugar, looks like we're good to go—let's make like a prom dress and take the fuck off."

As the subway rattled downtown Julia, smushed between a heaving construction worker who kept clearing his throat and an elderly lady with more shopping bags than a homeless person, thought about the strange turn of events that had occurred of late. It was really so amazing that she was living in Manhattan and working at Pelham's, let alone that she'd gone to Lell Pelham's wedding! When she called her friends back home and told them, they couldn't believe how glamorous her life had become. They already thought that she was well on her way to accomplishing her dream of designing glam jewelry—she had been making jewelry for her family and friends her whole life with macaroni, then beads, then handmade chain links. Somehow Julia didn't feel too close to her dream's realization. She wasn't sure that her sales position could catapult her into the creative side. She knew she had to be patient—and look for opportunities. In the meantime, her

Pelham's experience had been pretty fabulous. She felt she had Douglas to thank for everything—certainly for the place to live and hooking her up at Pelham's.

Douglas was her mother's best friend Marianne's second cousin. Marianne had only ever met him when he was seven years old at a family reunion, but she had no problem contacting him on Julia's behalf when Julia announced she was moving to New York, after putting in three years in the public relations department of a winery. She knew no one in New York, and although her parents were out of their minds with worry about her moving to the Big Apple, they fully supported her quest to design jewelry. They knew that she had to give it a shot.

Douglas's roommate had just happened to have moved out, and as hesitant as he was to take on a young girl from Northern California as his bunkmate, it was a quick fix for his rent problem. Their chemistry was instant. Douglas and his boyfriend, Lewis, took Julia under their wing. And aside from Julia's volunteering at Girls, Inc., teaching jewelry making and art twice a week (evenings or Saturdays, schedule permitting), the three had been inseparable ever since.

Although it was minuscule, Douglas and Julia had managed to insert a certain amount of glamor into the decor of their apartment through constant trips to the Chelsea Flea Market and smart choices of fabrics and paint. The coffee table was a Louis Vuitton trunk, found in a small store in Upstate New York. It was a little battered, but it had its charm. Douglas covered the floors with rugs from a trip to Morocco that he and Lewis had gone on the previous spring, and one wall was coated with his Majolica dish collection. Julia had splurged on two Ralph Lauren hurricane lamps, which rested on IKEA nesting tables, and every surface was covered in red lacquer trays meant to disguise all the clutter. It was small, but it was homey.

After exiting the subway, Julia and Douglas walked home to Seventh Street and entered their pad. Julia happily chucked her bag down on Douglas's chaise and flopped lazily on the couch.

"Aaaaagh!" shrieked Douglas. "Oh my God, it's a fucking Buick! Oh my fucking God!"

Julia jumped up when she saw the turbo-charged roach running across the floor. With a swift move, she took the heavy March *W* magazine off the coffee table and chucked it onto the megabug, stopping its sprint across the floor. Then, for safe measure, she gracefully stepped onto the magazine to seal its doom.

"Once again, fashion saves the day," said Doug, breathlessly.

"We're like reverse *Annie Hall*. Minus the sex," Julia observed.

"And the lobsters. Thanks, girl. What would I do without you? Lewis screams even louder than I do when he sees insects or rodentia."

"That's not possible, judging from my eardrums right now. What time are we meeting the new Vice Prez, by the way?"

"Let's chow first, then we can go dance on tables and make mischief."

After the takeout containers from the Indian joint a block away were cleared, Julia went with Douglas and Lewis to The

Cock, their favorite local gay bar. She always felt free—to shimmy, laugh, and fully be herself, without worrying about gold-chain-wearing cheezoids making a move on her.

After a couple of shots toasting Lewis's big promotion at work, Julia knew it was time to say good night, but Douglas, always the partier, coaxed her into another quick drink. And another.

When she woke up feeling as if someone had just chucked a cinder block at her forehead, Julia thought of calling in sick. But Douglas was all dressed and blaring his morning combo of Nine Inch Nails and Howard Stern.

"Come on, sweets, we're gonna be late, get up!"

"My head feels like a New York City manhole cover."

"No, sweetie," he teased. "I'm the manhole expert."

"*Por favor*. It's really too early for analmania."

Julia hauled her carcass out of bed, shoved a brush through her hair, threw on her black suit and high heels, her mother's old coat with a fur collar, and announced she was ready.

"You make me sick. What, did you spend like all of three minutes this morning? You look stunning!"

"I love you," Julia replied, bleary-eyed, giving her roomie a squeeze.

Back on the floor of Pelham's Julia was unwrapping a new shipment, when Douglas jabbed her in the side.

"Ow!"

"Colin Firth, two o'clock. Approaching."

By the time Julia looked up, a tall gorgeous man in a blue button-down was standing before her. Although obviously moneyed and attractive, he seemed uncomfortable and shifted uneasily, as if his own body made him feel awkward. She gave him a small smile of encouragement, which seemed to only heighten his embarrassment. She knew these types; they were totally unaccustomed to purchasing jewels for the women in their life, and just wanted to get the whole thing over with as soon as possible. She could handle that. In fact, this was her specialty.

Oscar Curtis was indeed in a rush. He had only ten minutes to jam down lunch and buy a birthday present for his mom. He had no clue what to get, figuring he'd seek advice from an employee. From a distance he saw two Pelham salesclerks who seemed to be free, so he walked over, thinking he'd ask for gift tips, but as he approached, he realized how beautiful the blonde was. He got too nervous to ask her even a simple question.

"Hi, um, so sorry to bother you—"

"Not a bother! What can I do for you?" she asked with a smile.

"Uh, my mom, it's her birthday tomorrow . . ."

His mom? That was sweet. Julia couldn't help but notice how handsome he was. Even better, he seemed intriguing.

"I've been working like a dog and forgot to buy anything—what do you think I should, maybe, get her?"

"Hmm, well, we have sterling on five, bracelets, maybe a simple initial necklace. Or china, maybe a Limoges-style box or a vase—"

"Oh, she loves flowers, that's a great idea."

"There are a whole bunch upstairs on the second floor, including the new Frank Gehry collection, very cool."

"Thanks, thanks a lot."

With a nod of gratitude, Oscar left for the elevators, while Douglas looked on in a daze.

"Oh. My. God."

"What?"

"That guy."

"Cute, huh?"

"I mean, beyond. Girl, he is to die. Kill me now. He was fully into you, too!"

"What? No he wasn't. He was into mommy."

"Oh come on, he's a good son. I love those smoking-hot types who don't even know their power."

"He was probably dorky in high school and blossomed late."

"I love that! Ugly duckling turned fox. The hottest."

Gisele Beauvoir stepped out of the elevators, looked around, saw the pair, and walked over at a brisk pace.

"Julia—can you come with me upstairs, please?"

The small white hairs on the back of Julia's neck stood up. Why did she need to see Gisele today of all days, when she looked like hell. She should not have had that last drink last night.

"Am I in trouble?" she asked, half joking, half worried.

"No! Why, should you be?"

Julia looked at Douglas and followed Gisele upstairs. But on the sixth floor, instead of making a left to the PR area, the two made a right and headed for the luxurious executive offices. Holy shit, thought Julia. I must have done something wrong. This is a big deal, going to the Big Boss's office. Julia gulped. She and Douglas had been invited to the wedding, hadn't they? They had all said come, bring a date, be part of the B group that comes later, right? Now Julia was in a panic that maybe she had heard incorrectly. Maybe she and Douglas had been supposed to be taking coats at the party or hovering at Lell's feet under the table to make sure no one scraped their chair on the train of her gown. Shit, shit. As Julia floated by Warhols and Lichtensteins on top of beautiful priceless Persian carpets, her head pounded. Every time she passed assistants speaking in hushed tones she was certain they were talking about her, and she felt like she was being led to her execution.

Gisele headed to the end of the corridor, pushing the grand door open. And against the snowy backdrop of Central Park, Gene Pelham was lounging back in his desk chair, swiveling around from the glorious view to face Julia.

"Well, here she is! Have a seat."

Gisele left the room, while Julia sat in the leather studded club chair her CEO was gesturing toward. Did she need a lawyer?

"Just got off the phone with Lellie—she's loving the honeymoon—and as you may know from our company memo, she's going to be my little right hand this year."

"Oh, yes—"

"So, as our new creative director, her first order of business is a new staff around her, and from the beach, she has asked me to bring you in to join our team up here."

No way! Julia was stunned. "Wow, really? I'm so honored—"

"Great. So we're doubling your salary and you'll start Monday when Lellie's back in the saddle. You'll have an office up here and Gisele will get you up to speed and all set up."

With a thousand fountain-coin tosses, stray blown eyelashes, and extinguished birthday candles, she never would have dreamed this could happen so easily. She was moving up. Moving from ribbon-tying drone to the rainbow world of Creative. "This is . . . amazing, thank you."

"Hey, kiddo, I'm thrilled. You're what we need at this company, you're the whole package. But don't thank me, thank my daughter." Gene got up to shake Julia's hand. "She's your new best friend."

chapter 8

Lell and Will both sighed with relief as the doorman unloaded their T. Anthony luggage from the cart and placed it gently on the Persian rug in the foyer of their apartment. Will immediately disappeared into his office to listen to the hundreds of voice mails that had been left by thrilled and wistful wedding guests, while Lell grabbed the pile of magazines that had accumulated since her departure and curled herself into a ball on the white sofa in the living room, tucked under a plaid Ralph Lauren throw. They were both glad to be back.

The honeymoon had been lovely; beautiful tropical weather, plush accommodations, and fantastic food. They played tennis, read the latest must-read bestsellers on the beach, danced the tango, even snorkled. But Lell and Will both craved the company of others more than the average newlyweds. Sure, there were some Australians passing through who they had a laugh with one night at the Tiki bar while tossing down blended drinks, and there was the couple in their forties from Chicago who were reasonably amusing for a day or two. But as the weeks wore on and the pace slowed, none of the sort of jet-setty glamorous crowd that Lell and Will were accustomed to arrived at the hotel. And intrinsic to both of their characters was the need to see and be seen by people whom they deemed worthy. Otherwise, what was the point? As a result of the dearth of boldfacers (even the Euros were conspicuously absent), ennui set in.

After a week and a half, Will became a champion backgammon player, challenging a local fisherman at every turn, and Lell started calling the office, becoming more and more interested in what was transpiring in her absence, putting on a faux-concerned voice at every turn. She never would have called one of her dear friends to check in, lest they think she was not having the most amazing time of her life, but work was a different story. She was now creative director, so of course she had to be concerned with what was happening at Pelham's. But because hers was a newly created post with still somewhat vague responsibilities, nothing was really happening that needed her attention. So, in an effort to battle boredom, she sat under her umbrella on the snow-white beach in front of the gleaming water, and turned her attention elsewhere.

She had seen Julia Pearce around the office and was intrigued by her. There are some people, regardless of class, who just have an aura, a sort of glow that attracts people to them. Julia was one of those people. When Lell walked around the ground floor of Pelham's, perusing the cases, making sure everything was in order, she'd spy Julia out of the corner of her eye: laughing effortlessly with tourists from Singapore or seriously advising a nervous groom-to-be. Something about Julia's confidence was attractive to Lell, and although Julia was a little rough around the edges, Lell decided she wanted her on her team. She reasoned to herself that it was because she needed an outsider, someone who had no allegiances, no contacts; and could be solely on her side. But the truth was, she was curious about this girl. Especially after she saw how Julia impressed Polly on her wedding day. Polly loathed most people, especially those who didn't have a 10021 zip code, and it was unusual that she paid any attention to an underling. So before Polly could swoop in and adopt Julia as her own, Lell called her father from Bali and had him put Julia on her team. She'd get to know this girl when she got back to the office on Monday.

As Lell was making her way through a tedious magazine interview of Angelina Jolie while snuggled on her couch the phone rang.

"You're back!" screamed Polly from the other end of the phone.

"And soooooooo bummed to be back. We didn't want to

leave!" lied Lell in a gloomy voice. Meanwhile, she was thrilled to be back on her home turf.

"Well I am so psyched you are back. It's been a total bore without you. Meredith is being the devil, literally, I can't deal with her. Nightmare. And Hope is sweet but sometimes I think she has no edge. I mean, say something mean about people once in a while, will you? She's like vanilla ice cream. I swear we need new friends. So how was the trip?"

Lell launched into the details of her honeymoon, peppering every verb with glowing superlatives and embellishing every moment. Polly listened patiently for the appropriate amount of time, while tending to errant cuticles and stray lint on her skirt, then abruptly changed the subject.

"So, what's on the agenda? We need to shake up this town."

"Well, I've missed three weeks of work so I really have to get back into the swing of things for a while. No long lunches for at least a week."

"Boring!"

"It is my family business. And I'm creative director now."

"So what does that mean? Do you like run the place?"

"No, no. I just have to be more visible. I will be the face of Pelham's."

"I thought Nicole Kidman was the face of Pelham's."

"She does our print campaign, but she's hired help. I need to be the ambassador, you know, at every important event and fashion show."

"Kind of what you do now."

"Sort of, except I'll have a much larger team under me."

"Minions? Cool."

"Actually," said Lell, bending to stir her chamomile tea, "I hired a deputy."

"*Deputy?* What are you, Boss Hogg?"

"No, you know what I mean. Remember that girl Julia, who brought me the necklace?"

Lell waited. She knew Polly would be jealous yet intrigued.

"Julia? No."

"You remember, the pretty blonde who my dad invited to the wedding?"

"Oh, yeah, her. Oh that's good," Polly said nonchalantly, through gritted teeth.

Hmmm . . . thought Polly to herself. Lell has beaten me to the punch. Polly's big plan—that she had been cultivating and nursing for weeks—had been to swoop in and take Julia under her wing. She wasn't sure how to do this, but she saw potential in Julia, and wanted to see if she could turn her into a society darling, just for kicks. And now Lell had gotten to her first.

"She'll be my gal Friday, really coming with me everywhere. I think she has an appealing image that will work well for Pelham's. She reads very well—people are taken with her style and she seems very savvy and cool. Fresh. She has that—"

"*Je ne sais quoi,* mmmm-hmmm, I know what you mean," said Polly thinking aloud. "But. There is the issue of her Downtown edge. I mean this is Pelham's we're talking about here."

"I know. That's my one petite issue . . . the East Village factor."

"I mean, the girl's got style, clearly. She's just not—"

"Refined."

Polly shrugged as if to say *oui*.

Lell thought for a minute. "We could easily buff that right out of her—"

"Totally!" agreed Polly. "We can beat the Alphabet City right out of her and clean her up. She could be an overnight social star."

"I think so," Lell agreed. "After we spruce her up with some designer threads, give her some pointers, she'll be a perfect reflection of Pelham's."

"It's true," said Polly, lost in thought. Perhaps with a heightened title of "deputy" that was just as fraudulent as Lell's title of creative director, doors would open a little easier for Julia, making Polly's efforts to integrate her into their clan a bit easier. Yes, this could be a good thing. "It's like at Polo," Polly added. "Ralph surrounds himself with little blond clones of his ad campaign models, people who fit the part and seem cut and pasted from that world. Julia can definitely be that for you."

"This is going to be great," Lell replied with rising excitement.

"You know, Lell, why don't we have lunch one day with your new deputy? I'd love to, you know, find out what's going on downtown these days. Maybe it can inspire my next theme party," said Polly with fake casualness.

Lell knew she had Polly hooked. "Good idea. I'll get it on the planner."

Both Polly and Lell were now of one mind. *Winter Project* equals *Julia Pearce*. Better than Mortimer and Randolph

Duke themselves! This was their Henry Higgins opportunity to change someone's destiny, re-create her, let her into their golden utopian world. It would be fun. A public service! Julia would officially be Eliza Doolittle. Who could it hurt?

chapter 9

Having dough is pretty easy to fake in New York. It's all an ordered graph of mysterious tall buildings rather than visible squat mansions where one could estimate a neighbor's square footage based on the site of a front lawn. No one's vroom-vrooming around town in souped-up Porsches (except drug dealers)—even the wealthiest of tycoons often hop in a cab or arrive at black-tie functions in a discreet town car. You can spy a young social butterfly in a beaded dress that would cost upward of five grand on the rack, and never know she was returning it to the PR department the next morning. That Kelly bag? A knockoff bought from a dealer in Sutton Place. Those emerald-cut diamond stud earrings? "Travel jewelry"—that is, cubic zirc from Erwin Pearl on Madison.

Hope Matthews never really cared about money. She grew up in an upper-middle-class family in Connecticut, went to Williams, and never thought about material things. She married her husband, Charlie, for love and love alone, but his wealthy family's miserly way of cutting off their son was getting Hope increasingly frustrated and nervous about their future. Loathing the trust-funded brats they spied running amok without careers, Charlie's parents literally took out scissors and cut up his Amex on his graduation day, pronouncing he was "on his own." With two young sons who would soon start private school plus a rental apartment with a noisy record label exec neighbor (who often had rockers and rappers chillin' 'til dawn, yo), Hope was a ball of stress. She wanted desperately to move to a co-op apartment, but she and Charlie were constantly chasing the market, and even teeny classic six spreads where the boys would share a room were seemingly always out of their grasp. Plus the board package they needed would surely require proof of a liquid net worth three times the purchase price of the apartment, which simply was not possible. Hope's parents would have given them the shirts off their backs, but after forty years of servitude at the office, her dad was living off his savings, having bought a modest second home in Sea Island, Georgia, where he and Hope's mom could live out their golden years. With their generous help, they could maybe afford half the down payment. The Matthews family, her in-laws, were loaded, but gave them zilch. But Charlie didn't want their help out of pride; he was eager to earn his own keep, which Hope respected.

While many husbands came home with heavy wallets, Charlie came home with a heavy heart. He was Les Miz at his "I-banking" job and detested his alcoholic boss. He was always so run-down at the day's end that he decided to take the bull by the horns and quit to seek work elsewhere, hopefully in private equity.

Hope wanted to pull a Tammy Wynette and support his difficult decision, but the idea of Charlie leaving his stable job was daunting, though on the flip side, she hated seeing him down after the workday. She felt so much pressure lately, she'd often wake up in the middle of the night, heart pounding and covered in sweat. And her friends were too clueless—they just assumed everyone had a few mill in the bank. Polly kept saying, "You have got to get out of that apartment! I am having Kirk Henckels call you tomorrow about new listings on the market."

Hope pretended she was in no rush and was simply waiting for the right place, when in reality she knew she could never afford the luxurious floor plans her friends had. She couldn't even dream of competing—Polly's digs were at least $3 million and the place Lell was about to close on, well, aside from the purchase price of $6.9 million, the maintenance in that white-glove building had to be at least seven grand a month. Argh! Hope hated it when she found herself counting other people's assets. It was loathsome and classless, and made her feel like she was drowning. Okay, calm down, she thought. What is my problem? She knew there were limbless cripples with gangrene begging in India, and gaunt starving Somalian children with flies on their faces and even in her country—her city—there were rape victims and rat-infested spider-hole studios and families whose tenements were ravaged by theft or gunshots or fires. What the hell was she freaking out about? That she was in a postwar rental a few blocks too far east? Big deal! She was blessed! People would kill to have her life, because the outward appearance was so flawless, but it was in fact cobbled together with the duct tape of borrowed gowns and invitations to the right parties and running with the rich.

But at least Hope had love. She loved her husband so much it hurt. Her college sweetheart, Charlie had always been her number-one best friend. She'd be in a frustrated sea of running boys, spaghetti sauce splatters and another shattered glass, and then Charlie would walk in and all the noise and chaos melted away in his hug. The boys would run to him and pounce, sticking to him like a couple of suction cup–Garfields, while Hope looked on smiling. He knew she was going nuts with little help and close quarters. And Hope knew he aleady felt enough pressure that he didn't need any from her. The poor guy was doing the best he could. He worked his hardest and he loved coming home. She smiled, feeling the warmth of her affections soothe her stress . . . for the moment. But lately, that *pavor nocturnus* always crept its way back. What was that expression? Love don't pay the rent. And love certainly don't cough up forty g's for tuition.

On Friday evening Charlie persuaded Hope to stop fretting about financial woes and enjoy herself at the intimate soirée that Polly was hosting "in honor of Will and Lell's return." The gathering consisted of a small group that had been carefully selected by Polly when she was in one of her less than benevolent moods. As a result, Meredith and her beau were out, and in their stead Nina Waters, who had given Polly a large discount on her trunk show linens, and Oscar Curtis, Henny's mother's godson who had recently moved back from the West Coast, made the cut. It was good not to have same-old same-old, thought Polly, as she surveyed the crowd assembling in her well-appointed drawing room.

"So tell us, Oscar, how the hell could you survive life in that giant Gap ad aka San Fran? It's so lily-white and boring there, the place is, like, covered in chinos. I swear I get claustrophobia the second I step off the plane," said Polly, taking a break from her hostessing duties to plop down on the sofa next to Hope.

Hope balanced her white wine glass on the monogrammed cocktail napkin in front of her, and glanced at Oscar Curtis with nervous pity. He was very handsome, but very awkward. He shifted uncomfortably under Polly's gaze and squinted as if he was in fluorescent airport bathroom light. The poor guy looked as if he would rather be anywhere else than this posh dinner party. Little did he know that Polly was just starting her Spanish Inquisition, and there would be no escape for him now.

"I worked all the time, mostly in Palo Alto, so I didn't pay much attention. Could have been anywhere," he mumbled, taking a gulp of his drink.

"Well if you could have been anywhere, why did you stay there? I mean, the Internet exists for a reason."

"It was easier. Everyone's out there."

"I just don't know how anyone can live anywhere but New York. I feel like I'm missing out on something when I'm not here. I mean, even when I'm in Europe, I'm like, get me out of here after a while. You just feel so irrelevant everywhere else," said Polly.

"The world is big and New York isn't the only place . . ." said Oscar, obviously wanting to end the conversation. Hope noticed his discomfort and tried to change the topic.

"Lell! Come over here and show us your gorgeous wedding band," said Hope, yelling across the room.

Lell walked over and sat on the arm of the sofa. Her Indonesian tan was complemented beautifully by the brilliant yet subtle sapphire necklace that she wore over her gray Prada cocktail dress. "I've only been away three weeks and so much has happened! I didn't even know Drew Vance was thrown out of the Union Club."

"Old news," said Polly, rolling her eyes.

"I didn't know that either," said Hope.

"He got totally wasted and threw up everywhere. Chunks, apparently. I think he's just suspended, there's no way he's expelled, his family practically founded the place."

"And Lila Meyer got engaged? Who to?" asked Lell.

Oscar rolled his eyes as the girls started to gossip. He stood up abruptly without excusing himself and walked over to the windows, where he stood alone gazing at the view. Lell shot Polly a curious look, but she shrugged.

"To some guy from some random place like Scotland or Australia. We'll see if she makes it down the aisle," said Polly.

"When they get old and desperate they always go for the accent," sighed Lell, now a full-on Bridget Jones smug-married.

"So true. He's probably from like, a trailer park in Essex, but everyone here is just dazzled by the fact that he calls trucks lorries," laughed Polly.

"I have to admit, the accent gets me every time," said Hope.

"Forget all that crap," said Polly, once again taking

charge of the conversation. "The big news is what Rosemary told me about Carlin Overland—"

"Which is . . ."

"You haven't heard?" Polly looked both ways and leaned in with a stealthy whisper. "Gingivitis."

"No!"

"Can you deal? That's pretty embarrassing."

"You're not kidding," agreed Lell, repulsed.

"Gingivitis is totally curable, isn't it? I mean, they advertise it on TV," said Hope.

"Yeah, well, they advertise STDs and they're not totally curable," said Polly.

"Isn't gingivitis like, herpes of the mouth?" asked Lell.

"God knows where Carlin's mouth has been!" said Polly.

"You guys! I can't believe we're talking about this, it's plaque or something! Anyway, I want to hear all the details about the honeymoon," interjected Hope.

That's my cue, thought Polly, rising. She couldn't bear one more Bali story. Enough about Lell and her three-grand-a-night beachside cottage. "I've got to check on dinner."

In Polly's cherry tomato dining room, amid the Matisse collages and the Bennison curtains, Hope found herself seated on a leopard upholstered Biedermeir chair next to the host himself. Polly always sat Hope next to Henny, and she always put herself next to Charlie. Sometimes Hope thought Polly had a little crush on her husband, although she would never admit it. She laughed really loudly and often at his jokes, and always compared her Henny unfavorably to Charlie. Whereas Charlie was easygoing and friendly, Henny was boring and uptight with a lead pipe lodged up his bum. People referred to him as "the cut-and-paste husband" because he was just an accessory in Polly's world, a cardboard cutout that literally could have been anyone with a weenie and a wallet. Well, anyone with the right credentials: lineage and four middle names.

The seat on Hope's other side remained empty for the first few bites of the goat cheese salad appetizer and Polly—with an eye roll—shouted over the guests that Hope's dinner companion was running late. Just as Henny was concluding his story on helicopter skiing in British Columbia, Hope felt the empty chair next to her being pulled out, and then the soft wool of a man's blazer brush against her arm.

"Hey, John, glad you could make it," said Henny, getting up and greeting his new guest with a firm handshake as he was introduced to the gorgeous girl he had brought with him.

"Sorry we're late."

"No problem, we started though."

"We couldn't wait all night, John!" yelled Polly across the table.

"I'm glad you didn't," he said with a warm smile.

"Do you know your dinner partner? This is Hope Matthews. Hope, John Cavanaugh."

"I don't believe I do," said John, extending his hand.

"Nice to meet you," said Hope.

Polly led John's companion to the other side of the table. She was big on splitting up couples, which always bothered Hope. Once she had asked Polly why she always split everyone up—sometimes at different tables across the room—and Polly sniffed, "Oh it's so boring to talk to your spouse all damn night!" Hope disagreed; after a long day of work, she missed Charlie desperately and hated parting with him for two hours while having to make an effort with new people. She hoped her dinner partner this evening was not the usual bore.

John Cavanaugh was extremely good looking. Not in that pretty boy way, but in a very masculine and solid way. His confidence was immediately apparent, and he possessed a gallant smile that could relax anyone at a glance. With his dark hair and dark eyes he even looked a little like the late John F. Kennedy Jr., God rest his soul.

Henny turned to Lell to continue his travelogue, and as Susan Wong, John's other seating companion, was engrossed in her conversation with Will, Hope and John were left to chat.

"Polly's going to kill me for being late," he said, leaning in and whispering.

"No, don't worry, it's a blizzard outside," she offered, comfortingly.

"She doesn't care, come on." He grinned with a raised brow.

Hope smiled. "Well, murder may be a stretch, but she may maim you."

"Maybe she'll just torture me. I guess I deserve a good lashing."

Before Hope even realized what she was saying she blurted out, "Why, have you been a bad boy?"

John looked at her and smiled. "Behave!" he teased in full Austin Powers cockney. "Naw, not really. Not too bad . . ."

Normally Hope would never tease a stranger or engage in any sort of flirty banter, but something about John made her feel audacious. Charlie was across the table deep in conversation about new tax laws, and as soon as she caught herself batting her lashes at this sexy stranger, she flushed a deep crimson.

"So how do you know the Mecoxes?" asked John.

"I went to boarding school with Polly. How about you?"

"I know Henny through work. I have a venture capital company."

"Oh, which one?" asked Hope, with interest.

"Greenwich Equity."

Greenwich Equity. Even Hope had heard of that. They had just done some megadeal with all the record labels. Charlie was dying to get into the venture capital biz. He should have been sitting next to John.

"I've heard of it. It's yours?"

"Yes, mine and one other guy. We started it a few years ago after we left Goldman."

"Wow." She wanted to say her husband was looking desperately for a job in that field, but that would seem a little tacky.

"What about you? Do you work?"

"I was running the jewelry department at Frothingham's—the auction house—but I'm on a temporary maternity leave. I have two sons under the age of three, so it just wasn't possible to keep it up."

"My sister has two kids, and forget work. I mean, she does more work than I do running after those boys."

"Do you have kids?"

"No, I'm not married."

"Oh," said Hope, glancing across the room at the woman John arrived with. She was spectacularly beautiful, probably a model, with short dark hair and olive skin. The antithesis of Hope, actually. Hope had a natural, fresh beauty—blond hair that swung just above her shoulders, large blue eyes and the clear smooth skin of an Ivory girl. She was the girl next door, if you lived in a nice neighborhood. Hope was approachable, whereas John's date—who oozed style—seemed remote and glamorous.

"Natasha is my girlfriend."

"Oh. She's very pretty."

"Yeah," said John with little enthusiasm. "But someday, I'd love to have kids."

"They're the best. You look in their huge eyes and it's a new lease on life, everything is so fresh. I feel like a new human since I had my little nuggets. They're so unjaded, you know? They're my best little pals."

Then Hope caught herself. "Sorry. Is it so deathly boring to hear a mom yammering about all her kiddie brood? Yawn."

"No, not at all! People these days are all so selfish," he said, looking into Hope's eyes. "It's refreshing to talk to someone who is nurturing and actually cares about something other than herself."

John looked at Hope intently and smiled. She smiled back.

In the cab home, Hope couldn't wait to tell Charlie about John.

"So he's from Greenwich Equity—"

"I know exactly who he is," said Charlie, giving the driver their address.

"Well, this could be good. I wanted to say something—"

"You didn't, did you?" asked Charlie, immediately anxious.

"No, come on. I can be subtle. Give me a little credit, will you please?"

"I know, it's just, it has to be done carefully when you meet someone in a social setting like that. They'll never think you're unhappy with your job and looking, so they'll never say, come in and talk to me."

"Do you want me to have Polly say something?"

"No. She has zero tact."

Hope was relieved. She didn't want Polly to know that Charlie was looking for a new job.

"We have to think how to do this," said Charlie.

"Yeah. Well, maybe we need to have a dinner party," suggested Hope.

"We don't have a dining room."

"Well, I can host one at the Links or King's Carriage. Or the small room at Orsay."

"That'll cost a fortune."

"But it'll be worth it. We need to put in money in order to make money. That's how business works."

"Thanks, my little Billie Gates. Let's think about it tomorrow," said Charlie, leaning his head against the window in the cab. "I'm beat."

Sometimes Hope felt so confined by their life she wanted to scream. Everything was claustrophobic and small. She and

Charlie needed a break. They deserved it, for Lord's sake. Please, prayed Hope, let something good happen.

She was feeling dejected until she got home and went in to check on her boys. She loved watching them sleep, they seemed so peaceful and trusting. Hope ran her hand across their cheeks and tousled their hair, and then sat on the edge of the bed to watch them. Who was she to complain? Something good had happened—she had these beautiful little babies. That was all that mattered.

chapter 10

"Good luck, sweet pea!" cheered Douglas, as Julia modeled the outfit she'd chosen for her first day as Pelham's special projects consultant at large. She had been installed in a killer office the Friday before and this was her official first day o' biz with her fancy title, as well as her first duties reporting to her even fancier boss.

"I just pray I'm not just Lell Pelham's butt boy—"

"Girl, who cares if you are? You got the engraved business card with that major fucking title! You are on your way. Two words: expense account. Hellooo? You could inhale soufflés at La Grenouille daily and no one would stop you."

"Except my expanding waistline."

"With your crazy metab? Impossible. Trust me, you're in such a good space right now."

"I guess . . ." she smiled, straightening the new jacket she had splurged on at Barney's after Douglas and Lewis railroaded her into slapping down her Visa. It was not something that she could afford at all, but they convinced her she needed to invest in her wardrobe to look the part. She had never worn anything so expensive, it seemed almost obscene. She felt quite conspicuous wearing it after work to Girls, Inc., where she usually volunteered in her normal low-priced eclectic getups. But on the other hand, she saw how those PR girls dressed to the nines, and knew she had to look good in order to compete.

"Lell seemed really nice. I just hope it goes well."

"You know what Lewis heard? Apparently at the bank there's this guy who went to some prissy fucking fancy-ass boarding school with Willoughby Banks and apparently he was, like, engaged to some chick who he fully bailed on when he met Lell."

"Oh, really?" She had locked eyes with Will at the wedding a few times; she knew from his piercing gaze that this dude definitely was a big-time heartbreaker. "That's sad. He just unloaded her?"

"The bitch was discarded like yesterday's *Post*. Some friend of his asked him about it and he just said, 'Lell Pelham. Ka-ching!' So creepsville."

"*No way*, you think he gold dug her? That makes no sense, isn't he loadissimo? I hardly think she and her family would go for some grifter."

"He has some bucks, but more importantly he's a full-on Social Register type, which they care about big time. That marriage was a perfect merger, like when all those rich Amer-

ican chicks married Brit royals so they could infuse the dilap-
idated castles with new world cashola. Symbiosis."

"Interesting."

Julia walked to her office and logged on to her brand-new
e-mail account—she was thrilled to be considered a real employee with a full cyber identity. It seemed her brown bow–tying days were over. If all went well, that is.

"Hi there," said Lell from the doorway. "How are you
finding the new office?"

"Oh," said Julia, surprised to see her boss. "So great, I
love this! I cannot tell you how excited I am to be working
with you up here. Thank you."

Julia paused as she saw Lell studying her from head to toe
with an appraising eye. She was now more grateful than ever
at having let Douglas and Lewis talk her in to the new jacket.
She shifted awkwardly under Lell's gaze, unsure whether or
not to acknowledge that she was being summed up as if she
was a contestant on *America's Next Top Model* or if she should
pretend to be busy with something. But what? It was her first
day. Finally Lell looked her in the eyes.

"Let's get started."

The morning was spent poring over the new collection,
discussing press, and setting up appointments for Julia to
meet with celebrity stylists. Julia was reticent and decided it
was appropriate to be quiet and not a know-it-all on her first
day. After all, she didn't want to be too audacious and opin-
ionated. Even though it did seem like Lell kept coaxing her to

give her opinion. But maybe Lell was just being nice? Better to play it safe and just nod at whatever Lell said, that's what the other lackeys were doing. Just listen intently and try to suck it all in.

Initially, she had believed that Lell's job was just a bullshit title, but she was discovering she was wrong. Although it seemed that Lell was just saying yes or no to everything, which in essence she was, Lell was also trying to update Pelham's image, and that was no easy task. Especially when people were bringing her some piles of jewelry that looked like they belonged in a Ross Dress-for-Less rather than Pelham's. A few times, Julia had to do everything in her power not to say something. That was one area she felt totally confident in: jewelry. She had studied and admired it her entire life, and she read every book and knew who had owned every important collection in the world. It had always been her obsession. Her dream was to be at the helm of her own company, designing jewelry that made its owner feel a little more glamorous. She wanted to make simple, elegant pieces that created sentimental attachments: a stunning but sleek mongrammed locket, an engagement ring with delicate old-world appeal, a bracelet that would make any wrist appear more feminine and sweet. She had a clear vision and taste that guided her all the way; she knew that she knew what people wanted.

After three hours of hard work, Lell and Julia strolled a few blocks to the Colony Club, Lell's cafeteria. Over arugula and endive salad, Lell probed Julia on her love life.

"So there's no one out there at the moment?"

"No, not really, you know, just adjusting to living here still, but I'm having a blast."

"And who was that guy you brought to my wedding? Gay, right?"

Julia didn't even realize Lell had spotted them at all. "Oh, Douglas? Yes. He and his boyfriend, Lewis, are my best friends here. Doug works at Pelham's also."

"He does?" Lell raised a perfectly groomed brow. Yes, he did kind of look familiar. She didn't really notice most of the worker bees on the floor. "Right. Well maybe we can involve him in our team, too . . ."

Julia felt a rush of excitement. "That would be fucking amazing!" Oops! How could she curse in front of her new boss? Yikes.

Lell made a grimace. "I hope you won't use language like that around the office."

"I'm so sorry," said Julia, reddening. Fuck.

Lell moved on. "Listen, Julia, I think it's important that we talk about some ground rules."

Shit. Fired on my first day, thought Julia, panicking.

"Don't get that face, it's nothing bad," said Lell, smiling.

"Sorry, it's just you sounded like my seventh-grade science teacher when he was about to fail me. I sucked at science."

"No, nothing like that."

Julia exhaled a sigh of relief that could have blown up a balloon. "Good."

"Well, I bet you're wondering why I brought you in on my team. As you can imagine, I get thousands of résumés a day. Thousands. From debutantes, trust fund babies, former starlets. Even girls with royal titles have applied to be my deputy. Everyone wants to work for me."

"I'm sure! It's like the coolest gig in town."

Lell meticulously squirted lime in her Perrier and paused to take a small sip. Julia was amazed that she didn't even leave the slightest hint of lipstick on the rim of the crystal glass.

"Anyway, my number-one priority is discretion. As you can recall from my wedding day, I don't like to have people who are loose-lipped working close to me. I don't gossip about my coworkers, and I expect—no, no, *demand* the same from them. Besides the fact that we have no friends in common, you don't seem the type to waste time on meretricious persiflage."

Meretricious persiflage? What the hell was that? "Of course not. I am like a vault, like that episode of *Seinfeld*. The buck stops here, with me." Julia felt stupid, but what could she say? And God, what had she told Douglas so far? She'd need to put a filter on that.

"I didn't think so. Because gossip is really just tacky and harmful," said Lell, dabbing her napkin on her lips. Again, no lipstick came off. Amazing. "In fact, there are two girls that I'm sort of friends with, and they have a book deal to write about twenty-something Park Avenue debutantes. I think it's really shameful and tacky."

"That's terrible."

Lell waved her hand in disgust and continued. "Doesn't matter. The point is, tight lips, tight hips, and tight ships. That's one of my mottoes."

Julia nodded because her mouth was full with salad. As soon as she swallowed she said, "Absolutely."

"So that's really rule number one. Another thing," said Lell, pushing the organic leaves around her plate. "It's not just that you're some random girl and that's why I hired you. I also think that you seem to have a certain *je ne sais quoi*."

"I'm sorry?"

"I don't know what it is about you. I mean, your clothes are not expensive, but you definitely have style. I've noticed it. And I've noticed customers noticing it."

"You have?"

"I have a camera where I can watch what transpires on the main floor."

Julia gulped. Holy George Orwell. She'd definitely have to warn Douglas. Maybe Lell had microphones everywhere also. Scary. Like that terrible Billy Baldwin–slash–Sharon Stone movie. Yuck.

"Really?"

"Yes. And the way you swooped in and styled the girls and my dress at the wedding—you have it. You could be a sittings editor at *Vogue*. You just get the look. But it's quirky. Cool. *Anyway*, what I'm trying to say is that I didn't hire you to be a mute in my office. I want to know your opinion on things. I don't need another yes-man in my life."

This last part didn't quite seem true. Although she probably was sincere and did want Julia to tell her the truth, she would bet her eyeballs that a girl like Lell could never have enough yes-men.

"I'm really flattered."

"You should be. This is a really great opportunity for you. I want you to come to me with ideas, information, things you think are problems, and, most of all, solutions. Another one

of my mottoes is, 'Don't only be a problem identifier. Be a solution finder.' "

"That's a good one." Weird that she has so many mottoes,
thought Julia.

"The rest, we'll just figure out as we go along."

"Sounds great."

It did sound great, but also nerve-racking. Lell was so
confident, and obviously had such a distinct idea about everything, yet she was so hard to read. Julia could foresee a lot of
these little chats down the road. And although she knew the
payoff would be worth it, there was something that made her
a little nauseous.

"Moving along. I'm going to host a dinner for my husband's birthday next week, and I'd love you to come, if you're
free." It seemed more of a demand than an invitation. "The
New York Times' Style section will be covering it for the
Good Company column so we should go get outfitted this
week."

"Okay, I mean, me too?"

"Of course. You're a representative of Pelham's now, and
I need you in designer duds when the press is around. I'll call
Monsieur de la Renta this afternoon."

"You're joking . . ." This was too surreal.

Lell looked at her quizzically. "No. You must look the
part, as they say."

"That's amazing, holy sh—oot!"

Lell bristled at the near-use of the *s*-word.

"Sorry," said Julia.

Whoops. Julia made a mental note-to-self to can the
curses. It was just that, except for the Barney's splurge, Julia

never wore anything but stuff she'd shopped for in Williamsburg or the East Village. The idea of actually donning thousand-dollar threads was almost too insane. She didn't even bother to salivate over the pages of *Vogue*; she knew she'd never be able to afford any of it. She just drank in the fantastic sexy images and let the styles enter her via osmosis. She'd later channel the candied visions into purchases that maybe evoked the glossy editorials but with her own stamp of downtown edge and vintage flair.

"Ohmigod! What have we here?" boomed Polly, who had just walked into the dining room. "A little ladies' lunch?" She glanced at Lell's plate. Arugula, natch. "You and your rabbit food! Could you please eat something? The honeymoon's over, no bikini for several months!"

Lell just smiled. She hated being monitored by Polly. She was always their group's food police.

Meanwhile, Polly was also looking Julia over head to toe, before turning to examine Mrs. Banks. "So, Lell, Henny and I are in for Will's party on Saturday. So psyched. What to wear? I have got to do Madison this afternoon. I am so busy I could die! Plus I have to buy a dress for Lila Meyer's engagement to that cockney person. And I need to storm Bonpoint to get Quint an outfit for Keeley Kincaid's first birthday party. I am swamped!"

Julia could not believe what these people considered to be work—she would kill for their chores!

"So, are you guys going to the FADD ball next week?" asked Polly.

"Willoughby and I took a table," replied Lell coolly. Of course she'd be at one of the biggest charity balls of the winter season. I mean, as if she would ever miss a Fight Attention Deficit Disorder, come on! Lell turned to her lunch companion. "Julia's joining us at our table."

She is? "That is so nice of you, thanks." She was so honored that Lell was extending such a generous invitation. Douglas would freak.

But the only one freaking at the moment was Polly. She decided to ratchet it up a notch.

"Hey Julia, that reminds me, I am cochair of the steering committee for the Junior Ball for FIBS, you know, Fight Against Irritable Bowel Syndrome, and we are always looking for new pretty young things to add to our gang . . . How about it?"

Julia looked at Lell, who made a small grimace despite her best efforts to maintain a poker face. Should she agree? Lell remained silent so Julia was forced to answer. "Um, okay, I mean what does it entail?"

"Nothing! That's the fun of it. Valentino's sponsoring this year so we all get dressed by Mister Garivani, and then we usually do a pre-party in-store event. It's really fun! All you have to do is buy two tickets." Polly failed to mention to her new recruit that tickets ran a thousand per head.

Lell knew just what Polly was doing. Julia had the exact knockout looks and fashion flair that would have Patrick Mc-Mullan and his posse snapping away with lights flickering as fast as fireflies at a New Canaan summer barbeque.

"Oh come on, Polly. Tickets are a fortune. Julia won't do that one," interjected Lell.

Julia felt herself redden, but she was thrilled that Lell

saved her. She wondered how much the tickets must cost for Lell to have actually noticed. Three hundred dollars?

"Well, actually, Polly," said Lell, "I'm just now in the process of sorting out Julia's charitable commitments. She can't appear out of nowhere and be omni; however, it is time to make a splash. I'm thinking of putting her on my benefit's committee—it's for the Prescott Museum." She turned to Julia. "You know, on Fifth?"

"Oh sure, the Prescott Museum," said Julia, certain she had never heard of it. And how much would this splash on the charity circuit cost her? Lell knew how much she made. "Gosh, all these lovely offers. I don't know how much I can help, I mean financially—"

"No, no, no, Will and I will take a table. You obviously would come as our guest."

Polly was turning red. She didn't have daddy's little fucking family foundation to purchases tables right and left, not to mention the Pelham's vat o' dough, which Lell could use as her personal purse for charitable sponsorships.

"Henny and I will take a table, too, for our benefit. Come as our guest, see if you're into it, and then you can be on next year if you want."

Julia smiled in polite acceptance, but as she saw Lell's jaw clench, she started to feel that it wasn't about her helping hand: she was suddenly feeling like a pawn in Polly and Lell's sidewalk-sized game of chess.

chapter 11

Polly had been sitting in the back of her town car for forty-
five minutes waiting for Julia to exit Pelham's. She was becoming increasingly annoyed and very impatient. But in order
to put her project into effect and to ensure that she had something to do this winter, she had no choice but to wait. Finally
she saw the employee door swing open and Julia exit the
building, looking around for a second to assess the cold, then
tucking her chin into her wool coat.

"Yoo-hoo! Julia!" called Polly out the window of her car.
"Over here!"

Julia looked up, surprised, then waved and approached
the car.

"I was just passing by and saw you come out. I'm on my
way downtown to an important appointment, do you need a
lift?"

"Sure, I'd love one, if it's not out of the way."

"Hop on in."

Julia opened the door and got in the back of the car. She
smiled gratefully and unwrapped her scarf. "It's freezing.
Thanks so much for the ride."

"No prob." Polly looked at Julia appraisingly. She really
was eye-catching. The society photographers would love her.
But she definitely needed some of Polly's sense and coaching,
in order to maneuver her way through their world.

Julia felt Polly staring at her and tried to chat to break the ice. But she had no idea what to say to Polly. "So um, do you go downtown a lot?"

"Not really. Just when I have this appointment."

"Oh."

Silence. Julia attempted again. "So, what do you think about Julia Roberts and—"

Polly waved her hand and stopped Julia before she could finish. "I don't follow celebrities. They're overpaid and should become extinct. That's why I only watch reality television."

"Oh, I love *The Apprentice*."

"Me too. But I really prefer *The Bachelor*. It's so much fun watching these guys play with the minds of these idiotic girls. They're so easily manipulated. Most of them are in mortgage brokerage or pharmaceutical sales. What the hell is that?"

"Yeah, I guess they have to be in some rando profession so they can take a leave of absence in order to move to Malibu, back stab each other, and find the man of their dreams. It's beyond bizarre and totally hilar-y."

"You have such a funny way of talking, Julia. All those abbreviations and shorthand. Very clever."

"Oh, thanks."

"You really speak your mind."

"I guess."

"So how's your job going?"

"Great. I love it."

"Good, good." Polly studied Julia closely. She really was like Silly Putty, just prime for molding. This would be easy.

"Listen, Julia, as you probably know, you're now playing with the big boys. And Lelly is great, such a super friend, and so pretty. But sometimes she hurls people into the ocean and it's like, sink or swim, and they have no lifeboat."

Julia nodded, unsure where the conversation was going.

"So, I want to help you swim, Julia. I will be your lifeguard. I will help you make it through those choppy waters," said Polly, touching Julia's arm to emphasize her point.

Polly felt a warm and cozy sensation envelop her when she realized how charitable she was being. Forget giving money to firemen or African orphans, *really helping people*, real people, was what it was all about. And Julia needed help. She was green, and left to her own devices, might not be able to handle the social strata she was about to be launched into.

"That's so sweet, Polly. Thanks."

"So if you need any help, when we're out and about, like where to get your bikini line lasered—don't let anyone tell you to get waxed at the J. Sisters, that is like, so 2001—or if you need to know what forks to use when we're at a fancy dinner party, just give me a holler."

"Thanks."

"So, where do you live?"

"I'm on Seventh Street, but you can just let me out anywhere it's convenient—"

Before she could finish, Polly interrupted her. "Driver, pull over on this corner." Polly turned back and looked at Julia. "I'll let you off here."

"Oh, okay." Julia looked around. They were in Nowheresville, on lower Fifth, not near any subway that could remotely take her to her destination. "Thanks so much for the ride."

"No prob. So listen, don't hesitate to ask for *anything*."

"Thank you so much."

Julia exited the car, and was left standing on the curb as the car lurched away.

After the whirlwind of her newly catapulted placement at Pelham's, as well as budding new "friendships" with the likes of Polly Mecox, Julia was more eager than ever to be with the girls whom she volunteered with. So on Saturday morning, she darted out of her apartment Mach ten and leapt on the subway to a place she could always be herself.

Once through the doors of Girls, Inc., Julia immediately felt warmth and friendship and zero competition. It had been one of her first priorities when she moved to New York to find a place where she could volunteer, preferably working with young underprivileged women. She had always volunteered back home and during college, and her parents had instilled a sense of civic duty in her starting at an early age. The Pearces were the type of family that spent Thanksgiving doling out food in soup kitchens, and Christmas gathering presents for the poor. Her parents had always been extremely active in promoting the rights and health care of migrant workers. In fact, Julia's mother, a registered nurse, volunteered her services three times a week at a Medical Mobile, which made the rounds to various wineries offering to treat workers for whatever ailments they had.

Julia had been referred to Girls, Inc., by a colleague of Lewis's, and at once felt that, not only could she be of use, but the girls who attended could also be helpful to her in keeping her sane in this crazy city. The programs were designed to help inner-city girls build self-esteem through a myriad of classes from arts and crafts and theater to computer science. Julia tried to go as often as she could, but work was sometimes an obstacle.

When she burst through the large red doors, Purva, her department head, greeted her with a hug.

"Hi honey," she said, giving Julia a big squeeze. "Josie and I missed you! I know you're working hard, though."

"Yeah, sorry I missed the other day," Julia replied with a nod.

Julia followed Purva into a classroom at the end of the hall, and the girls immediately greeted Julia with enthusiasm.

"How's your new job?" little nine-year-old Josie asked, plopping on Julia's lap, touching her ponytail.

"Crazy," Julia replied. "But being here balances everything out."

Julia helped the other teacher set up the arts-and-crafts tables, and then rolled up her sleeves to get started. As she gathered the girls for an hour of beading bracelets, she smiled, knowing this was a haven where the only games were board games and the only pawns being played were on the chessboard.

chapter 12

"Alice, don't break my heart. What will I do without you?"

"Oh, Mr. Banks," laughed Alice. "You'll survive."

"I don't know, Alice, I don't know," said Will, shaking his head. "You'll be very missed. Please send me a postcard."

"Yes, Mr. Banks," giggled the fifty-year-old waitress in a manner more befitting a twenty-year-old waitress. "I will."

"Promise?"

"I promise."

"Good, well have fun in Ireland. Give my love to the folks."

"Will do, sir."

Will smiled as he watched the heavyset woman lift her drink tray and walk into the kitchen. She was a doll. He loved all the Irish waitresses at the Badminton Club. They were such fun to tease. And Will knew that he was also one of their favorites. That was one of the things he had going for him: he was able to seduce anyone. He was a consummate flirt and everyone from serving staff to cabdrivers to CEOs of Fortune 500 companies to old ladies, even to his tough-as-nails mother-in-law, were unable to resist his charms.

Everyone, that is, except his beloved wife. She presented a constant challenge to him. When he first met her, he didn't realize what a tough nut to crack she would be. He thought he knew everything about her, hell, he had read enough about her, and he didn't even read *fashion* magazines. But when you see enough party pictures of someone, you think you know them. He had made assumptions. Well, he was wrong. In fact, every time he thought he knew Lell, she surprised him.

Will remembered the moment he first realized that Lell was a total enigma. They had been dating for five months, and he still felt like they were in that get-to-know-you phase, even though they were together practically every night. He'd never experienced that with women, usually by date number two they were picking out china patterns and doing everything possible to sink their claws into him (which only made him run faster for the hills). But with Lell it was different. She was always so distant that he couldn't discern if she was interested in him at all.

But on this particular night, they had been at the Central Park Zoo dinner-dance, seated among the monkeys, when Lell made an offhand remark to Polly about how thrilled her mother would be when she and Will married. He was floored. It was the first time Lell had expressed any sort of desire about their future. In fact, it was the first time she had let him know her desires beyond what restaurant to book for dinner or which charity event she hoped to go to on Saturday night. And it was not out of character that the way she informed him of her feelings for him—that she wanted to *marry* him—was by allowing him to overhear her tell someone else. That was his problem with Lell; everything felt thirdhand. And even once he had her, she was still the girl he couldn't get. It was frustrating, but also deeply intriguing. It was the first time that anyone had made him work for not only their approval, but their love. It had always been so easy, and with Lell it was not. And that excited Will.

At least it excited him at the time. But now that they had been together for several years, and had gotten married, for God's sakes, he thought it would get easier. But it hadn't, and in fact, it was beginning to frustrate him to no end that his wife didn't seem happy with him. What's more, she seemed to have developed a bitchy air of superiority that was driving him crazy.

"Hey, there, Mr. Banks, what was the score?" asked Henny, plopping down on the chair across from Will.

"I killed him."

"No shit?"

"He was toast. It was pathetic. I told you I've been practicing."

"I'm impressed," said Henny, grabbing a large scoop of mixed nuts and cramming them all into his mouth. "Alice!"

Alice turned around with a smile, but her face darkened when she saw Henny. "Yes, Mr. Mecox."

"Get me a whisky sour. What do you want, Banks?"

"I'm all set. Thanks, Alice."

It was clear from Alice's demeanor that she much preferred Mr. Banks to Mr. Mecox.

"Hey, did you get the Ferrari?" asked Henny, loosening his tie.

"Yeah. I ordered it. Should be here in two months." It was a wedding gift from Lell. Will had hinted how much he liked Ferraris when they were visiting the Della Marco's estate in Capri, and Lell got the hint.

"You dog, you!" hissed Henny.

"Dude, I need nice wheels." No more two-year-old BMW for Will. Thank God his wife and her father were as status conscious as he was.

"So, listen, is your ball and chain dragging you to the Frick tonight? 'Cause if I have to step foot in one more fucking museum for one more fucking snooze-ass benefit, I'm going to freak out," said Henny, cramming more nuts into his mouth with his fleshy hands.

Will watched Henny with disdain. Henny's face was flushed and bloated, and his blue eyes looked watery from all of the alcohol he had consumed in his life. His reddish-blond hair was receding, and his stomach was bulging. He had that look that suggested he could be thirty-five or forty-five, and he was not even thirty-three. Will was proud of his own lean and muscular physique. Just a few sessions a week at the Badminton Club hitting the ball around, and he was bathing suit ready. He was like a girl that way. Always watching his figure.

"We're going tonight," sighed Will.

"Sucks. And Polly is in such a pissy mood these days. Totally on the rag or something. I'm so sick of her nagging shit."

"That sucks."

"You're still in the honeymoon period, you lucky dog. Still getting laid, still wanting to spend time with your wife. She's having fucking parties for you. Me, I can't wait to get out of the house."

"What about your kid? Aren't you psyched to hang with him?"

"Quint? He's a baby. Fast-forward me to when I can get

the kid with a baseball in his hand and we can relate. I don't do diapers."

"Harsh."

"Come on, don't tell me you're going to be changing shitty diapers. I can't even see Lell changing them. Hell, I can't even see your wife pregnant. She'll probably have someone do it for her."

"Hey, watch it."

"Kidding, dude!"

Alice came and placed a drink in front of Henny. He immediately took a swig, and when she started to walk away he grabbed her arm. "Another one," he ordered.

"Take it easy, dude," warned Will.

"No thanks. It's the only way I can get through this life," said Henny, sitting as far back in his chair as it would go.

Will hoped his life wouldn't come to that. It seemed so depressing. But it couldn't, he was nothing like Henny. Henny was a big, fat, overgrown frat boy, whose wife had him by the balls. That was not Will. That would *never* be Will.

chapter 13

The waitress at Jackson Hole smiled patiently as Gavin recited his order. "Umm . . . French fries."

"Right, sweetie, we got that already," prompted Hope. "How about something a little more nutritional?"

"Um, a milk shake?" asked Gavin.

"We'll just get an order of chicken fingers for them, with the fries, and I'll have a tuna salad, please."

"And a milk shake!" reminded Gavin.

"And a vanilla milk shake," added Hope, smiling.

"No prob," said the waitress, sauntering to the counter.

Gavin and Chip were dressed adorably in matching blue Ralph Lauren cable knit sweaters, and little Gap cords. Hope was always so proud when she was out with her boys. She knew she was biased, but people had confirmed that they were just deliciously adorable. She couldn't argue with that.

"So how was school, bunny rabbit?" asked Hope.

"Good," said Gavin. He was busy trying to drink water from two straws she'd cobbled together for him.

"Me, too, Mama," said Chip, who handed his mother two straws. These days he wanted to do everything to emulate his big brother.

Hope took two straws and hooked them together and handed them to her son. As her sons slurped their drinks, the voice of two girls next to her caught her attention.

"Oh my God, Orlando Bloom is *so not* cute. He's like a dog. His body is just so skinny and he has no muscles."

"No way! He's so hot."

"Brad Pitt like blows him out of the water."

"Gross. Brad Pitt is like my dad's age."

"So what? He is the most gorgeous man on the planet. Ask anyone!"

Hope turned to the girls and smiled. "I agree," she said.

The girls, who were both probably around fifteen, looked at Hope blankly.

"Sorry, I couldn't help but overhear. I think Brad is definitely the sexiest man alive."

The girls exchanged looks and then mumbled, "Yeah," before turning back to their food.

And suddenly it was as if a ton of bricks hit Hope in the face. Oh my God, she thought. *I am old.* Here she was, listening to these girls, totally relating to them and their conversation, totally hip to the whole Orlando versus Brad debate, and yet these teenagers saw her as a mother, some uncool adult, someone they might address as "ma'am." It made her so sad.

How could she not see the warning signs? Lately, every time she picked up *Us* magazine there was more and more focus on stars like Lindsay Lohan and Hilary Duff—seventeen-year-olds, for Lord's sake! She was getting a little old for reading trash like that. And come to think of it, she hadn't been carded in years, even when she wore her hair in a ponytail. When was the last time she went to a nightclub? Literally, not in this century. Pathetic.

Hope looked at her boys, and although she loved them dearly, she realized that life had become their story now, not hers. Now she was the supporting player. She knew who she would marry; she knew what her wedding dress looked like; she knew what sex her children would be; she knew where she would work. All of the questions that she wondered about when she was a teenager had been answered. Although she was only twenty-eight, that was it. Nothing exciting was going to happen. She loved and adored Charlie, but she'd never experience falling in love again. She'd just get older and crinklier and wrinklier and less and less attractive. It was so unfair that men aged well and only got more desirable as they got older.

Hope glanced at the girls next to her. They were still in their school uniforms, although they'd rolled up the skirts as far as the school would allow, and they had accessorized their white shirts with jewelry and scarves so they could have some identity. They were casually munching on onion rings—of course they didn't worry about weight yet. Ah, the arrogance of youth. They didn't realize how lucky they were. She remembered her dad always said to her, "You don't realize." And now she knew what he was talking about.

I wish I could have one more turn, thought Hope. She didn't know quite at what—to feel young again, to feel attractive again, to be surprised again. Just one more chance to not think about all the stupid stuff—like where to order takeout from or who to seat next to whom at a dinner party or will the boys get into a good after-school program—but one more chance to think of something that didn't matter. One more chance to be reckless. Without consequences, preferably. But that would never happen, sighed Hope. She was used goods.

chapter 14

Dearest Penny and Brooks,

Henny and I had such a lovely time at your dinner party last Wednesday that it was absolutely worth missing the second to last episode of The

Bachelorette *(thank God for TiVo, right?). Your apartment couldn't be more charming and I really admire the way you've done up the place. How clever to have those nesting tables! They really do make the space feel so much bigger. And you totally compensate well for the fact that you don't have a separate dining room. The Chinese screen is a nice touch, and you would never notice the scratch. It is so nice to have friends with good taste, and to be able to go to those friends with good taste's homes and digest their wonderful choice of decor. We simply must see you soon, and we are so thrilled you are joining us at our table for the EAT (Erase Acne Today) Benefit. It is such an important cause for us, especially since Henny's youngest sister Dorothy has been battling this gruesome affliction for years. (Cystic.) Thank you again.*

    Fondly, Polly

As the Mecoxes exited their building into the brisk March evening air to the comfort of their heated town car, Polly handed her doorman the thank-you note to her former college roommate, written out in practiced cursive on her ivory monogrammed Mrs. John L. Strong stationery. By the time the car lurched from the curb, en route to Doubles for Will Banks's birthday fête, the doorman had snapped shut the mail slot and the note was nestled deep down in the bowels of the brass postal box, awaiting an early-morning pickup.

From the sheer opulence and extravagance of the party that Lell was hosting for her new husband, one would never know that her family had recently spent several million dollars on a wedding. Marcus Harrington, the party planner of the moment, had been enlisted to "work his magic" and was given carte blanche to make the affair memorable. Lell had dismissed several suggestions of having the party be Moroccan-themed or forcing guests to wear costumes, complaining that costumes were so passé, much more to be expected from the older society gang—Rosemary Peniston and Olivia Weston's set. Those gals had had their moment, and now the younger generation was movin' on in for the flashbulbs. With that in mind, Lell was determined to create a night that was beyond compare. Having just returned from an exotic land on her honeymoon, Lell immediately concurred with Marcus's idea to go tribal.

As guests walked into the ballroom, they made their way through two long rows of twenty of the most chiseled, handsome, and fantastically fit African-American male models (booked from the top agencies in New York) dressed in loin cloths. All of the men were holding long flaming torches, and stood stoically, staring straight ahead, their dark skin glistening with oil. African music thundered overhead, and the beat of the drums coupled with the models' gigantic shadows dancing on the walls against the flickering candlelight was both impressive and frightening.

As soon as the Mecoxes made their way through the gleaming bodies, and hacked their way past the hundreds of palm trees and other foliage that had been flown in from Senegal for the evening, Henny headed to the bar to pick up a coconut drink. Polly scanned the crowd for her friends. It was hard to see where anyone was through the thick bush. After pushing her way past the limbo stick, she at once zeroed in on Julia Pearce, who was reaching for a canapé and chatting with the waiter. Polly studied her from head to toe. Although obviously solo, she seemed totally at ease. She was wearing a beautiful lacey pearl dress that only she could pull off, with a dramatic ruby necklace, probably on loan from Pelham's. Polly made her way over.

"Are you alone?"

"Yes, my friend Douglas couldn't make it. It's his four-year anniversary with his boyfriend, Lewis."

"Then we'll be Velcro tonight. Henny is going to station himself at that tropical drink bar for the next three hours and I have no patience for that. Let's do the rounds."

Polly linked arms with Julia and guided her around the room. She was like a peacock preening before the crowds, showing off her beautiful feathers.

"Wow, what the hell is Meredith thinking in that outfit? She looks ten months pregnant," sneered Polly, turning her abruptly away from a girl Julia recognized as one of Lell's bridesmaids.

Julia thought it wise not to comment.

"What do you think about these male models?" asked Polly.

"It's a little—startling." Julia knew she had to be diplomatic, as it was her boss's party, but she was actually repulsed. It was beyond racist and she was sickened by the objectification of all these men. This was money put to the most bizarre use she had ever seen. She was a bit surprised that all the guests were white (with the exception of two Asian couples who were later pointed out as belonging to "big Hong Kong families") and those male models were just standing there watching everything. She shuddered.

Polly didn't even pick up on the weirdness. "Well I just hope that they used extra virgin olive oil on their skin. Because there will be some ladies licking it off by the end of the evening."

What era are we in? thought Julia. She glanced back at the models, who were literally doing a better job at standing still and averting their eyes than the guards at Buckingham Palace. "How did Lell conceive of the idea?"

"It was Marcus. He booked every black male model in the city. The top guys are all here. So chic."

"Who's Marcus?"

"Marcus Harrington? He's the party planner, you know, all the biggest events in the world. He's from Norway. He won't talk to you for like less than half a mill. I think he's dated like half of these models."

"Wow."

"Oh, there's the birthday boy!" said Polly, steering Julia toward Will.

Julia recognized him, too. He was very handsome, like a movie star, and he clearly knew it. She watched how he tilted his head back when he laughed at something his friend said, flashing his perfect white teeth. He was all ease and effortlessness, and totally relaxed in his role as man of the hour. In fact, Julia would bet that he liked to be the center of attention.

"Happy Birthday, Willoughby!" shouted Polly, leaning in to kiss him.

"Thanks, Poll," said Will, returning the kiss. He then

turned to look at the woman accompanying Polly and couldn't believe his eyes. It was the girl from the wedding, the one standing in the corner who had fixed Lell's dress.

"Will, have you met your wife's deputy–slash–new best friend yet?" Polly asked, then added, "*Muse* is probably a better word."

Will stared straight at Julia. She was gorgeous, with buttery blond hair and crystal blue eyes. He was riveted. "No, I haven't," he barely managed, and stuck out his hand to shake hers. "Willoughby Banks."

Although Julia wanted to remain cool, she blushed when she reached for his hand. "Julia Pearce."

Just as Julia and Will were clasping each other's hands, a waiter carrying a large tray tripped and knocked into Julia, pushing her straight into Will. Luckily, the very reflexes that made Will an ace on the squash court assisted him here, so he was able to adeptly catch Julia in his arms and break her fall without so much as disturbing her dress or coif.

After the waiter profusely apologized, Will kept Julia in his arms a little longer.

"That waiter should watch himself!" snapped Polly.

"Are you okay?" asked Will, concerned.

"Totally," said Julia, straightening up. "Just a little embarrassed." Mortified, more like it. She smoothed her gown and pushed a piece of loose hair behind her ear.

"Don't be. I adore catching damsels in distress."

"Oh, well, um, I don't adore being a damsel in distress. But thank you. You saved me from splattering all over the dance floor. And with this jungle theme going on, it might have been hours before they found me in the bush."

Will laughed. "Don't worry. I'd notice if you went missing."

"Oh, thanks," said Julia, smiling at Will.

And although it was just a flash—a flicker really, Polly
saw it too. Something in Will and Julia's eyes betrayed them.
Something you can't fight. Chemistry.

"Well, Will, you'll be seeing a lot of Julia from now
on. We simply can't get enough of her," said Polly, egging
them on.

"Really? That's great," said Will.

"She's the next big thing, already has millions of suitors
lining up."

Despite being a married man, Will felt a pang of jealousy,
and, almost, competitiveness. Who was this girl? How come
I didn't know about her earlier?

"Oh, please," said Julia, embarrassed.

"It's true. Tongues hang when you pass. I mean, hellooo
saliva carpet? Don't you agree, Will?" asked Polly. She knew
Willoughby Banks well, and one thing she knew was that you
can't teach an old dog new tricks; he loved the ladies. Even
when he was supposedly with someone, his head always
turned for any beauty waltzing by. Until one day that looker
was Lell and then gal-pal went the way of the woolly mam-
moth.

"If Polly says it's true, then it's true," he said, his eyes subtly studying Julia's body.

Julia didn't know how to respond. It was weird, but she
was fully in the middle of an accidental flirt-fest with her
boss's husband.

Susan and Dennis Wong approached and pulled a reluctant Will away for salutations. Polly and Julia stood in silence for a moment. Polly could tell that Julia had that flushed look that a girl gets when she's been making out in the backseat of a car with a guy sporting two-day-old Don Johnson growth. Red and prickly, and guilty. Somehow guilty. Polly watched with glee as Will, now with his back to them, concentrated hard on what the Wongs were saying. But she could already tell that he was mentally curled up naked with Julia. How delicious! Miss Perfect Lell's husband, not two weeks off his honeymoon, already has the hots for someone else. Here was the winter scandal that Polly had been looking for.

chapter 15

"Shut up. No. You lie."

Lewis and Douglas were agog.

"She booked every black model in New York City from Ford to be her torchières? I am gagging." Douglas was horrified. "That is vile."

"What possessed her to do such a thing? I always think of Lell Pelham as the pinnacle of taste," added Lewis, confused. "I mean, she's on the *Vanity Fair* best-dressed list again."

"Oh please. She's an heiress! She can afford to dress impeccably. Plus, she borrows. The blackamoors must have been a Marcus Harrington lightbulb," said Douglas.

"They were," confirmed Julia in her boss's defense. "He

was friends with some of them, which makes it even weirder. Anyway, you guys, I have to go, late for work!" Julia gathered her coat as the guys wrapped up breakfast.

"Yeah, the chick's been getting to work at like seven-thirty these days!"

"Well I have a big day—lunch avec the *New York Times*—I have to get prepared."

"Go girl, have fun," said Lewis, kissing her forehead.

"See you later, cutie," added Douglas as she closed the door.

She was running through the details of Lell's party over and over in her head. She had never seen anything like it. But besides all the opulence, there was something nagging at her. Something that excited her. And against everything in her bones, she knew what it was. There had been weird energy she experienced with Will. She couldn't deny it, and she could tell Polly sensed it as well. And she was totally flattered, against her better judgment. It was probably the absence of someone else alluring. But his gaze throughout the course of the night—a sideways glance during dinner, or the way he seemed constantly aware of her coordinates on the dance floor, or the way he said good night with a look that lingered a nanosecond too long—penetrated her.

She felt herself walking faster and faster down the street. Having a flirtation in one's life adds a spring to the step, even if it's a forbidden fruit you know you'll never sample. The jolt of a stolen smile, the flickering buzz that makes you feel like a woman. Not in the cheesy Shania Twain way, but in the fierce, sexy, pheromones-blazing way. Julia would never go for another gal's husband. Ever. She was way too morally centered and detested predatory girls who pounced on taken guys—there were enough dudes to go around after all, and she could never stomach being a home wrecker. Plus, she was smart and knew damn well that what goes around comes around—if they are capable of flirting with you, then they'd do it with someone else later when you're the one holding their hand. But she decided to allow her head to go wild just for this morning. That's all, and then she'd forget it, she promised herself.

On her subway ride she remembered how Doug said some guys make more money in two minutes at the altar than in fifty years at the office—could Will really have married for the money? Maybe the limelight? Who knew?

His bride, Lell, was at the office when Julia arrived, and the two gathered the new collection for Cathy Horyn, who was coming to scope out the new goods for a profile on the jewelry house. This time, Julia took Lell at her word, and decided not to be a meek cow.

"What do you think of this bracelet?" asked Lell.

"Something my grandmother would wear," said Julia.

Lell paused, shocked at first. Julia could tell Lell had liked it and feared that it was based on her designs. But what could she do? Lell told her to give her opinions. Had she gone to far? Finally Lell broke the ice.

"You're right. It is a little grandmotherish."

"No offense."

"None taken. It's business. What about this one?"

"Rockin' robin. Seriously cool and totally perfect for lunch at La Goulue or Chateau Marmont."

"Good."

They worked their way through the entire collection with Julia giving her opinions and Lell discarding her rejects. Julia had never had more fun at work.

At noon, the veteran reporter entered and Julia and Lell walked her through the pieces. Following Lell's lead, Julia explained in expert detail why the chosen pieces were important and how successful they would be, and she saw that both Lell and Cathy were impressed.

At lunch at the Four Seasons afterward, Julia excused herself to hit the ladies' room.

"She's adorable," said Ms. Horyn. "Is she new?"

"Yes. She's terrific. We're quite pleased."

"Now, Pearce, is that . . . the one and only glassblowers in Vermont?"

"The heiress, yes. And she's so natural about it. Never brings it up."

"Hmmm . . . where has she been hiding?"

"Downtown. Oh, here she comes!"

"Hey, Julia, do you want to come play bridge with Nina Griscom tonight?" asked Lell. "We're doing a last-minute thing. I'm thinking we should start a club."

"Oh, um . . . well I actually volunteer today. After work, of course, just at this after-school program."

"Oh my God, you're amazing!" said Cathy.

"Really," said Lell, who then remained silent. Julia was unsure if the really was a bad or good really.

Just then, the check was delivered and Lell slapped down the corporate platinum card without even looking at the grand total.

When the girls returned to Pelham's, Lell's window-facing desk chair had a familiar mop of brown hair atop the back.

"There you are," said Willoughby, who saw the pair approaching in the mirror. "I decided to drop by."

His gaze struck Julia, who chose to look away rather than wither. Willoughby looked at Lell with a big smile, then subtly scoped Julia out of the corner of his eye. "Hey, Julia."

"Hi," said Julia, shyly.

"Oh, sweetie, hi. What a treat," Lell said, sounding only half psyched for the midday rendezvous.

"Hey, babe. I decided to stop by 'cause I just had lunch with Binny Jones and he gave me the info on the ski château in Gstaad. I want to get on that, babe, before it's all booked up."

"Right. I forgot you wanted to go skiing."

"The whole gang's going. But Binny said the house he rented was the best and we better act fast."

"I can't do it right now," said Lell with irritation. Her face looked tight and annoyed, but as soon as she remembered Julia was standing right next to her she changed her tone. "But darling, later. Right now I'm heading back out, I'm swamped."

"Oh, I didn't realize—"

"I have a fitting for Balmain couture this afternoon. I absolutely need something to wear for the FAF event next week—"

"Which one's that again?" he looked at Julia with a bold smile. "I can't keep all these things straight."

"Fight Anal Fissures."

"Right—"

Julia broke a smile, shared with Will, while Lell, dead serious, wore on. "Mr. de la Renta is on his way to the Lowell so I really should go right now. Julia can hang out with you—"

With that, Lell gathered her things and walked to the door.

"Oh, and Will, I invited Julia to Polly's in Southampton."

"We're going to Polly's?"

"Yes, in two weeks."

"What for?"

"To gather, regroup."

"Right. Our *Big Chill* get-together."

"Minus the dead body," said Julia with a grin.

"Yeah, let's hope," added Will.

Lell didn't get it. "See you later." Lell disappeared in a flurry of shahtoosh and tweed, and left in the debris of her glorious exit was her husband. And the woman he could not stop thinking about.

"Should be a fun weekend," Will said, breaking the silence.

"Yeah, I'm so psyched to be included. Thank you so much."

"Me? Naw, it's the Mecoxes' place. Lell and Poll have been doing it for years. It's pretty mellow and cozy this time of year."

"Oh, right. Must be nice." Julia wasn't exactly a Long Island fan, but when the boss asks . . .

"I can't stand the Hamptons myself. I prefer the city. I get a little—"

"Stir crazy?" Julia ventured.

"You know the feeling?" he said, unseaming her with his now openly penetrating gaze.

"When you grow up on a vineyard surrounded by miles of grapes, you definitely get the twitch." Just thinking back on the endless afternoons of being housebound made her shudder. From her first trip to New York at age ten, she remembered looking out the rear window of the cab, watching the dizzying collage of lights and people and glass buildings. And now that she lived in the pulsing heart of the action, there was no going back—even on the worst days, she preferred chaos to crickets. "That country mouse thing was so yawn. I guess I'm a city rat now," she laughed.

"Girl after my own heart. Lell digs the country—well, not the real country, as in, dirt on your boots, but the *country house* country. But I hate it. I need the motion and noise, I guess."

"It's weird, when I moved here, I couldn't sleep at first— the sirens, the voices from my walk-up, the haze of all the electricity . . ." she trailed off as he nodded.

"But now you can't live without it."

"Right! And when I go home—"

"The crickets keep you up."

"Yes."

"Noisy little fuckers. Worse than fire trucks."

"Yup."

Their shared stare filled the silence so that the air was thick with the wattage of their locked eyes.

Julia caught herself abruptly. What the hell was she doing? She could have kept paddling off into the water of his sloshing blue eyes, but she had to jump ship before the undertow caught her. It was time to get out before she was dragged out beyond her control. Fast.

"Well, I should be headed back to work, it was great seeing you."

Now frazzled, she gathered her things to go back to her office, but even as her face was down as she reached for her handbag, the slight but blooming blush on her cheeks did not elude Will. "See you," was all she could offer as she walked through the door.

Will turned back to the vista of Central Park spread out before him. His pulse quickened as he reexamined the trees and rooftops in front of him. The surge he felt after moments with Julia made the taxicabs look yellower. The oxidized roofs looked greener. And the fact that Julia Pearce would be with him for a whole weekend made his blood feel redder than ever.

chapter 16

It was a particularly packed lunch hour at the perpetually bustling La Goulue on Madison. Crossed legs with Jimmy Choo knee-high boots lined the sidewalk in outdoor chairs on the unusually warm winter day, as ladies inhaled the intermingled scents of Chanel and the exhaust from the M4 bus. The air was hot; the groundhog hadn't seen his shadow weeks earlier, and on this sun-kissed day it seemed spring had definitely sprung. Polly was the first one there, dabbing dew from her brow and anxiously looking at her Cartier watch wondering where everyone was. This was why she usually chose to be late; she detested waiting alone. Plus she had no magazine to whip out, no voice mails to listen to (the Verizon box was empty, she'd checked moments ago). She just had to sit alone and sip her water with lemon wedge. Polly had the kind of face, though pretty, that always looked like she had just sucked on a lemon wedge. Her sour stance scared many from the second they met her.

"So sorry I'm late, Poll!" Hope rushed over nervously, chucking her mom-ish giant bag that could fit two diaper sizes, A+D ointment, squeaky toys, and sippy cups, along with her sunglasses, keys, cell, and wallet. "I have been so crazed. Ugh, trying to get everything settled for the weekend. I just hate leaving the boys."

"Well you have to do it. Henny and I take vacations all the time. It's very important."

"I know, I know. It's just . . . I miss them so much! I almost feel like I can't have fun without them."

Polly didn't answer. Because she didn't know what that felt like. While she loved Quint, she didn't have the connection Hope had with her sons. There wasn't that pull.

"Ah, finally," Polly said, looking over her friend.

Lell, outfitted to perfection in a Michael Kors coffee-suede belted shirtdress, Malo cashmere cardigan, Louboutin heels, and custom-tinted $500 sunglasses from Robert Marc, sat down next to Hope. Behind her was Julia, who smiled to greet the girls and followed Lell in putting her handbag on the chair and sunglasses on her head.

"Hi, how are you guys?" Julia asked.

"Just grand," Polly answered, studying her.

"*Bonjour, Gustave. Une grande bouteille d'Evian et de Badoit, s'il vous plaît,*" Lell ordered in a perfect French accent.

"*Tout de suite, Mademoiselle Pelham.*"

Polly hated that her friend was constantly treated with kid gloves. Whenever they lunched together Polly noticed the extra dessert, compliments of the chef, or the well-dressed women who whispered and subtly pointed Lell out to one another. She was A list. Decorators, designers, PR flacks, everyone was practically falling over themselves to stop by and say hello, scope her threads, or even just catch a glimpse of her.

"So Julia," said Polly. "Lell tells me you volunteer uptown—*way* uptown—a couple days a week?"

"Oh, yeah. I work with girls, we do art projects, jewelry making—"

"Whoa," said Polly. "Could you *be* more perfect? What, are you home polishing your halo?"

Julia smiled uncomfortably. Was that a compliment? Or not?

"So," said Lell, looking at her gang, changing the subject. "How excited are we for the weekend? I can't wait."

"It's going to be a blast. Party central. Full-on posse weekend, sans Meredith, who I've kicked out of the posse. But everyone else is going out this weekend," announced Polly. "Everything's heating up for a really fun season."

Julia was super-psyched but slightly apprehensive. She looked over her fellow lunchers and then at her own duds. "What should I pack?"

"Julia," Lell carefully treaded, looking to Polly for support. She had been wanting to have this conversation with Julia for some time. While she admired Julia's unique style, sometimes she felt that it bordered on sloppy. There was a very fine line between grunge and edge. You can dress eclectic, as long as the eclectic means Marni instead of Prada.

"Now that you are a face of Pelham's, maybe there are certain things you might want to think about with regard to image . . ."

Gulp. "Okay, sure . . . I'd appreciate your advice. I know I'm not exactly the country club set."

Hope looked at her friends nervously as they rolled up their sleeves to jointly launch their makeover tactics.

"Okay," started Lell. "First of all, those flip-flops you wore to work the other day during the freak heat spell? You need a heel. Even just a kitten heel. Yours looked too . . . beach."

"So I should save them for this summer?"

"Well, no," said Lell. "I don't think they'd go over in Southampton."

"But I thought the Hamptons was the beach. You guys always say, We're going to the beach."

"We all call it the beach," said Polly, rolling her eyes, "but it's not really the beach."

Lell shot Polly a look, implying she'd take it over from here. "Julia," she said, as if talking to a four-year-old. "It is a beach. It's just not Venice Beach. We don't actually go running in the waves. Especially not in March. But even if it were July, we just basically walk Main Street, shop around, maybe drive to Southampton, go to the Club, have lunch, stuff like that. But people really do dress up."

"Okay. So no flip-flops. Do heels."

"Well, you can do flip-flops or flats, but maybe go for a Jack Rogers or a fun Manolo flat. Something cute and stylish. Sigerson Morrison. Kate Spade, you know," offered Polly.

"Another shoe thing," started Lell, taking a deep breath. "Those," she said, looking at Julia's chunky platform slides, "are maybe too clonky."

"These?" Julia looked down.

Polly studied the horrendous footwear. Like Steve Madden exploded. "Here's how I like to think of it. Women's feet should be dainty. Small. Feminine. Not like two cinder blocks strapped onto them! What's delicate about that?"

"Another thing, speaking of feet . . ." started Lell, looking at Polly. "It's about the anklet."

"You gotta lose the anklet. And the toe ring," Polly interjected. "I know it seems hip and stuff, but there is no room for toe rings. Our feet are not hands. They are feet. Don't try to fingerize them."

"Okay," Julia nodded, gulping her water. Sheesh.

"And the pedicure . . ." Lell ventured.

Julia studied the deep almost black shade of blood red that was visible through her stockings. "Too dark?"

"I know maybe Wicked is really downtown and vampy and all that, but it looks a little violent," Lell explained. "I'd go with Ballet Slippers or Like Linen only."

"I always get Mademoiselle," said Polly, sticking up a perfectly pummeled, scrubbed, polished foot. "Dark is too scary. We aren't goths."

"But Lell," Hope said, feeling horrible about this superficial assault on Julia, "you totally had red once. Red is fun. I get red."

Polly shot Hope a silencing look. Clearly she was trying to make Julia feel more comfortable, but she was interfering with their Eliza Doolittle intervention. "Hope, that was for a theme party, that's different," she chastised. "It was a Latin-Chic event, remember? The Red Hot in Rio ball for the Young Committee to Fight Rosacia."

"Even then, the darkest we'd go is maybe a cherry red," Lell told her with earnest eyes. "But only for two days and then you have to go get a change of polish. Back to Ballet Slippers."

Polly nodded in agreement. "The red can chip. There's nothing worse than that. You don't want to have that prostitute-in-San-Juan vibe."

"It's like what I was saying about some of your clothes," said Lell softly. "There are ways of looking edgy without looking dirty. Go with the groomed choices."

"Like with your hair," added Polly, as if giving a killer stock tip. "A bun should be always be sleek, not too thrown together and messy. Maybe use some Fekkai shea butter balm."

"Okay," said Julia, now looking at the menu to distract herself from the barrage of rules. Oooh, hamburger. Perfect.

"If you want to go messy and windswept," said Lell, "then you can go to Frédéric Fekkai to get it looking windswept and messy. It's just done with more precision. On purpose. You know, like I said, put together."

Gustave the waiter came with his pad and looked at Julia. Great. Finally chow time.

"Hi, um, I'll have the burger please, medium rare."

The girls all looked at each other. Shock. It was as if she had ordered a plate of fried maggots.

"I'll have the Salade Folle, please," said Polly with a smirk. "Dressing on the side."

The waiter looked at Lell. "Same," she said.

"Same," said Hope.

After the menus were collected the four sat in silence for a second. Oops. Did Julia get the wrong dish? They all clearly liked this salad. "So, is this salad like the specialty of the house or something? This must be one badass pile o' leaves!"

The girls looked down. "Julia," Polly started. "Why French fries and burgers always?"

"I . . . like them, I guess. I know, it's so bad, right?"

"Terrible for you," said Lell. "I always say, keep it clean and lean."

"See," said Polly, "it's like what we were saying about feet. Dainty. Elegant. Small shoes, small portions. Yes, you are thin now, but I am looking at you, not your DNA. I can't see your ancestors! Were they skinny? Scandinavian? Were they fish eaters? These things matter. Your genes are the forecast for your thighs. But because we can't see backward and see portraits of our forebearers, we must be careful. It's just not worth it. There's nothing worse than being fat."

"Except chipped red nail polish," said Julia.

Lell and Hope laughed. Polly flared her nostrils and looked at Julia. "No," she said coldly. "Fat is worse."

"Excuse me, sir," Julia said, stopping Gustave on his way back to the kitchen. "Make that four Salades Folles instead."

chapter 17

It was the painful, tragic blight of the MTV generation of quick editing, strobelike images, and a remote control that could power through a hundred channels in a single bound. It was tearing through homes—ravaging even in the upper crust of New York Society, breaking hearts and shattering dreams: Attention Deficit Disorder had to be stopped. Now.

The tearful, hopeful plea came from the chairman of FADD, Vaughn Tiverton, who interrupted the light conversation and clinking of sterling silverware on china plates to give his imploring speech on behalf of the cause. The bow-tied and dressed-to-the-nines glittering crowd stopped eating or fake-eating, an art mastered by those at Lell's table, who expertly pushed the food around, managing to eat only the decorative greens, somehow making the rest of the food magically end up on one side of the plate.

"Ugh, the speeches are the worst part about these things," said Polly, in a loud whisper to Julia.

Julia made a nice half smile–slash–grimace to acknowledge the comment, but she didn't want to speak while the chairman was talking. Polly paid no mind to the podium, continuing on as if she were in her own living room. "See that girl with that tacky body glitter? She's the worst. She's obsessed with us, such a climber. Her name's Pansy von Oppenslauffer. *Everyone* knows she added the 'von.' Pathetic."

Julia recognized her from the floor at Pelham's. She was very statuesque and always seemed incredibly sweet, even to a little nobody salesgirl like Julia.

"She thinks she's so great, but she lives in a postwar Trump horror show."

Hope overheard the comment and winced. What kind of bitchy things was Polly saying behind her back? Hope looked at Julia, who was bristling in a similar way. *If Polly could only see the dump Douglas and I share, sheesh.*

"Anyway," said Polly, looking at other women around the room. "She's not nearly as bad as Sommersby McClintock. She is such a raging self-promoter! Look at her scanning the room for Mary Hilliard to photograph her. She came out with that retarded coffee table book on designer tree houses in the Hamptons and now she thinks she's an author. She even got new stationery made at Mrs. John L. Strong with an engraved *quill* on it! I mean, *as if* she's William Shakespeare or something! What a joke. It's self-published! It's literally Shady Oak Press. Who are we kidding here?"

"Shhh," Lell said, across the table. "Poll, we can't hear."

Polly's blood froze. Then boiled. How dare Lell admonish her in front of everyone. What a goody-goody. Christ, she was only whispering!

Finally the speeches were wrapped up, with the delivery of the fantastic news that the evening had grossed a whopping $2.3 million.

Charlie always rolled his eyes at these grandiose numbers. "But what's the net? They never tell you the net," he said to Hope.

"It's still major, though," she answered, always the optimist.

"Yeah, but how much do the caterer and flowers cost? A shitload."

Julia imitated her tablemates' golf-claps as the band resumed playing. A beret-wearing Bill Cunningham snapped the floating gowns of women spinning on the floor of the Burden Mansion with their husbands. That was Lell's cue. Cameras flashed and she had to go get some of the action—that's what Daddy would want. Ahhh, work. It never ended. She had to go promote the company! With that, she took her husband's hand. But even as he rose from his seat, Will's eyes were locked on Julia, who was almost too gorgeous to behold without panting.

As all the other couples rose from their seats, Julia realized she would be left alone in their wake, with empty Champagne-flutes and full plates of food.

Hope caught sight of Julia not budging as Henny took Polly's hand and Lell took Will's. "Julia, do you want to come dance with us?" she asked.

"Oh, no, it's okay, you guys go."

"Are you sure?" asked Charlie. "We can all go—"

"No, no, you guys go ahead, I'm fine!"

As the couples hit the floor, Julia looked around the glistening ballroom. This was so incredible. It was more dazzling than the fanciest wedding she had ever attended—before Lell's, of course. The three-course meal, the twenty-piece orchestra, the lighting, the decor, the flowers, it was all so stunning she felt like it was a royal ball. And this was just any night of the week for them! What lives they led. How amazingly fairy tale–esque.

Just then, she saw tons of lights flicker as Lell stopped dancing to pose for the hordes of photographers that swarmed around her to snap her couture Balmain gown. The beading alone must have taken ten people a hundred hours. It fell to the floor in a wave of shimmering tulle, and her hair swept her bare shoulders in a perfectly coiffed, glossy mane. Very few people knew the facts of her nightly preparation, but Douglas had heard through a friend who worked at a hair and makeup artist agency, that she had Miami Papadam on retainer, and he'd come blow out her locks and apply makeup for $2,000 a night. All expensed to the company, of course, since she had to maintain "a look" for Pelham's sake. Douglas always dumped on the fact that she was spending like this, but now that Julia saw how much attention she got—as if an invisible red carpet was laid out just for her at each of these engagements—maybe she *did* need to look a certain way. Maybe there were always two sides to every story.

Meanwhile, amid the blinding flashbulbs, one thing was constant: the gaze of Willoughby Banks's eyes on Julia. She looked away from his piercing stare, then subtly back again to find his wide pupils still inhaling her. Then, never breaking his gaze, he walked over to her.

"Sorry you've been left here. Lell is occupied at the moment," Will said, glancing at his preening wife. "Shall we?"

Julia nervously took his hand and went out on the dance floor. They shared barely one measure of a waltz together when Lell came back, finished with her spontaneous photo shoot. "Oh, Will, you are too sweet to take care of Julia. Thanks, dear."

Patrick McMullan, who had been snapping Lell, had followed her to this mysterious, gorgeous creature. "And who have we here?" he asked.

"Patrick, this is Julia Pearce, our new special projects consultant at large for Pelham's Important Jewelry."

"You're a knockout, sweetie!" He started taking her picture. And one thing is for sure: flashbulbs beget flashbulbs. Within seconds, ten paparazzi were snapping away. Julia shyly smiled and looked to Lell for some kind of coaching. Her look said "this is so weird," but her stunning face and bod were born for it. Lell and her society cronies had the perfectly positioned pose they struck on these kinds of occasion—like young up-and-coming starlets trying to be glam divas at the Oscars—always trying to channel the old-school glamor-pusses of yesteryear. It was the one foot in front of the other with a hip twist, always accentuating the waist, and therefore bust, with a peek at the slim calf coming out. It was an art. One that was not too hard to master. Julia had seen Lell do it, and every actress at every movie premiere she'd read about in *Us Weekly*, so she gave it a try.

One foot out, twisting slightly. Flash.

"Give us a smile," Cuddy McGill said. "Right here!"

Flash.

"Who *is* that pretty young thing?" Joan Coddington whispered.

"It's the new head of something or other at Pelham's," said Wendy Marshall, watching her grow more comfortable in her stance before the lenses.

"Hmph. I'm sure Gene Pelham and his wandering hands are going to try and find their way up that skirt."

"You know it. She's really something. Could be a model." Flash.

By now, Julia was getting a little buzz. *Pictures?* She thought to herself. *Of me?* It was all too surreal.

Polly, who was dancing with Henny, was barely looking at her husband's stupid dance moves. In fact, he often embarrassed her so with his scotch-induced *Dance Fever* steps that she wanted to die. He flailed his limbs and looked like a mosquito getting electrocuted by a porch-hung zapper. *Well, well, well,* she thought, watching Julia get blinded by the cameras. *Lell's little slave may overtake the master.* Yes, Polly was jealous. From time to time she had her picture in *Quest* or *Avenue*, but never in the fashion pages of *Vogue* or *W*. And now that Lell's little protégé was out "representing Pelham's" just like Lell, she was in head-to-toe designer threads. Borrowed, naturally. She studied Lell's face for a reaction as she looked over her husband's shoulder mid-dance, just as Polly was doing with Henny. And there it was: the look of pride. Pride ever so slightly tinged with a hint of wanting to keep this newfound darling in check.

chapter 18

"Okay, sweetie, you are about to worship me for the rest of your life. I just stood on line for thirty solid minutes at Tower Records to get you this, and I know you'll freak," said Douglas, slamming the Yeah Yeah Yeahs latest CD on Julia's desk.

"Oh my God!" shrieked Julia. "You rock!" Julia grabbed the CD and started reading the liner notes.

"I am too good to you, I swear. You owe me big time!" boomed Douglas.

As Douglas continued rattling on in his loud, dramatic voice, Julia glanced out the door of her office. The secretaries in the hallway were giving her curious looks, and she realized that Douglas's voice was reverberating through the entire floor, which was usually as quiet as a library. Shit, she didn't want Lell to hear.

"Thank you so much," whispered Julia.

"No prob, sweetie. We have to get tickets for their—"

"Um, Douglas," interrupted Julia. "Could you keep it down?"

Douglas looked flummoxed. "What, did someone die?"

"No, it's just, um, people are working."

"Oh, okay," said Douglas. "Sorry. I'll come back, later."

"Um, maybe it's better if I come down to see you."

Douglas gave Julia a curious look. "Why?"

"I don't know, I just feel weird having visitors—"

"I hear you."

"Don't be offended, I just don't want to ruffle feaths."

"Got it," said Douglas, heading for the door. "I'm off like a prom dress."

"Catch you later. And thanks for the CD."

Just as Douglas reached the threshold of the door, Julia's buzzer rang. "Julia, could you come in here a second?" crackled Lell's voice over the speaker.

Shit. She hoped Lell hadn't heard Douglas. But knowing that Lell had those cameras everywhere, she probably had.

Lell was seated behind her immaculate glass desk, which held the most exquisite arrangement of calla lilies in a clear crystal vase. Everything was arranged perfectly, from her pencils to her silver accessories to her monogrammed notepads to Lell herself. Clad in a charcoal gray suit, a fitted blue-and-white striped oxford, a knotted Hermès scarf, and little tortoise-shell glasses perched on her nose, Lell was a posterboard for how a sophisticated modern woman should look. Julia immediately felt like a slob, even though she had ironed her blouse three times and had even shined her boots to a mirrorlike shine. She sighed and wondered if Lell's glasses were just for show.

"Hey, sit down," said Lell, motioning to a chair.

"What's up?" asked Julia.

"I was just wondering why I didn't see you at the Burberry party last night," asked Lell, taking off her glasses and putting them on the table.

"Oh my gosh, was I supposed to go?" asked Julia, worried.

"Well, you were invited, and it was a store opening."

"Oh, I didn't know, I just thought it was a store opening so—"

"Well, store openings are important. Paparazzi cover those things. We're trying to get our face out there, we want Pelham's representatives everywhere. The Tiffany people were there, the Swarovskis."

"Okay, I'll definitely go next time. I'm sorry, Lell. I just, well, since I'm going to the Hamptons—"

"Southampton."

"Southampton. Sorry. Since I'm going there this weekend, I knew I would miss time volunteering at Girls, Inc., so
I thought I'd make it up by doing an after-school class yesterday."

"Yes," said Lell, staring at Julia carefully. "This Girls,
Inc., seems to take up a lot of your time."

"I don't ever let it get in the way of work, though. I promise."

"Oh I know, but I just think, hmm . . ." said Lell, picking
up her silver letter opener and fondling the edge. "Maybe you
should rethink it for now. You're doing a lot of meaningful
charity work by going to these benefits. I don't want you to be
overcommitted. There are going to be projects that will require help and more benefits to go to. Sometimes I need a
fourth for bridge and poker, and I just want you to be available. Why don't you push back the Girls, Inc., for now?"

Julia gulped. This wasn't a request; this was a command.
She had no choice. "Um, okay—"

"Great," said Lell, smiling. "Now, I want you to help me
with something fun. *Vogue* just sent over a fax. They want me
to answer questions for their June summer vacation issue.
Here it is."

Lell handed Julia a sheet of paper and a pen.

"Oh, so I'll ask you and then write it down?"

"Yes," said Lell, giving her a quizzical look.

So she can't even write down her own answers? thought
Julia. Whatever.

"Okay, number one, what is your favorite travel destination?"

Lell leaned back in her chair and folded her hands. "I love going to our family's house in Jamaica, which we have owned since the seventies, before Jamaica became a popular travel destination. I have so many wonderful memories of the island. It's the only place where I can truly relax."

Julia scribbled as quickly as she could. Lell turned to her. "Oh, and you can just type it up when you're done, and you know, correct all the mistakes and put in any good vocabulary words that you think of. You're a good writer."

"Okay. So question two—"

"You can just ask them, you don't have to number them."

"Right. So, what do you bring on the plane with you?"

"I always bring my Hermès Birkin bag as a carry-on. Inside, I have my iPod with my favorite songs downloaded, my DVD player with the latest films—I get screener copies from my friends at the Academy. I have three giant bottles of Yucca water, which is from the Himalayas and is really the only water to drink, it's so chock full of vitamins. I bring my Evian spritzer, to spray my face because the plane is so dry, and also my Kiehl's lip balm and Crème de Mer, for the same reason. I apply the Crème de Mer religiously throughout the flight. I have cashmere slippers to keep my feet cozy and my shahtoosh to prevent chills. I always have the latest books and magazines, especially *Vogue*, because I never get a chance to read unless I am on vacation. I am simply too busy."

"Wow, that seems like a lot of stuff in one bag. How can you carry it?"

Lell gave Julia a look. "I don't."

"Oh, right. And uh, don't you have to go to the bathroom like a million times with all that water?"

"It's really important to keep hydrated, Julia. Water is soooo good for you. And I have no problem peeing out all those toxins."

"Well, airplane bathrooms are so gross, I try to avoid them."

"Julia, I don't fly commercially."

"Right. Good point."

"Next question?" said Lell, arching her eyebrow.

"Um, well, you sort of answered that one, what are you going to read on vacation?"

"No, I didn't."

"Oh, I thought, the magazines and latest books—"

"No. Call the director of publicity at Knopf, tell them to send over whatever will be the big summer books and tell them it's for me. Then put in the titles."

"Okay," said Julia. "What do you bring to hotels to make the room your own?"

"Well, I always travel with Diptyque candles. Red Currant is my favorite scent. I bring lots of scarves, which I put on all the lamps in order to make the lighting my own. I also bring some coffee table books to put around the room, as well as pictures of my husband and family—in Pelham's silver frames, which I put next to my bed."

Wow, thought Julia. She must travel with trunks.

"Who is your favorite travel companion?"

"My friend Maria de Barca," said Lell quickly. "We met

at camp, and when we were in college we took a Eurail through Europe—wait," said Lell, stopping herself.

"What?" asked Julia, looking up.

"How silly. I mean, obviously *Will* is my favorite travel companion. Scratch the Maria thing."

"Do you want to put both?"

"No, where was my head? I mean, the *best* vacations of my life were with my husband. We went to the fashion shows together in Paris and Milan, to visit the Greeces in London, Felipe's wedding in Madrid."

Julia squinted her eyes at Lell. "Any trips just the two of you?"

"Just the two of us? You mean, where we didn't see anyone we knew?"

"Yes."

"Well, our honeymoon. Is that a question?" asked Lell, defensively.

"Sorry, no. I was just wondering."

"I mean, we're alone together every night after we get home," said Lell, her voice trailing off. She was quiet for a second. "What's the next question?"

As Julia continued on, posing questions and furiously scribbling Lell's answers, she couldn't help but wonder about Lell and Will's marriage. He seemed like such an afterthought to Lell. Maybe it wasn't as rosy as she wanted everyone to think. Definitely interesting.

chapter 19

The slushy ice crunched under the wheels of the dark blue Mercedes as it turned the corner onto Dune Road. Although the heat was blasting in the car, the frigid winter air managed to penetrate inside and nestle deep down into the bones of the passengers. There had been a heat wave the whole week— until now, naturally. Julia leaned her head against the steamy window and glanced out at the perfectly manicured hedges and trees. Even stripped of their foliage, they managed to look stately and proud. As the car sped by all of the mansions, Julia half expected to hear Robin Leach over the sound system, giving an informative tour of one of the richest zip codes in the United States.

Julia had been to East Hampton for a party for one of Douglas's friend's and had even spent a very long August night at a summer share in Quogue once, but the houses in those hamlets were nothing compared to the grand, Gatsby-esque estates that lined the ocean in Southampton. One was bigger and fancier than the next, and Julia couldn't help but wonder what the hell she was doing there. She glanced at Lell, seated next to her, who had her eyes closed, and asked herself for the millionth time why Lell had taken such an interest in her. She had sensed some sort of rivalry between Polly and Lell. She had a feeling that she was some sort of chip on their board. But as Lell included her in more and more facets of her social and business lives, Julia found it harder than ever to believe that this was just a product of a seventh-grade class-mates' competition gone too far. Of course, Julia was thrilled with the new job—she felt she worked really well with celeb clients and her ideas for some promotional events had been very well received. But despite the fact that she was basically a constant presence at Lell's side, she realized that she knew very little about what made her tick. Was she so insecure that she needed Julia there as a professional best friend? Did she just hate to be alone? If that was the case, why did Lell barely talk to her when they were alone? She was so hard to read. Sometimes Julia felt Lell must be extremely smart, and that she had some clearly defined master plan that Julia couldn't even fathom. But there were other times, like when Lell was asked a pointed question by some top client and she would have little to offer, that Julia felt maybe Lell wasn't so sharp after all. Or maybe she was just playing a game. The jury was still out. But the fact was that for all the time they spent to-gether, they were not any closer than they had been the first day they met. There was still an air of formality between them that Julia felt would never dissipate.

Lell's husband was another story. Where Lell was distant and distracted, Will came on strong with all the magnetism turned up to eleven. Julia had been trying not to think of him since she last saw him, but knowing that she was about to spend the entire weekend with him at Polly and Henny's house made her excited. And she felt terrible about it. Being attracted to a married man was against everything she stood for. But she couldn't help it.

"On the left, Ivan," said Lell, opening her eyes and pointing to an enormous three-story shingled mansion. Her driver turned the car into the gravel driveway, past the giant flagpole that exhibited both the American flag and another that Julia assumed was the Mecox family crest.

Julia looked closely at the sign in front of the house, which read "Dune Cottage."

"Dune Cottage? Is that meant to be ironic?" Julia asked with a laugh. This was no cottage.

"It's one of the oldest houses out here that hasn't been totally eaten by the hurricanes. It started as a cottage, but then Henny's family just kept adding on to it."

"It's beautiful."

They walked into the celadon-colored front hall and a maid rushed forward to help them with their coats. Julia took in the place. The house was truly enormous. There were views of the Atlantic from every window. Julia had never been in anything like it in her life. This was like some Shangri–la she'd only read about in the glossy pages of *House & Garden*. But although the scale of the house was impressive, the decor was decidedly subdued. Julia found it disappointing. She expected something more grand. It seemed very lived in, and there was the faint smell of old dog and mildew. Before Julia could get her bearings, Polly came rushing down the sweeping staircase, tailed by her two King Charles spaniels.

"Hooray! I'm so glad you guys got here early," said Polly.

"Thank you so much for having me," said Julia, as she tried to fend off the yapping dogs that were nipping at her heels.

"Please! It's going to be fun. Guess who's coming?" said Polly, stopping and staring directly at Lell.

"Who?"

"Alastair Keach."

For someone who never betrayed her emotions, Julia finally saw Lell's face light up. She quickly recovered. "Really?" she said in a feigned disinterested voice. "How'd that come about?"

"Ran into him at Nello's last night. Don't tell me you're not psyched?"

"Why would I care?"

"You may be married, but you're not dead," said Polly, wagging her finger at Lell. She turned to Julia. "Alastair and Lell had a thing but then she met Will."

"Please, Polly, that was years and years ago. He's a total playboy who has a 'thing' with just about every woman in the world. Now which room am I in this weekend?" asked Lell, intent on switching the subject.

As Polly guided them upstairs, past citrus-colored room after room of sun-blanched chintz curtains, fading toile wallpaper, and rickety wicker furniture, Julia got more of an idea about how well-to-do Wasps spent their weekends. She followed Polly into a small corner room, which looked out on the stormy ocean slapping waves on the sand, and plopped down on the Laura Ashley comforter as soon as she was left alone. So Lell has a secret heartthrob. Things were getting interesting.

Julia didn't realize she had napped for so long until she sat up in bed and saw that it was now dark out. She threw on her sample sale–purchased Stella McCartney pants and a cashmere fitted sweater and made her way through the maze downstairs via a rickety servants' staircase.

She walked through the kitchen, where a maid and cook stood chopping vegetables and animatedly chatting in Spanish until they noticed her and froze. They exchanged nervous glances, then directed her to her right. Julia was mortified. She wanted to say, "Hey, I'm one of you! I'm hired help also!" but she feared that they wouldn't understand her and it would all be misconstrued. Instead, she turned into a darkened pantry and heard voices coming from a room down the hall, but before she could open the swinging door, which promised light on the other side, she felt a tap on her shoulder. She turned around and was face-to-face with Will, who, before she even registered recognition, had pulled her into an embrace and giant liplock. Stunned, Julia reciprocated for a second before pulling away.

"What are you doing?" she whispered.

Will smiled. "Oh, sorry, Julia, I thought you were my wife."

Julia stared at him, unsure of what to do. Holy shit, she'd just inadvertently kissed her boss's husband. Was he serious? Had he really mistaken her for Lell? It was dark in there. Whatever, this was bad, bad, bad. She was no home wrecker. But hell, he was a good kisser. With so many conflicting thoughts racing through her mind, she felt it best to take him at his word, or just pretend to. Even though they both knew he was lying.

"Okay, um, where is everybody?"

"In the library. I'm just getting more gin," said Will, leaning down and looking through the pantry cupboards.

Julia was paralyzed. Should she say something else? Before she could speak, she heard Polly's voice calling from the other room. "Will, where's the booze?"

"Let's go," said Will, holding a bottle in one hand and gently placing his other hand on the small of her back. He pushed open the door with his shoulder and led her through the breakfast room to the dining room, past the living room, into the library where all eyes settled on Julia and Will at once, the most daunting pair belonging to Lell.

Polly was seated under a tartan throw on the dimpled leather couch in front of the roaring fire. "Good, you finally made it down. Will, give Henny the booze pronto, I am dying for a drink. Julia, sit down. Do you know everyone? Probably not. You know Hope and Charlie, and this is Alastair."

Alastair, who had a thin pretty-boy face, and a smattering of blond hair that wouldn't see him to forty, was dressed in perfectly ironed chino pants and a Thomas Pink button-down. He rose and stuck out his hand.

"So nice to meet you, Julia," he said in a clipped British accent. So this is Lell's type, thought Julia. An Oxbridge fop.

"Nice to meet you."

"Oh, and that's Oscar," said Polly, motioning to the attractive dark-haired man sitting awkwardly on a bar stool. Julia walked over to shake his hand and realized that they had already met.

"I know you. You came into Pelham's to get your mother a birthday present."

In spite of himself, Oscar flushed. "Right, right. Nice to see you again."

"Well, did she like it?" asked Julia.

"Yes, thanks, yep." Oscar was once again flustered by Julia's beauty; he was instantly tongue-tied.

Julia realized that she wouldn't make more headway with Oscar, so she turned to her host. Henny stood behind the bar, mixing martinis.

"Shaken or stirred, darling?" Henny asked, feigning a British accent.

"Oh," groaned Polly. "Will you please stop that, Henny? Is that like your only joke?"

Henny laughed and continued mixing drinks. He always took on the role of bartender, no matter if it was his home or someone else's.

"When you're done, Henny, go tell Rosario that we need more cheese and crackers," ordered Polly.

After she got her drink, Julia went and sat down on in a plush checkered armchair. She looked around at the group. Polly was holding court with Lell and Alastair, waxing eloquent on the merits of Percy Sinclair, the child-care expert, whose work Polly had never read, but whose virtues she extolled nonetheless. She at least wanted to put on a front that she was somehow involved in little Quint's life, even though he had been tucked away in the nursery all day and had not even so much as laid eyes on his parents. Lell and Alastair were pretending to listen, but Julia could see the sparkle in their eyes as they glanced at each other. Whatever attraction had once been between them seemed easily rekindled now. Julia nervously glanced over at Will, who was sitting on a bench, his hands clasped and his body leaning forward as he chatted obliviously with Hope and Charlie. He had a way of talking to people that made them feel as if they were the only ones in the room. She

watched him laugh his confident laugh, and saw how his audi-
ence responded to his jokes, and felt almost proud—and a little territorial. *Stop it, Julia! He's not yours.* He was Lell's, but
there was something so exciting about being coveted by someone whom everyone liked and admired. Despite herself, Julia
had always gone for those guys who were center-of-attention
types. They were so magnetic and alluring, and also often the
eye of the storm. Just as Will finished up his conversation and
gave a small smile to Julia, an indication that he was on his way
over, Julia felt someone next to her.

"So how do you know these people?" said Oscar, plopping down on the ottoman.

Her plans for tête-à-tête with her secret flirt foiled, Julia
tried not to be cross with her unwitting foiler. "Oh, I work for
Lell, and she introduced me to everyone."

"Oh, right. Right."

He stared at Julia, as if unsure of what to say next.

"How do you know them?" she asked in response.

"Um, Henny's mom is my godmother. We're old family
friends. We call each other cousins, but we're not really re-
lated."

"That's neat. Did you grow up together?"

"Yeah, but more recently I lived in Northern California
for years."

"No way, I'm from California," said Julia, excited.

"Yes, you are," said Will, bursting into the conversation.
He came and sat on the arm of Julia's chair. "But you made
the right decision and moved east."

Oscar was annoyed. He'd met Will several times through
the years and he'd always seemed like such an idiot to him.

But, for some reason, the girls loved him. His act was so transparent to Oscar. He was such a player, and he just lucked out and hit his jackpot with Lell Pelham. He was sure she would one day regret it. Irritated by the interruption, Oscar got up abruptly and walked back over to the bar to get another drink. Will raised his eyebrows at Julia as if to say "What's with him?" and Julia smiled.

Polly finally had to get up herself and go check on the cheese and crackers (that fucking Rosario!) but not before surveying the room. She was thrilled. In one corner sat Lell and Alastair, talking about nothing important but sinking deeper and deeper into each other's eyes; it was just like old times. It helped that Polly had whispered to Alastair that Lell was miserable in her marriage. She wasn't sure that was true, but she had been miserable her first year of marriage, so why shouldn't Lell be? Alastair, the international womanizer, made a living out of defibrillating pretty young brides into hopeless romantics who harbored pulse-pounding crushes on him. Rich brides, that is, so he was more than game for the challenge. His trick: tapping into their fears that their marriages had flatlined their desirability to other men. And in another corner Julia and Will were chatting away. She had the vibe that Julia had Middle America morals. She might be tough to seduce, but Polly didn't doubt Will's metal-melding magnetism. This was fun, thought Polly. And after a few more drinks at dinner, who knew what would happen on this tempestuous night in the country?

chapter 20

Hope felt hopelessly adrift. After dinner, as most of the houseguests went to play Scrabble in the Mecoxes' parlor, Charlie excused himself, saying that he felt tired after a long week of work and adding that, aside from Oscar Curtis, he was probably the only one there who really busted his ass during the week. Hope understood but was disappointed. He was right, of course, but she wished he would stay up and hang out for at least a little while. He couldn't. With her husband tucked off to bed, her kids with their nanny in the city for the first time in ages, Hope found herself with the now double-edged luxury of something she so often desired: time alone. And silence.

In the city, there was always someone around her or something making noise: the whir of the fax machine spitting out papers for Charlie, the piercing ring of the phone that sounded not unlike an Amazonian endangered bird (she had to change that darn ring), or the squeak of one of her sons' toys she'd step on around the house. Yet here she was, feeling somehow unnerved with only the mollifying mix of crashing waves and flickering fire. What was her issue?

She decided to bundle up and hit the beach with her thoughts. She snuck out the back of the kitchen and hopped down the steps to watch the black beating ocean stir up its waves and cough them out onto the shore. She'd have a nice, quiet walk. Thank goodness she was among friends and could disappear, instead of at her bitchy sister-in-law's house on Lily Pond Lane where every second was scheduled, army-style. She always felt beholden to Charlie's sister Diana—who'd married a Rockenwagner—and meandered through their huge halls like she needed a visa to be there. They always lorded their wealth over Charlie, which added even more pressure than he already felt, and Hope hated being their "guest" and not feeling free.

Here at Polly and Henny's she was at least able to do what she wanted without straying from some fixed grid of events. Henny was sort of a schmuck, though. Hope couldn't put her finger on what it was about him that bothered her, but there was something assaholic about how he was quizzing Charlie about work at dinner. Like he was tabulating his salary or something. Sorry, we're not all trust-funded. Hope guiltily exhaled the mean thoughts, calming herself with the crashing waves. Her mind had been like a dry sandy tide, carrying her feet farther away until before she knew it, the mansion she'd strayed from was only an orange glow in the distance over her shoulder and she turned to make her way back.

Charlie sat up when Hope walked in. Though she'd tried to tiptoe, the energy she exuded was vibrant enough to ring louder than a siren for a five-alarm fire.

"What's going on?" he asked, alarmed.

"Holy moly," she said, crawling into bed in her sweats with her spouse. "Charlie, you're gonna die," she said in an urgent whisper.

"Why?" he said with curiosity. "Hope, you are freezing!" He ran his arms quickly over her to warm her up.

"Never mind that, I'm wigging out."

"What happened?"

"Okay. I just went on a walk," she relayed breathlessly.

"Alone?" asked Charlie, concerned.

"Yes, I didn't expect to go far, but then I just kept walking and walking."

"Isn't that dangerous?"

"Come on, we're in Southampton, for God's sake. Anyway, as I was walking back, I saw this pair, like in silhouette. Making out."

"Uh-oh," groaned Charlie.

"Wait. So I go 'Hey! Who is that?' and they quickly break the liplock."

Charlie put his head back on the pillow. "Okay, I can't wait to hear what happened next," he said, teasing.

"And so I walk up until the tiny sliver of moonlight makes them visible and it was Lell and Alastair!"

"No way," said Charlie with disbelief.

"I swear. It was Lell and Alastair."

"What a slut. She's married, for chrissakes."

"She always had a thing for Alastair."

"Really? I don't see them together at all."

"What are you talking about? They used to hook up on and off for years, and every time she had a breakup, they'd reunite."

"But she didn't have a breakup, she got married. Are you sure they were making out?"

"Full-on tonsil hockey."

"But it was dark."

"I know what I saw."

"Wow," said Charlie, rubbing his eyes.

"They played mellow when they saw me, but I clearly interrupted something. And then I said hi, and, just isn't the ocean pretty, blah blah blah, and we walked back. It was so awkward."

"Where was Will?"

"I don't know. They said everyone else was still playing Scrabble."

"Is Lell crazy? Why the hell would she cheat on Will?" asked Charlie. He never really held Lell in high regard.

"Lell is just weird that way. I don't know . . . but I always had sort of the suspicion that she was never really that *into* Will. Everyone just sort of said, 'Oh this is the right guy for you' and she went for it."

"But Will is a great guy."

"He is, but he isn't her type. He's nothing like all of her previous boyfriends. She always went for those skinny blond types who look like they've been shooting heroin."

"Then why the hell did she marry him?"

"I think she felt she had no choice. Once her mother met him, he was the anointed one. There was no backing out."

"That's stupid. But whatever, I'm exhausted, the last thing I care about is what's going on between Lell and her lovers. Let's go to bed."

"I can't believe you can go to bed when you just heard what I told you! I'm freaking!"

"Then please do an internal freak," said Charlie, fluffing up his pillow. "I'm beat."

Charlie put his head back down and closed his eyes. He wasn't really into gossip. Hope got undressed and ready for bed. She couldn't believe Lell would have the guts to be cheating on her brand-spanking-new husband so flagrantly. He was a hundred feet away! But that was something that always struck her about Lell, she had sort of a sense of entitlement, as if she was saying to everyone, 'Why shouldn't I have my fun? I deserve it.' The rules somehow didn't apply to her. If Lell wasn't happy with Will, Lell was the type to do what she had to do to make herself happy. She'd been raised that way. She was more than a little spoiled. And she also got bored easily, which was never a good combination.

Hope pulled up the comforter and got in bed next to Charlie, who had already fallen back to sleep. She could never cheat, no matter what. That just wasn't in her mind-set. Although, that said, one side of her was secretly jealous of Lell. Lell was the type who would marry and divorce and have affairs and make it all look so glamorous like Pamela Harriman or Slim Keith. People would write biographies about her and her jet-setty life, anecdotally recalling the men she discarded along the way—dashing Europeans with well-cut suits and cigarettes hanging out of their mouths—and it would all seem so harmless and chic. She was such an icon in the making that the path of destruction that she left in her wake wouldn't resonate.

Hope thought about what it would be like if *she* were to cheat. Pathetic. She was hardly old, but somehow having two kids made her feel over the hill. She turned to look at Charlie, who had his back to her. Thank God for him. He was such a cutie. She turned and cuddled him, pulling her knees up and tucking them into his. She drifted off into a quiet slumber.

The other Scrabblers were wrapping up a heated game, rife with tension and placements of *blithe* (Julia, 14 points), *zenith* (Oscar, triple word score, 48 points), and *whore* (Henny, 12 points). Will was draped Adonis-style, feet up, on the nearby couch, reading the *Financial Times*, staring at Julia's letters. He gazed at her unabashedly, but she shook off his glance, ensconcing herself in the spelling tasks at hand.

Will faux-read the stocks, but the tiny numbers blurred and danced on the peach paper as he thought of the girl on the floor. As she casually twisted a piece of hair in her fingers deciding what word to make, Will looked at her leg then looked back at his paper, and the Dow Jones wasn't the only thing that was rising. He wondered what everyone would do if he suddenly got up, hurled the game board across the room, alphabet flying, and made love to Julia right there on the coffee table.

Across the board, Oscar Curtis watched the way Julia bit her lower lip while she was trying to craft her next turn. It was adorable beyond measure. He liked Julia. A lot. At first he had been intimidated by her beauty, but took solace in the fact that he could dismiss her as being as frivolous and superficial as Lell and Polly. He knew the gang she ran with, those bitchy gaggles of pretty, primped girls who just want to appear in party pictures and run with the jet set. But throughout the course of the evening his opinion had changed. He had to admit to himself that his criticism of Julia was unfounded. Everything about her actually seemed uncrafted and genuine, especially compared to the rest of this crowd, which he found so artificial. He was impressed with her knowledge of current events at dinner, and the way she unabashedly shared her opinions on politics. She definitely held her own, and she didn't seem so bogged down by all the girly stuff. But what was she doing hanging with Lell and Polly? She seemed so above them. She was in danger of being corrupted. He felt protective of her, like he wanted to take her away to a safe place. He wondered what everyone would do if he suddenly spelled out *I love you Julia* across the whole Scrabble board.

Polly wondered where in Satan's holy house of hell Lell and Alastair had gone; that was an awfully long trip to the cellar for more Niebaum-Coppola Rubicon.

In a heated turn where Henny was practically bursting blood vessels coming up with his word (which turned out to be *young*), Julia let out a sneeze, interrupting the silence.

"Bless you!" shouted Oscar and Will in unison.

"Thanks," she said, wiping her nose. "Oh, Polly, where are the tissues?"

"There're some in the powder room, through the pantry and the hallway, the third door on your right."

"I'll get them," offered Oscar politely, jumping to his feet.

"No, no, no. Thank you, though," said Julia, rising to hit the wallpapered labyrinth for some Kleenex.

She found her way down the botanical print–covered hall, blew her nose in the powder room, and exited to her right instead of left, ending up in the sun room. But before she could turn around to go back, she heard a giggle through the window. She looked out and, below her, in full embrace, were Lell and Alastair. Shocked, she quickly stepped back from the window so they couldn't see the unwitting witness to their smooch. Julia darted back to wrap up her game.

Upon her return, as she plopped back down Indian-style, Will looked her over with a sly smile, which she now chose to return as she felt her temperature rising despite the crisp chilled air. And this time, she let herself enjoy the fever.

chapter 21

This was surreal, thought Julia as she rolled over in bed and lifted up the shade to check out the early-morning sky. She felt like she was in Gosford Park, or more accurately, an episode of *Melrose Place*. What was up with all the illicit sex or potential illicit sex that was flying in the sea air? One thing Julia knew was that this was not going to end well. The best thing to do was to just try and have a good time, and avoid Will at all costs. There was no reward to be had in joining this crazy circus. She felt like she was on *Dynasty*. If this was what life was like for the rich, then no thanks.

After showering, Julia made her way down the back stairs to try to sneak in a cup of coffee in the kitchen before having to greet the others. She was pretty sure most would still be snoozing, since it was only seven o'clock, but didn't want to take her chances. As she approached the kitchen door she heard Rosario chatting away in Spanish and assumed she was talking to her husband. So when she opened the door and saw Oscar sitting at the table, looking uncharacteristically relaxed and animated, you could have knocked Julia over with a monogrammed dickey.

As soon as Oscar saw Julia his countenance changed, and his face grew more serious and strained. Rosario noticed the change, and fearing that Julia was another demanding diva like her employer, turned her back to them and quickly made a dash to the flower room for a vase, leaving them in peace.

"Good morning, I didn't expect to find anyone else awake," said Julia. She walked over to the coffeepot and poured herself a steaming mug of French roast.

"I can't sleep late," said Oscar. "I-I guess it's just a rhythm, going to work so early and everything."

"Did I hear you speaking Spanish?" asked Julia, sliding the *New York Post* over to the side so she could place her steaming mug in front of her. "Are you fluent?"

"I guess. I spent a lot of time in Chile."

"Really? Doing what?"

"I worked in international banking for a while. Before I got bored and went into the software business."

"And as I understand it, you did really well. Didn't you invent something?"

"I . . . yes, I invented a piece of technology that I got the patent for last year. All the wireless carriers were infringing so we sued and . . . It's—well I'm sure you'd think it was all very geeky."

"No, no! Geek-chic. You know, the geek shall inherit the

earth, right? Polly said you invented something kind of revolutionary."

"Whatever. It's boring."

Oscar looked down at the croissant crumbs on his Villeroy & Boch plate. His anxiety seemed to make them dance around. Julia made him completely inarticulate. He knew he came off as nervous, maybe even rude, but he didn't know how to talk to her. If they had met in other circumstances, maybe, but what the hell was she doing here? The fact they had met here of all places completely unnerved him.

"I heard—" he started, then looked down. "That you volunteer in Harlem."

"Oh. Yeah," she said, looking out the window. A pang hit her chest. "I . . . did."

"Not anymore?"

"Well, Lell wanted me more available for socializing with important Pelham's clients, there's a bridge game she particularly wanted me to join so . . ."

"Hmmm."

Julia looked away. Oscar looked out the window. They sat in silence.

"You know, you're kind of hard to talk to," said Julia, smiling.

"You think?"

"Do I rub you the wrong way somehow?"

"You? No."

"Okay," said Julia, biting into a sugar-coated brioche. "I thought I'd done something wrong. Something to put you off."

"No."

There was an awkward pause, which Oscar finally broke. "I just don't understand why someone like you is here with all these people."

"What do you mean?" said Julia, feeling the blood rush to her face. "Is that some sort of class comment?"

"No, no. But . . . I just feel like all the people here are . . . kind of assholes. You don't seem that way to me."

"Well, I don't think they're assholes."

"I guess you have to say that. You work for Lell. You have to do what she says. Quit community service, play bridge."

"I resent that. I'm not here to kiss ass to my boss and her friends. I genuinely like everyone here, they have been totally welcoming of me. And I'm frankly having a good time."

"Okay . . . I'm sorry," said Oscar, slinking back to his croissant.

"And if you feel that way, why are you here?"

Oscar shrugged. "I don't know. I thought maybe I should spend some time with . . . people instead of my computer."

"Well, give them a chance," said Julia, getting up to look out the window onto the crashing waves. "People may take longer to penetrate than a hard drive, but they're usually worth it."

Oscar stared at her blankly, tongue-tied.

"I'm going to go take a walk," said Julia, now feeling bad for him.

"Good idea. Mind if I join you?"

"Why not?" said Julia. "I'll go get my coat."

While Julia and Oscar ambled along the sandy beach in silence with the cold wind slapping their faces, Polly was nestled under her duvet dreaming about Brad Pitt. Just as she was about to lean in and lick Brad's adorable nose, something woke her with a start. She opened her eyes and looked around the room.

"Henny?"

There was no answer. Polly sat up and looked at her watch. Where the hell was Henny? It was like seven-thirty. He was usually so hungover, hardly the type to jump out of bed and start his day early.

Polly threw on her robe and walked through her dressing room to the bathroom.

"Henny?"

Still no answer. She opened the door to her bedroom and looked both ways. The coast was clear. She didn't want to run into anyone before she'd put on her face.

Polly crept along the sisal-carpeted hall toward the small office that looked out on the backyard. The door was ajar and she peeped in. Henny was hunkered down at the walnut desk, peering at his laptop, his face inches from the screen.

"Hen?"

Henny started and slammed down the cover of the laptop. "You scared me!"

"What are you doing?" demanded Polly.

"I'm doing work. Jesus, Polly, don't come sneaking up on me."

"You're doing work on a weekend?"

"I have stuff to do. Could you please leave me alone?"

"Fine," said Polly, her tone suggesting it was anything but.

Since when did Henny do work? He usually just hung out

at the Racquet Club and played chess. Polly didn't know he even knew how to use a computer, he was so retro. But then she remembered that he had been talking to Oscar about the Internet last night, asking him about eBay. Maybe he was researching something to get Polly for her upcoming birthday.

"So what did they name the kid?"

"Thaddeus."

"So ethnic."

"Yeah, but they have some foreign ancestor who was like Greek and was a prince or something, so they want to make the connection. Even though it was like four hundred years ago."

"That's just odd."

Hope, Lell, Polly, and Julia had gone to East Hampton for the afternoon to check out Ralph Lauren and pick out some cute ribbed cashmeres to go with the rest of their country outfits. Well, really the rest of Lell and Polly's outfits. Neither Hope nor Julia could drop seven hundred for a casual sweater.

"Did you know that Jaden, Caden, and Aidan are the most popular boys' names in the U.S.?" asked Julia.

"No way. I don't know anyone who named their kids any of those names," said Polly.

"It's true."

"And isn't Brianna one of the most popular?" asked Hope.

"Yup," said Julia. She'd just read the list in *People* magazine.

"No way! I never even heard of that name," said Polly. "It's made up."

"No, it's true," nodded Lell. "It's reaaaaally popular. If there's a hurricane in some random state, with, like, trailers flying around and stuff, chances are a Brianna was hit."

"Hello, ladies," said a smooth male voice behind them.

All of the girls turned. It was John Cavanaugh.

"Hello, John," said Polly, giving him an air kiss. "What are you up to?"

"Just walking around, seeing what stores have survived the winter. Every time I come here, a new store has come and an old store has gone."

"It's so sad. The malling of America," said Lell solemnly.

"If Granddaddy was alive he'd have a coronary," added Polly, with a hand to her heart. "These used to be such sweet little towns and now they're total tourist traps sans personalities. It's disgusting."

"Remember the days when you could drive into town in the summer and find a parking space?" recalled Lell with sadness.

Lell and Polly stopped and stared at the sky with glassy eyes, remembering the good old days when they had their summer towns to themselves and the locals. They paused as if taking a moment of silence, while Hope smiled at John, who grinned back. Julia observed their exchange with curiosity.

"So are you just out for the weekend?" asked John.

"Yes, we're all staying at Polly's in Southampton," said Hope.

"You should come by, John," said Polly.

"I'd love to, but I have to run back to the city tonight."

Hope didn't know why, but she felt disappointed.

"You work too hard," admonished Polly.

"What can you do?"

"Where's Natasha?" asked Lell.

"Oh, well, we broke up," said John, looking at Hope.

"You're terrible, John. You are such a womanizer!" said Polly.

"That's not true."

"You have a different babe on your arm at every event."

"I'm just looking for the right one."

"Well, this is Julia Pearce. She's single," said Polly, pushing Julia to the forefront.

"Polly," said Julia, embarrassed.

"Nice to meet you," said John.

"Isn't she gorgeous? She's like a sister to us."

"She is gorgeous," said John, nodding.

"Okay, now I feel literally like a piece of meat," said Julia, feigning jokiness to cover her embarrassment. "Um, shouldn't we be heading back?"

"Yes, it's time to get ready for dinner. So much to do," sighed Polly.

"Are you cooking?" asked John, amused.

"Hardly. But it does take an effort organizing the menu. I mean, try explaining the difference between green beans and haricots verts to someone who barely speaks English. Such a hassle."

John laughed and waved goodbye to the girls, who wandered off down the street.

"Julia, you shouldn't have done that," reprimanded Polly.

"What?"

"John Cavanaugh is a true catch. You shouldn't have dismissed him like that. He'd be very good for you." Something about the way Polly said this made Julia bristle. As if what she really wanted to say was, You'd be lucky to get him.

"Sorry, Poll. I just like to be a little more subtle."

"Well sometimes you can't afford to be subtle," said Polly, again in a scolding tone that rubbed Julia the wrong way.

"Give her a break," interjected Hope vociferously. "You were practically whoring her out."

Polly turned and stared at Hope, surprised at her outburst. "I'm just trying to help Julia," said Polly. She turned and gave Lell an eye roll and then clicked on the keys of her car to unlock the alarm.

As they packed into the car, all four of their minds turned to men. Lell was excited that she'd see Alastair when she got back. He was so much more entertaining then show-offy Will. Julia, despite herself, was excited to see Will. He just commanded attention, and she couldn't look away. Hope was disappointed that John couldn't come for dinner. She told herself that it was for Charlie's sake, of course. She really wanted him to offer Charlie a job so they could finally get the classic eight in the Seventies or Eighties. But was that really the reason? Or was it that John was the only guy in the six years she'd been with Charlie who made her feel like she was still a catch herself? Polly was most looking forward to seeing Charlie. She didn't know why, but there was something proper and gentle about him, unlike her idiotic husband.

All four sat in silence for the twenty-minute ride back to Southampton, their secret desires burning through them, keeping them warm despite the chilled air.

Unfortunately, everything was turned upside down when they got back to the house. Hope's nanny had called to say the kids were sick, so Hope and Charlie had to rush back to the city. Alastair had mysteriously left the house early, claiming an important engagement in the city but leaving no message for Lell. Furious, Lell insisted that she and Will return to the city, seeing no reason to hang out any longer at Polly and Henny's drafty old house. That left Julia with Polly, Henny, and taciturn Oscar to suffer through a rather boring and overcooked dinner. Julia was thrilled to head back to the city early the next morning, eager to dish with Douglas on all of the scandals that had arisen.

chapter 22

"I honestly might keel over," said Douglas, sitting down to brace himself. "He kissed you and said, 'I thought you were my wife'?"

"What a load," said Lewis. "He clearly wanted to sample your goods. So then what happened."

"Nothing. We had this weird eye contact all weekend and then—"

"What?" the men shouted in unison.

"I saw Lell Pelham making out with Alastair Keach."

"The hotelier?"

"Yeah. Weird, right?"

"Holy fucking shit!" said Douglas, practically giddy with shock. "Get out!"

"I swear."

"You know . . ." Douglas trailed off. "I did hear that she used to do him. For like years."

"I know. But this whole vibe seemed . . . strange to me. At first it was like this big fun weekend bash and then I just felt guilty and gross by the end."

"Well, we're glad you're back," said Lewis, giving her a squeeze.

"I am, too," replied Julia while she unpacked. "At the end, I was starting to max out on Polly and Henny Mecox. Something about that guy rubs me the wrong way. And then there was that guy Oscar, who was practically mute. I think he hates me."

"Wait, is this Oscar Curtis, the entrepreneur?" asked Lewis.

"I think so."

"There was a huge article on him in the *Wall Street Journal*. He is major, you know."

"I know. But totally awky."

"But hot," said Lewis. "I saw his picture in *Fortune*, too. He's adorable."

"I guess . . ." Julia trailed off. Oscar was definitely cute but so . . . lacking in confidence. So insecure. Will, on the other hand, was a rakish Valmont-type who unseamed her with a glance. Just thinking of him now made her so weak she wanted to lie down. With him. She was in a caught stew and needed a lifeline ladle out.

As she got on the subway with Douglas, he sensed the tension boiling behind her blue eyes.

"C'mon. It's me. You know I'm not gonna judge your ass," Doug coaxed. "Talk. Did you fuck him?"

"No. I swear. I would tell you."

"No, you wouldn't."

"Douglas! Yes, I would. Plus I would never sleep with a married guy. Ever. That is just so not me."

"But his wife is cheating! It's a sham marriage."

"I know. That's the only thing that's letting me justify thinking about him all the time."

Henny was perfecting his bow tie in the mirror when Polly appeared behind him in the reflection.

"Hello? I said seven! It's now seven-twelve, come on!"

Henny rolled his eyes but obediently turned on his John Lobb heels to follow his wife down to the car. Chaffeurs Unlimited had sent the usual driver, Ricardo, who was downstairs waiting in the Mecoxes' navy blue Mercedes. Henny always sat in the front with the driver since his wife's black tie gowns took up the space of a whole person. After sliding in and making sure her silk Valentino ball skirt wasn't getting smushed on the backseat, Polly opened her Estée Lauder makeup stash in the armrest and began powdering her T zone.

"I'm so thrilled Hope and Charlie could join us," Polly said aloud, not that anyone was really listening. "I think the

Burgundy Society could be a good match with them. Charlie really seems to know wine."

In front of the Waldorf Astoria, an armada of limos lined Park Avenue. Polly was annoyed she had to walk from the corner of Forty-ninth Street as the shiny car drop-off zone was now three automobiles thick.

She walked in ahead of Henny and saw the giant banner for the BSNY: Burgundy Society of New York, a hundred-year-old oenophile bastion.

After selecting her calligraphied table card, Polly burst into the ballroom, which was swarming with immaculately dressed couples and lined with tables, each place set with a staggering twelve wineglasses. After every three tables there was a microphone stand, where guests, after reflecting on the small pool of red wine that had been swishing inside their mouths, could make a comment if moved to do so by the overwhelming flavors on their maxed-out taste buds.

Across the room Polly spotted Hope with her arm through Charlie's and happily headed over.

"Hello, you two!" she said while air-kissing and scoping Hope's outfit. Hmm. The same Kors she wore to the Fight Against Dysentery ball last year. "Table eight?"

Hope nodded. "I'm starving."

"It's not about food tonight, my dear," said Henny, looking around. "It's all about the vino."

The foursome arrived at their table to find John Cavanaugh seated to Hope's right. She gulped. That was weird, she didn't know this guy before and now she was running into him everywhere. She tried to suppress her excitement. Why was she excited? She didn't have a crush on him, no. She was married. That's it, she thought, internally snapping her fingers. It's because this was a perfect opportunity for him to talk to Charlie about the job; Hope was thrilled. She was just looking out for her man, she sighed, relieved. But then John looked at her in a deep way that made her feel like she hadn't felt in years as he got up to pull out her chair and she realized that she was fooling herself.

"Ladies and gentlemen," the emcee interrupted. "Before we begin, I'd like to introduce you to our esteemed wine panel for this evening. Miss Charity Frothingham of Frothingham's Auction Gallery, wine division chair. Mr. Lucas di Carolo of Brunspire Imports, Dolly Lecompte of *Eats and Wine* magazine, and Emelia Sorrell of *Wine Connoisseur*. Let us begin with the first glass. By now you have all sampled your amuse-bouche of turnip cappuccino garnished with caramelized shallots kissed with white truffle. So take a sip from the first glass, close your eyes, and disappear into the wonderful world of Burgundy."

Hope looked at Charlie, who smiled, reaching for his glass. They looked around and watched the entire ballroom sip in silence. After what seemed like a full two minutes, one guest broke the silence.

"It's funny," he started, as hundreds of heads turned to the mike stand near Table 31. "This seventy-four is gutsy and amusing—so much like an eighty-six, it's almost unabashedly woodsy and with an oaky thread, so much like our trip to Château Laseurat in that crisp fall, right, Sharon?"

A woman, presumably Sharon, nodded with a wistful

smile while wiping a tear from her glistening eye. Ah, memories.

Suddenly, the entire crowd, in unison, shouted, "Long live Burgundy! Burgundy forever!"

Hope was stunned. She looked at Polly, who smiled but seemed fully into it and not at all weirded out by the group chants.

Next, a small intellectual bespectacled man rose to take another mike stand.

"I sampled the year before, the seventy-three, recently, and what is so absolutely hysterical is that just one fall before this vineyard had the audacity to release such a vulgar, fruity wine; it was as if the grapes themselves had little boxing gloves and were punching me in the mouth. Just loathsome and manipulative. But this seventy-four, ahhhhhh! So subtle yet so alive, precocious, dancing on the palette in swift, bold steps. A sweet French kiss from Dionysus himself."

"Long live Burgundy! Burgundy forever!" yelled the crowd in synch.

Gimme a break. Hope was already tuned out of the whole crazy wine thing. She felt like she was in some weirdo *Eyes Wide Shut* party. Hell, she loved a nice glass of red wine, but these people were freaks.

"It's kind of cultish, right?" said John, leaning in and reading her mind.

"Yes! I was just thinking how over the top this is. Making out with Bacchus? I mean, I think we can can it with the Greek mythology."

"I agree," John agreed.

"What are you doing here anyway?" asked Hope, the

wine now going to her head. "I didn't picture you as the sort of guy who would take this stuff seriously."

"I don't. One of my clients is on the Burgundy Society board of trustees so there was no getting around it. This is unusual, but honestly it's nothing compared to the ATS event two weeks ago."

"What's that?" asked Hope, looking into John's sparkling eyes.

"You know, the New York chapter of the Adventure Travel Society."

"Oh, yes, with that amazing Gothic mansion on Fifth?"

"That's it. They have their annual ball here every year. I sat next to this octogenarian who looked like he was about to keel over, but in fact, had just returned from his seventh attempt at Everest."

"Get out."

"No. It's over the top. I'm not kidding, they serve monkey brains and dog spring rolls and all this crap."

"Shut up!"

"Yup. And do you know how the Board of Governors enters?"

"No—"

"They have these harnesses and start on the roof of the hotel and rappel into the ballroom through those windows."

"You're lying," said Hope.

"Hey, are you talking about the ATS thing?" asked Charlie, overhearing. "I heard about that, they all climb down in their tuxes."

"It's out of control," said John, launching into another anecdote.

At first Hope was happy to have her husband stop talking to Polly so he could get in with John but then she realized John's attentions weren't just focused on her anymore. Wait. What was she thinking? She loved Charlie! She was happily married and plus, this guy wasn't into her! She stood up to go to the ladies' room and John got up to go as well.

"I have to go myself, I'll walk you."

As they meandered through the red sea of wine obssessors they smiled at each other and finally made it to the hallway.

"So this client roped you in and wouldn't even let you bring a date?" Hope asked.

"Naw, they offered but, hey, the best ones are all taken," he said with a flirty wink. That wink was a hot pink arrow and Hope was pierced.

"Plus," he added, "I have to wait for you to leave your husband. Maybe next year." He smiled, rendering the comment a joke, adding, "See you back in there," before hitting the men's room. Hope felt herself swoon.

Back in the ballroom, eleven wines and twenty-nine speakers later, not to be outdone, the auction wine queen herself rose to the panel podium.

"This wine was actually looted by the Nazis from the cherished cellars of the elite Rossini famiglia, and it was stored by the SS in an underground cave for many many years by the estate where there was also a trove of gasoline. Now if you all just humor me, close your eyes."

Hope closed her eyes. But she didn't picture dark red liquid, she pictured John.

"Now taste the Burgundy on your tongue, let it slide back

and forth. See if you all do not detect an ever so faint lace of petrol." The crowd ooh'd and aaah'd, amazed. Aghast. Why, yes! There was gas in this wine, how divine! As the crowd waxed rhapsodic at the discovery, Charlie yanked Hope and said they had to bolt.

"Why?"

"Sweetheart, it's midnight. I have work tomorrow."

"Fine."

"Thanks so much, Poll and Hen," said Hope, as she rose and grabbed her pashmina. Hope looked around. John had gone over to chat with another table and was totally out of sight. She didn't want to leave without saying goodbye, but Charlie was giving her the impatient eye roll.

"Tell John we said goodbye," said Hope.

"Sure," nodded Polly, totally absorbed in her reverie of Nazi Germany and wine pilgrimage.

Hope and Charlie politely excused themselves and waded out through the jammed limos and Benz-fest to their own golden chariot home: a hailed New York taxicab.

chapter 23

"Okay, I think I just broke my arm carrying your mail, your highness," said Douglas, dropping a thick stack of invitations on Julia's bed with a thud.

Julia, still sleepy, lifted an eyebrow to see what Douglas was talking about.

"Judging from some of those return addresses, you're either being confused with a Rockefeller, or there's a Julia Pearce somewhere out there who is looking for all of her charity ball invitations."

Julia sat up in bed and sifted through the pile. There were letters from the Fight Obesity Ball, the GROG (Get Rid of Gangrene) Women's network, the American Ballet Company, the St. Petersburg Ballet Company, the Miami Ballet Company, and the Ladies Against Female Circumcision luncheon. Were they kidding? There were personal dinner party invitations from couples whom Julia had barely heard of: Franny and Monty Corcoran? Brooke and Stone Lutz? Rupert and Amanda Wingate? Who were these people?

"Darling, you've gotten very fancy," said Douglas, ripping through the invitations with Julia.

"Oh please, I just have a fancy job."

"I don't think so! Oh my God!"

"What?"

Douglas put his hand to his heart dramatically. "You're fucking *on* this invitation. You're on the junior committee!"

"What? Let me see that," said Julia, grabbing it out of Douglas's hand. And sure enough, there she was. Between Lydia Parth and Rosemary Peniston was her name, Julia Pearce. She was asking people to come to the Fight Xenops Extinction Ball.

"No one told me!"

"Oh my God, you are so major! *Major!*"

Julia was at first annoyed that they'd put her name on without asking, but then flattered. Wow. She was on a committee? She was getting noticed! That *was* pretty major!

"Just don't let it go to your head, sweetie."

"I won't. Obviously, it's no biggie."

But when Julia was taking a shower, she indulged herself a little and did let it go to her head. Things were happening. This was *major*. She was hanging out with some of the most elite and powerful girls in town, she was getting designer clothes thrown at her, she was now on charity committees. What was next? She could definitely get used to this life. The fun was about to begin. And let it. Why shouldn't she take advantage? All of the girls seemed totally genuine, nice. She'd of course watch her back, but why not jump in?

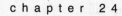

chapter 24

There are few relationships more complicated and delicate than that of mothers and daughters, and Lell's strained and competitive relationship with her mother, Emily, was no exception. Lell considered herself a daddy's girl from day one, whereas Emily deemed her daughter an opponent for her husband's attention from the minute she came out of the womb and refused to latch onto her breast. (Thank God, really, because Emily had no interest in breast-feeding whatsoever. Too bohemian, too California.) Throughout the years Lell and her mother had engaged in a constant but unacknowledged array of battles, which resembled such toddler-level games as emotional tug-of-war, capture the flag, and dodgeball, and where the prize was always dear Papa. As they both got older, Lell grew more powerful and beautiful and her mother grew more bitter and became marginalized, making the stakes higher and the risks more reckless.

Regardless of familial hostilities, Lell still had dinner with her parents every Sunday evening at Elio's, rain or shine. Lell's mother usually spent weekends at the house in Connecticut, with or without her husband, getting her knees deep in dirt in the garden or spending hours training her award-winning Airedales. Because of her intense dislike for Connecticut, landlocked country houses, and dogs (especially the very ones she suspected her mother of loving more than her), Lell rarely ventured to Connecticut. Instead, she spent her weekends in the city or with friends at "the beach," where the stiletto-balanced beauties teetered down main street with shopping bags and never actually saw sand. Despite their having very different weekdays, Lell and her mother's reunion on Sunday was not met with lighthearted catch-up banter. In fact, they had very little to discuss. Therefore Lell turned her attention to her father, and Emily to her daughter's attractive husband.

"Mom and Dad were just appalled. You can imagine," said Will to his mother-in-law, between bites of veal parmigiana.

"I can imagine," said Emily dramatically.

"Just chock full of low-class characters who look like extras from *The Sopranos*. So there they are, standing in the entrance of this club—and this club was not really a club. You just need a few hundred grand to join, money talks, and then anyone's in, I mean, anyone."

"Shouldn't even be called a club. More like a meeting place."

"Exactly. And they don't see anyone, I mean, anyone. My mother is giving my father daggers, because she does not see why the hell he brought her there—"

"You said these were business associates of his?"

"Well, sort of. The guy who was having the party just gave like five million to the Philadelphia hospital, and since Dad's head of the board, he felt he should go to their cocktail party. In and out. That's what Mom agreed to anyway."

"Louise is such a trooper."

"I know. So they're looking around this tacky ballroom, looked like Donald Trump's casino designer did it, just so gross—Mom said it was like a disco nightmare—and they are thinking, How quickly can we get out of here?" Will sipped his scotch and ran a hand through his hair as he painted the unsavory scene. "They thought they'd see at least one person they knew, but it was totally used-car dealers, dressed in like, brown suits. And then finally they see a guy in a tux, who looks kind of normal, so they go up to him and introduce themselves, you know, 'Hi, I'm Carlton Banks and this is my wife, Louise.' And the guy says, 'Nice to meet you, can I get you something to drink?' Turns out he's a waiter. The only normal-looking guy there was a goddamned waiter!"

Emily shuddered. "How terrible for your parents," she sympathized while putting a hand on Will's wrist.

It reminded her of the first time her parents had met Gene's family. Main Line meets New Money had not gone down well. Now Willoughby was exactly the type of guy her parents would have adored. Smart, charismatic, and from a good family. They had a special connection.

On the other side of the table Lell was engaged in a serious discussion with her father about whether or not to introduce a new specialty flatware line by Crimson Matisse at Pelham's. It was often this way at dinner, where Will and Emily would immediately break off into a separate conversation where they made snobby remarks about everyone they knew, and Lell and her father would talk about business. Then either Lell or her mother would turn on the other and accuse her of something or reprimand her for something.

"Lell, before I forget, Kitty Hancock called to see if you received her wedding gift," said Emily sternly.

"Of course I did. It was these hideous cachepots with birds all over them."

"Well, why haven't you written her a thank-you note yet?"

"I have a year. I literally just got back from my honeymoon."

"You've been back for weeks. People spend a lot of money; they want their gift to be acknowledged."

"I think it's so tacky and annoying when they call and say, 'Just wondering if you got the gift.' It's so lame. Like, give us a break, we'll write you a thank-you note when we get to it."

"Well, don't you have a team of assistants now at work? I'm sure one of those young ladies has good penmanship. Have her write it and send it ASAP."

Lell took a deep breath and rolled her eyes. Then she had an idea.

"Actually, I could ask Julia, my deputy."

Will looked up from his green beans. "Isn't that sort of beneath her?"

"Why? She works for me."

"Is that the blonde young lady?" asked Gene, knowing damn well that it was.

"Yes, the really pretty one who brought me the necklace at the wedding. You met her, Mom."

"I don't remember," said Emily, taking a sip of her wine.

"Which reminds me, Dad," Lell said, watching her mother. "I should bring Julia to our lunch tomorrow. Just to get her up to speed on things."

Lell was not unaware of her father's roving eye, and rather than try to avoid it, she had actually tried to insert herself into the situation on various occasions. It was a way of getting back at her mother and controlling her father. Paging Dr. Freud.

"If you think that's a good idea, sure, sweetie," said Gene, feeling a pang. He remembered Julia and how nicely she filled out her tight sweaters.

Emily could already see her husband's mind racing. She coldly inhaled and turned her attention back to her son-in-law.

"So, Will, tell me all about your meeting at the Racquet Club. How did it go?"

The following day, as promised, Lell brought Julia to lunch at 21 with her father. Once a week father and daughter broke bread at the renowned former speakeasy, in order to catch up on business and to see and be seen.

Julia was a little nervous at the last-minute invitation, but had been put at ease immediately. Mr. Pelham was really nice and jovial, and he seemed very impressed with all of her ideas.

"Oh, and tell him about the stationery idea," prompted Lell.

"Oh, okay. Well, I just thought since Tiffany's does it, there's no reason why Pelham's shouldn't—"

"I mean, why should everyone order Mrs. John L. Strong? We should try to corner that market," interjected Lell.

Gene nodded. "You're right."

"Julia has a whole proposal drawn up. It's all about letterpress these days."

Gene looked impressed. "Why don't you bring it by my office?" he suggested.

"Sure. It's only in the preliminary stages . . ."

Julia had actually spent a lot of time on the stationery proposal, enlisting Douglas and his amazing artistic abilities to help her come up with something both classic and unique. She had worked hours on it and was thrilled that she'd have a chance to present it to the Big Boss.

Lell excused herself to go to the bathroom.

"So, Julia, how do you like working at Pelham's?" asked Gene, taking a bite of his 21 burger.

"I love it. Lell is so great to work for."

"She's a great worker. Such an asset to the company. She sees great things in you as well."

"Well she's been really supportive."

"I think you're perfect for Pelham's," said Gene, sliding his hand on Julia's knee. Julia almost choked on her water.

"Thank you," she said, staring at her boss with alarmed eyes. *Holy fucking shit, he's coming on to me.*

"And if you need anything, just let me know," said Gene, rubbing her thigh carefully.

"Thanks."

Lell returned to find her father grinning like a cat and Julia sitting up rock-straight, looking very glad to see her. *Good,* thought Lell. *Daddy never lets me down. Fuck Mom.*

chapter 25

Hope was so nauseous she swore she had vomit mid-esophagus. Not because she had eaten too much Chinese food or had watched a gory movie. It was because she had to go to her sister-in-law's Sip 'n' See for baby number five. Jeez, she thought, who had five kids these days? I mean, it was 2005 for chrissake—isn't the planet, like, bursting with humans? Between the four (now five) cousins' birthdays plus Christmas plus friends' babies' parties and showers, Hope's monthly stipend was out the door on gifts alone. First there were weddings, which meant bridal showers and dresses (mostly awful looking) and bachelorette parties and wedding registries. Now it was babies: showers, birth presents, and then, the newest me-me-me phenom: the Sip 'n' See, an afternoon gathering to sip tea and see the tot. Oh, and take in more gifts. Not that Diana Matthews Rockenwagner needed it—aside from having free-flowing tidal waves o' greenbacks, she also received countless generous gifts from other trust-funded femmes. Many wealthy climbers lavished goodies upon Diana so that they could get in with her charity set, which ran the social circuit for the thirty-fivish group—sort of like an older version of Lell and her party photo-op gang.

But Hope was tired of it all—playing catch-up, not only with her friends but also with her family. She remembered how, the year before, she and Charlie and the boys had flown down one brisk weekend on Jet Blue to West Palm Beach to check in on Hope's Aunt Edna. Diana and her clan were all on South Ocean Boulevard and "couldn't place" quite where Edna's condo was when Hope described it. But Hope knew what her sister-in-law was thinking—that her aunt was in some sad cheezoid condo.

So it was with heaps of anxiety that Hope buttoned her jacket and headed to Park Avenue for Diana's latest self-celebration. She swallowed hard as the crisply uniformed doorman rang up, and her heart beat through her suit as she slowly ascended the floors. A blue balloon was on the door, marking the fête from the other apartment on the landing, but anyone could already hear the din of well-wishers and baby worshippers.

"Oooooh! Ford is so cute!" gushed one of Diana's friends.

"Are you guys going to call him Ford?" asked another.

"Yes," said the mom proudly, while patting his powder-blue cashmere fitted cap. "Rutherford just sounds so formal, you know? Oh! Look, it's my sister-in-law, you all know Hope Matthews."

"Hi," Hope half waved, shyly. She entered the room and

immediately Diana's butler offered her a selection of teas. After helping herself to jasmine, she sat on a nearby settee on the outskirts of the pearl-wearing primped ladies-who-liquid-lunch as they faux-nibbled crustless quartered sandwiches.

"Hope and my brother have two kids," Diana said to the group, who then began the Spanish Inquisition.

How old were they? Where did Gavin go to preschool? What classes would Gavin go to? What percentile was Chip's weight? Height? Head circumference? What were Chip's first choices for kindergarten?

"Well, thankfully, kindergarten is three years away," laughed Hope, unable to believe the competitive vultures feasting on her insecurities. She hated moms! These vipers had all this displaced anger because they didn't have work environments in which to rise through the ranks anymore, so they used each other as flesh-and-bone steps to make themselves feel higher.

"Oh, it's never too early to start networking!" said one. "Tonny, my son Weatherington, goes to Buckley and we're just so happy there. Such nice families."

Hope knew this woman had once been a big shot at Skadden Arps and saw that she was a perfect example of the kind of ambitious Newtonian energy that did not cease to exist when someone quit their job: it simply got rechanneled, funneled into the fetus. This was the horrifying breed of Type-A Momzilla that Hope abhorred. And their carnivorous species was the dominant life-form at the party.

Diana, on the other hand, had zero ambition—she had arrived, as they say, the day she wed into the Rockenwagner family at age twenty-four. Though part of this American aristocracy, she seemingly always returned to money, which, as Hope mused to Charlie, was decidedly unclassy.

"Oh, the Andersons, such shameless press-whores!" Diana laughed, while partaking in her daily ritual of schadenfreude voodoo after a group discussion of the *New York Post*'s gossip round-up. Hope always found it interesting that the only analysis these well-educated women ever did was over whom the blind items on Page Six were about. "You know," continued Diana in a fake whisper designed to make what she was about to say less disgusting, "They don't have a dime! They went to that special big donors dinner at Daniel for the new wing at the hospital, and they totally invited themselves and then sent in a few hundred lousy bucks!"

"She borrows everything and plays it all like they're so big," chimed in another powersnob, "and meanwhile they live in a rental on Second Avenue!"

Diana shot the girl a look and then glanced down, embarrassed. Then she looked at Hope. The other girls all quietly looked down at their teacups, realizing that Diana's brother and his wife lived in a rental, too. Oops.

After a very pregnant pause, someone looked at Hope to break the silence and said, "I mean, not that that's bad . . . there are some very nice family rentals—"

"Oh, it's fine!" said Hope with a good-sport smile, "we love our little place. You know what they say, there's no place like hovel," she smiled, disarming the group with her humor. Diana shot her a look, however, which meant, in no uncertain terms, can it. If you don't make bank, don't advertise it.

———

Outside in the misty April afternoon, Hope was partly relieved to be out of there but partly riled up in a frenzy of hatred. She loved New York so much, and yet there were times where she wanted to pack it all up and haul ass to Duluth and start anew, where her husband's income would make them the mansion-owning richest family in the town. But then again, she'd never really do that; it was all a fleeting fantasy she didn't even truly want. She remembered how after September 11 Diana dramatically swooped up her kids at their school, preschool, and pre-preschools with the chauffeur, and headed home to pack. As soon as the United States airspace reopened, she headed straight to Teterboro and hopped the private jet to Palm Beach, where she decamped for eight months until the Defcon alert was lowered to Code Mauve.

She told her brother Charlie to do the same, but, hello, he had to work! Plus Hope said in no uncertain terms that she would rather eat her spleen than move in with Diana down south, no matter how big their oceanfront estate was. It was still fucking Florida. And after all, she'd rather die of anthrax than die of boredom.

"Hope? Hi!"

Hope's musings were halted by a familiar voice. She turned to find John Cavanaugh walking out of a lunch at Daniel.

"John! Hi, oh my goodness, sorry, I could not be more spaced out. What are you doing in town, isn't your office in Greenwich?"

"Yeah, but I had an investor lunch. Hey, and I just was thinking of you."

Hope blushed. "You were?"

"Yeah, I had a great talk with Charlie this morning—he's a great guy. I'm hoping he can join our team, there may be a position opening up."

Oh. He thought of her because of Charlie. Not because he was dreaming about her running toward him in a bikini, Phoebe Cates–style. "Great!" was all she could muster.

"Yeah, he's a great guy." He looked at her warmly. "Not to mention a lucky guy."

Yes! Ridgemont High fantasy alive and well. "Oh, thanks," Hope smiled, heart racing.

"I was just going to check out the Whitney Biennial since I'm in town. I have another meeting at the Mark right by there at four, so . . . would you care to join me?"

Mrs. Matthews would be delighted. They strolled up Madison to the hulking charcoal gray museum, which Hope often called the Shitney due to certain exhibitions that weren't her cup of jasmine tea. The last few biennials she had attended seemed dead set on eschewing all connections to the canons of figurative art. Instead they were weird political works she couldn't relate to: angry word paintings or violent blobs and video installations of screaming moaning people. No thanks. But then this exhibit was . . . well, divine. Not because there was a new exciting man by her side but because the art did what it was supposed to do: inspire. They walked in silence by many of the clearly skillfully made works, charged with an overpowering, warm surge from the color and dimension of the sometimes obsessively handmade sculptures and the brilliant draftsmanship of crosshatched graphite lines on hundreds of squares of paper.

One installation had a guard outside, who sealed the

viewers inside the room for thirty seconds, one by one, but John quickly snuck in with her. It was called *Fireflies on the Water* by Yayoi Kusama and was a room with mirrored walls and floor and ceiling with thousands of tiny pinhead-sized bulbs that reflected infinitely off the glass and the watery pool below the lucite platform they stood on together. The two were floating in a lilting sea of heightened sensory awareness, finding a fleeting beat of quiet in a bustling museum in a bustling city; their only responsibility to drink in the glistening silence. It was a perfect, delicate moment, of twinkling light in inky darkness and the subtle sound of water below. Hope didn't know where these ethereal fake fireflies began or ended, but she did know one thing: she never wanted to leave.

chapter 26

"I feel really bad telling you this, but, you've become one of my best friends, and I just think you ought to know . . ." began Polly, with a serious and concerned look.

"What is it?" asked Julia, a pit growing in her stomach.

"Well, it's just that, you know how I'm going down to St. Bart's next month for vacation? We've chartered a yacht with Henny's brother, and anyway, we each get to invite some guests. Well, I of course asked Lell and Will long ago, and there's one other room, and Hope has to go see her dreadful aunt in Palm Bitch, so I said to Lell, should I invite Julia or Meredith? And Lell said . . ." Polly leaned in, "Meredith."

Julia had a sinking feeling. "Oh, whatever, I totally understand. I mean, you all have been friends forever, I totally didn't expect to be invited—"

"See you're just too nice, that's the problem. I know that you don't care, but I just think it's weird."

"Not really," said Julia, uncomfortable with the whole topic. "I mean, I do work for Lell. Maybe she wants a break from office peeps."

Polly shook her head and clucked her tongue. "I don't think that's it."

"You don't?" asked Julia, gulping.

"I think . . . well, I'm sure you've figured Lell out a little now. She likes to control things. And I think she feels like she can't control you if you're on the boat with us in the Caribbean."

"That seems weird . . ."

Julia watched as Polly's perfectly manicured hands circuitously rubbed the belly of her slobbering spaniel. Polly was always dressed so immaculately and obviously spent a fortune to look good and smell good, it seemed so odd that she'd let some dirty little dog shed and drool all over her.

"No. I think she's worried about her hubby."

Against every fiber in her being, Julia turned bright red. "Why?" she gasped.

"I don't know," said Polly, turning to her closet and pulling out a dress. "You tell me."

Before Julia could answer there was a knock on the dressing room door. Polly's two yippy spaniels jumped off the sofa and started barking furiously.

"Shush, Valentino. Be quiet, Armani," reprimanded Polly.

As Julia bit her cuticle nervously, Polly flung open the door. It was Scott Kelso, the society darlings' hair and makeup man, who performed his magic for $500 a house call before every black-tie event.

"Scott! Thank God! First of all, I look beyond puffy, like the biggest alien in the world today! I desperately need every cucumber on the earth's crust to lie in wait on my eyebags. And my hair! It's like, disquishious, total greaseball city. But before anything, I know you just did Brooke Lutz so you have to give me all the juice on her retarded child."

Scott, a slight man in his early thirties, parked his suitcase on wheels by the door and laughed. "He's not retarded, Polly."

"Well I heard he didn't get into any nursery school. Not a one. Not even the one in the basement of their church!"

"He's wait-listed at Hail Mary. Word is he tried to jam the square block into the round hole in his interview. Now that's just sad."

"Now that's just embarrassing."

"Oh, darling, I saw that relative of Henny's," said Scott, running his hands through Polly's hair.

"Carl?"

"No," said Scott, taking a bobby pin out of his mouth. "That handsome guy who kind of skulks around. The computer guy."

"Oh, Oscar," sighed Polly, disinterested. "Such a bore."

"He may be a bore, but he is very charitable. You know my boyfriend Ken? Well, his sister—the fat one, but such a sweetheart—she is a teacher at a public school. I mean, how noble is that? Anyway, she was honored and everything and Ken and I had to go to like this ceremony at the school—I brought Purex and Lysol to scrub down my seat of course—but anyway that hot cousin was there and he had donated like, five hundred computers to the school."

"Oscar did?" asked Julia, interrupting.

Scott turned and looked at Julia as if he had forgotten she was there. "Yes, the head of the school gave a really gushing tribute to him. Apparently he does a lot."

"That's really nice," said Julia. Wow. Unlike this gang who just goes to the parties, Oscar really gets involved. She was surprised, and yet it made sense.

"He's a weirdo," said Polly, wanting to change the topic. "I try to fix him up and save him, but it's useless. So, what else is new?"

Julia wanted to hear more about Oscar, but Polly and Scott had moved on.

"Hey, Polly," Scott asked curiously. "What ever happened to Avery Hoffs, you guys seen her lately?"

"TBD *plus tard, chéri.*"

Julia stood up. She wasn't fluent in French but she knew Polly was telling her brush boy she'd discuss it later. She, if anyone, could take a hint, even if it was in a foreign language. "I have to head out," Julia said, gathering her jacket.

"Sorry, Jules, you know Scott, right?"

"Yes, nice to see you."

"You too," said Scott, smiling.

"You don't have to go. Stay! Scott is the eyes and ears of this city. You'll know everything in twenty minutes. It's like 1010 WINS but without all that boring crap about the Middle East."

"I'd love to but you know I promised Lell I'd stop by before."

"Right," said Polly, giving Julia a meaningful look. "I hope it's okay for you there, at Lell's. After what I told you. And I'm sorry about St. Bart's."

"Don't even sweat it," said Julia. "I'll see you later."

Even though she had to walk four blocks in the chilly evening air, Julia was thrilled to be outside. She hadn't wanted to go to Polly's or even Lell's for that matter, and watch them get decked out in millions of dollars' worth of jewels just for an evening at the ballet where everyone would sit in the dark anyway, but they had both been insistent. And at first she had been flattered, especially when they had insisted, 'Oh, I need your advice on this dress' and 'Oh, I want your help picking that necklace.' But now that she thought about it, they never actually asked her advice. They knew exactly what they were going to wear. They always used these little getting-ready sessions to bring up some little point or topic that stressed Julia out. And she felt like she was a lady-in-waiting to royalty. Pathetic.

As Julia crossed Sixty-third Street she discovered newfound clarity. Polly and Lell had their little routine down pat. They'd make Julia feel like their best friend, one of the gang, an insider, and then say some sort of offhand remark to diminish her to a quivering idiot. She had to stop falling for it. She had to remain in her own private Idaho, she thought to herself as she turned into the green-canopied limestone building where Lell and Will had moved the week before.

On her way up in the elevator, Julia vowed to make a conscious effort at self-preservation. *Don't let the turkeys get you down,* she self-coached as she pressed Lell's doorbell. This was all worth it in the end—she was immersed in an amazing world, designing jewelry for the glamissimi people around her and was living the dream. So why did the dream give her a pit in her stomach? She took a deep breath. *Just be casual and focus on fun stuff, and totally ignore Will so Lell doesn't get any wrong ideas.*

A uniformed maid answered the door and let Julia in. Although Lell had been complaining for weeks that the apartment was nowhere near completion, Julia had a suspicion that it wasn't true, and her first glance told her she'd been right all along. In the interest of time, rather than have one decorator to handle the whole eleven-room project, Lell had hired Lionel Barclay to do the public rooms and Lilly Saint-Pierre to do the sleeping quarters. And Lionel had certainly done his job well. The black-and-white marbled floor in the foyer held only a circular Regency table with a gorgeous floral arrangement perched on top. Hanging from the ceiling high above was a Russian chandelier whose crystal reflections danced along the taupe walls. As Julia followed the maid down the Stark-carpeted hall she peeped in rooms. It was unbelievable. Everything about this place was eye-popping, and Julia was taking mental notes so that she could share with Douglas. Lell had a very distinct taste, one that would suggest someone older. Chintz and bright colors were banished, and instead heavy dark wood antique pieces, thick damask curtains, and dark paneled walls were favored. The art was important, but in lieu of flowery landscapes there were grim-faced portraits and reaping scenes replete with hearty farmers tilling the soil. But lest one think the Bankses were too uptight, she'd thrown in a leopard print ottoman, just to spice it up.

"You're here," said Lell, popping unexpectedly out of her dressing room. She was still in her Lora Piana cashmere robe, her hair wrapped in a towel.

"Yes."

"You're early." Something about her tone made Julia feel on edge.

"Sorry, should I come back?"

"No, it's just, I want to give you a tour myself, but I have to take this call. Why don't you go into the library and wait for me there. I'll just be a minute. Sorry, I'm running late."

"Are you sure? I can run out and come back later—"

"Don't be silly."

"Okay . . ." Julia felt immediately ill at ease. Why the hell was she there?

"Let me see what you're wearing," said Lell. "Cute! So you called Michael Kors. I knew he wouldn't let you down. Such a sweetie."

"He is so nice, and I love this dress. I just feel bad borrowing all the time. I mean, it's not like I'm a potential customer."

"Don't worry about it. He loves having his stuff on pretty girls."

"And thanks for okaying the Pelham's baubles. They really make the outfit."

"You're out there representing our company. Of course

you have to wear our stuff," said Lell, looking at Julia appraisingly. Her eyes lingered on Julia's chignon. "That's very clever how you put the Waterbury brooch in your hair. Was that your idea?"

"Yes," said Julia, touching her hair.

"I'm liking it," said Lell, nodding.

"Thanks. Anyway, I know you have to make a phone call, so I won't keep you."

Lell dropped Julia off at the library and disappeared. Julia tried not to wrinkle her dress as she sat in a $210-a-yard upholstered fauteuil, and glanced around the room. It was cozy, with bookshelves lining one wall, and a big dark green sofa and a black lacquer coffee table stacked with books on the history of Pelham's. Julia leaned closer in to the wall and ran her hand on it. Holy shit, the walls were adorned in red cashmere! That must have cost a fortune. Just as Julia was admiring the series of twelve dog prints (although she was hardly a canine lover), she heard a door slam down the hall. Angry footsteps made their way toward the library. She heard Will's voice mutter "Bitch" before he turned the corner into the room.

"Hi," said Julia, embarrassed.

"Oh, I didn't know you were here," said Will, who looked momentarily flummoxed. He walked over to a bar stand in the corner and poured himself a scotch. Julia had never seen him so unsettled. He was usually Mr. Smooth.

"Sorry, I'm so rude to pour myself a drink before asking you. Can I get you anything?"

"No, I'm fine."

Julia felt awkward. She wished she had bagged the visit. First Polly tells her there's weirdness, then Lell makes her feel creepy for being five minutes early, and now there was clearly something going on between Lell and Will that Julia did not want to get into the middle of.

Will, already clad in his black tie, rubbed his face with his hands. "Let me just chug this and get in a better mood."

"No problem."

Julia waited while he downed his drink, then refilled an even larger highball and plopped down on the sofa.

"So, you psyched for whatever shit we're being dragged to tonight?"

Julia laughed nervously. "Yeah, I guess. I like the ballet."

"I'm so fucking sick of these things. And the ballet is the worst of all."

Julia didn't know how to respond. Will took a swig of his drink, and they sat in pensive silence.

"I love your apartment. It's going to be great."

"Yeah, right," said Will gloomily. His eyebrows were furrowed and he looked deeply agitated. Julia had never seen him like this. Usually he was suave and flirty, but tonight he didn't even seem to notice she was there. And all along she had talked herself into thinking that they had some sort of secret connection. Obviously not.

"Sorry, Jules, I'm just in a pissy mood."

"No problem, really. But hey, do you think it's better if I meet you guys there?"

Will looked up and finally looked as if he was noticing Julia for the first time. His eyes brightened.

"No, not at all. I'm glad you're here. In fact, come sit here."

"Oh well, I'm fine here."

"Seriously, please come sit next to me."

Julia had no choice but to get up. She sat as far away on the sofa from Will as she possible could.

"Listen, we're friends, right?" asked Will, leaning in.

"Of course."

"Good, because friends give each other advice. And I need some advice."

"Sure," said Julia, not wanting to get in the middle of this at all.

"What would you do if you found out your wife—well, I guess husband in your case—was fucking someone else?"

Julia was stunned. She really didn't know what to say.

"Let's say," he continued, "you're getting ready to go out to another fucking charity ball you're dreading and you hear her on the phone talking to her pansy-ass Eurofag lover."

"Maybe it's a mistake."

"No mistake. And say this bitch has you by the balls. What do you do?"

Julia had no idea. She felt her pulse speed up as she tried to find a response. "I-I guess, just make sure and then try and talk things out."

Will laughed. "Not possible."

"You know, I think I should go," said Julia, rising.

Will grabbed her arm and pulled her down toward him. "Don't leave. I don't even know you, but somehow . . . you seem to be the only real thing around in this stupid world. Everything else is all bullshit. I don't know why but there's something about you. Stay with me."

Julia felt the blood rush to her head and heart. "Will—"

"You don't have to say anything. We have a connection. Let's face it, we're both owned by spoiled, rich Lell Pelham. The only difference is you can get out."

Julia stared at him in silence. How could Lell cheat on this man? He was so sweet and so gorgeous, and even though Douglas had tried to convince her that he was shallow and opportunistic, here he was being honest and open with her: he was as vulnerable as anyone.

"You don't have to say anything, Jules. In fact, don't. But just stay tonight. Come with us. And when I look at you across the room, just know that we are the only two people in the room who get it."

Julia stared at him, heat rising in her chest. He was everything she ever salivated over and beyond. Every knight, every Prince Charming, every dragon-slaying hero. Shit, why did he have to be married to Lell? Before she could say anything Lell entered the room.

"I'm ready, Jules," she said, purposely ignoring Will. "Now let me give you *la grande tour.*"

Julia got up and followed Lell out in the hallway obediently. She felt Will's eyes casting daggers on Lell, and then turning to her and softening. Now that their deep-seated affinity had been spoken aloud, it was as real as ever. If only.

chapter 27

Dearest Hope,

There are no words. I cannot begin to tell you how incredibly sorry Henny and I (and the whole gang, for that matter) are about the tragic loss of Charlie's job. Layoffs are just everywhere these days! I can only assure you that whenever people have been whispering about it, I have told them in no uncertain terms that you and Charlie will land on your feet. Do not worry about your unstable financial future in this city with two kids, and do not worry about what people are saying; as they say in the South, this, too, shall pass! I just want you to know we are all thinking of you during this extremely difficult time, and you are in our hearts.

Much love, Polly

Hope didn't know whether to laugh or gag when she opened her supposedly dear friend's note of grave condolence. It had been only two days since Charlie walked in the door, despondent, hugged his sons and looked over their little shoulders at his wife with a solemn face. And she knew. As she stood in the kitchen doorway with her oven mitts still on, she knew. Later that night in bed they talked about what they were going to do—thank goodness he had already sent out résumés.

Hope didn't really give a shit about what people thought, in fact, she'd barely thought about gossip until she received Polly's hand-delivered note. That was what made her freak out. People were talking? Plus, if that weren't enough, she came home, after gulping at the $314.73 scanned tally at the Food Emporium, and found an angry message from her Aunt Edna in Florida.

"Hope! I got your message about not coming down here this weekend. I depended on this visit! I have been looking forward to seeing you. You can be away from the boys for one lousy weekend. You come down here!"

But even with the Jet Blue fare, it would be hard. Plus, she didn't want to be apart from her boys. Hope felt adrift in a swirling sea of hopelessness, as if at any moment God might pull the plug and her whole world would wash down into an abyss. Okay, stop, she said to herself. This is so not the end of the world. You have four limbs and your kids aren't dwarves and you don't have Lou Gehrig's disease. You are not clinically depressed and your husband isn't a closet gay and you aren't a size 16. You don't have rats and roaches and you've never been robbed or attacked or raped. What are you freaking about? You'll get through this.

After an interior pep-talk monologue, Hope checked plane tickets online. We may be headed for broke, but family is family. Aunt Edna was all alone and Hope needed to see her. No matter the cost.

After talking on the phone with her aunt to resolidify her plans to travel down for the weekend, Hope went into the living room. It was weird having her husband there all day. She felt like a schizo because when he was at work she was constantly calling him wondering when he'd be home because she missed him. But then when he was camped out on their couch all day, she felt like he was somehow violating her domain.

"Sweets," she started nervously. "I know everything's going to be tight and stuff, but—"

"What, Edna is making you fly down? I heard her message."

Hope got anxious, waiting for him to tear into her for being such a pushover wimp. "Kind of—"

"No prob. I'll watch the boys. You deserve a fun weekend in the sun."

"Honestly?" she brightened. How great was he? "Sweetie, that is so nice. You swear?"

"Swear." He opened his arms wide, signaling a hug was needed, and she happily obliged.

"Well, well, well. Seat Fourteen-A."

Hope looked up from her *Us Weekly*, astonished. What the hell was John Cavanaugh doing on a flight to Palm Beach? It had been three weeks since their museum jaunt and it had taken exactly two and a half to get him out of her head.

"John!"

"What? Visiting grandparents?"

"Close. My Aunt Edna."

"Aha. Me too."

"All she does is beat up on me but hey, blood is thicker than apple juice." She lifted her cup of cider and smiled.

Just then, a tall Asian guy carrying a violin case appeared as Hope's apparent row-mate. John asked if they could trade seats, serving up a boarding pass and a smile. The musician happily agreed.

"So, answer me this, Hope. Any interest in a drink tomorrow after we tuck in our octogenarian relatives? I don't know about you, but we dine at five-forty-five and by eight, I have no idea what to do with myself."

Hope paused. Of course she'd want to meet him. How many Nick at Nite reruns can one human endure beside a snoring elder? But what about the way John made her blush? Feel? Dream? No way.

"Okay, sounds good," she said. Fuck. Brain one direction, heart another.

"Where you goin'?" asked Hope's crotchety Aunt Edna after she'd called the boys to phone-tuck them in.

"A friend's in town. Um, we were going to meet up. Since you're going to bed—"

"A friend, huh?" she said, looking over Hope's cute outfit and newly glossed lips. "Just don't be stupid, ya hear? Charlie's a good man."

"Auntie E! My God, you're crazy!"

"Am I?"

Hope closed the door behind her and headed into the beachy air.

Two hours and forty-five minutes later, John and Hope had finished a bottle of wine and enjoyed a hearty meal at Café L'Europe.

"So why did you dump her if she was so gorgeous?" probed Hope with a flirty edge. Somehow John's talk of other women made her a little jealous, but it was all safe territory, 'cause hey, she was taken.

"I told you, she was dumb as a post. I was picking her up from a bus at Port Authority and told her the people on her trip looked like plebeians and she asked if that was a family in Boston I knew."

"Come on."

"Yes. Like, hey, meet my old pals, Lisa and Lauren Plebeian."

"Retarded!"

"That's not even the worst."

"You can't top that."

"Oh, I can. We were driving on the Cape and we were talking about the cost of raising kids in New York and I said, 'Well I don't want my children living in squalor.' And she goes, 'Where's that?' "

"Oh my God," said Hope, practically choking on her Merlot.

"Can you believe that? Welcome to Squalor, Mass. Population 1,206."

"Hilarious." They shared a guffaw and then quieted down. It was as if both suddenly realized how much time had flown by and that most of their hours had been spent laughing. "Though in all seriousness," Hope said with a new tone, "with Charlie out of a job now, we might be headed for a new abode in Squalor, Mass. We'll up the population to 1,210."

"You guys'll be fine. Don't worry," he said, touching her hand comfortingly.

Hope felt a surge of heat where his fingers met hers and looked up at him, using words about Charlie as empty vehicles which were loaded with "I am obsessed with you."

"It's just hard, I get scared sometimes. There are just no good jobs."

"He'll end up okay. Trust me. I'll look into that position on Monday," he said, now rubbing her hand more suggestively. "We can make it happen."

"That would be amazing."

"Yes it would."

After paying the check and strolling into the now crisp air, Hope put her arms around her shoulders and the two walked in silence with only the sound of the wind blowing through the large palm trees. She wanted so badly to kiss him, to sleep with him, to be with him. He was larger than life, everything she had ever fantasized about. She had met Charlie when she was eighteen and, while he was her best friend and truly felt like family to her, she never thought she'd meet anyone like John, who was a matinée idol to Charlie's teddy bear. He had it all: looks, success, mega-confidence, and still wanted a smart woman as opposed to a blithering bimbo.

John sensed her feeling because he again used an innocent gesture—warming her cold arms with his hands—to gain access to her body. The arm warmage morphed into a hug, and then to her head momentarily on his shoulder. By the time they got to Hope's car a block away, the idea of making that Volkswagen rock in a parking lot somewhere teen-style would not have been so far away, the energy between them was that intense.

But amid the sea of Harlequin Romance flickers of John throwing her on the nearby sand and ripping her clothes off, Hope had an image. It was Charlie laughing. Holding her sons, reading Dr. Seuss to them in bed while she was gone. And she broke away.

"Well, this is me. Thanks so much for dinner."

"It's not that late. Why don't we go and get a drink somewhere?"

"I'd better not."

"Hope," he said, taking her hand again. "Come on, it's just a drink."

"I wish I could, I really do."

"I'll be honest with you, Hope. I ran into Polly and she told me you were coming down here this weekend. That's why—"

Hope held up her hand to stop him. She couldn't do this.

"I'm married, John, and while there is most definitely something drawing me to you again and again and . . . again, I can't do this. Not in a museum jewel box, not on this desolate street in Florida. I just can't."

And with that, she got in her car and drove off without looking back. As her heart pounded though her blouse, she floored the accelerator: back to Edna's, back to wifehood, back to a less elastic moral realm. She drove to safety, to the phone to call her husband, and away from John Cavanaugh. And probably away from Charlie's one real job opportunity.

chapter 28

Julia had managed to avoid Gene Pelham since the knee-grabbing incident, but after receiving a message from his assistant that her presence was requested by her employer in his office on Tuesday morning at nine a.m., there was little she could do to get out of it. She had dressed conservatively, in a dark blue suit with a white blouse and pearls even, more demure than her usual look, but one that she was certain would not emit any sexy vibes that would elicit lascivious moves. As she made her way down the sage-carpeted hallway to the grand corner hallway, she straightened her hair several times and took a deep breath. She was relieved when she opened the door to find not only Mr. Chester Molester, but also Pierre Luques, the chief designer for Pelham's, pouring over the new catalogue.

"Good, good, you made it," said Gene, waving Julia into a chair. "You know Pierre," he added.

"Hello," nodded Julia, who had only seen the reclusive middle-aged Frenchman from a distance. He was known to be quite the diva, and Julia was often warned to steer clear. Pierre barely acknowledged Julia.

"So, listen, Julia, the reason I asked you here is you're young, you're hip, you get it, and we need a new line. I want to work on something really big, and I thought maybe you could give Pierre here some of your ideas."

Julia was stunned and flattered. She looked over at Pierre, whose beady blue eyes shot daggers at her, and realized she had to be beyond diplomatic in order to finesse this one.

"Well, first off, Mr. Luques, I just want to say that I am such a fan. The reason I came to work at Pelham's was because I thought your designs were—are—so spectacular."

"*Merci*," nodded Pierre, obviously used to hearing this.

"And what I particularly love is that traditional element. Whereas some of the other jewelry houses have tried to go trendy, I love that Pelham's has always stuck to their guns and gone with the elegant classics."

"It's true, what you say, but the numbers need to count also," said Gene. "We don't want to just be your grandmother's jeweler. We need to bring in the young kids. The Asian tourists with their Vuitton bags and bottomless wallets. The rock stars."

"Well," said Julia, hesitating. She didn't want to piss off Pierre, but she did have what she believed were some good ideas. Should she go for it? Fuck it. "I was at the Met the other day, looking at the Egyptian jewelry—"

"Psshhhhh," interrupted Pierre with a snort.

Gene shot him a look. "Go on."

"And I saw some interesting ideas for cuff links and bangles, and I just thought, no one was really doing these sort of Egyptian-inspired King Tut things, and there's going to be a huge exhibit in the fall on Egypt, and I just thought, maybe if Pelham's sponsored some event and we did a tie-in and had like a benefit at the Temple of Dendur—"

"I'm loving it," nodded Gene.

Pierre sat quietly seething.

"It's just a thought."

"And a good one. Can you sketch?"

"A little bit," said Julia sheepishly.

"This gal can do everything!" said Gene. "Well, get over to the Met, get some info, sketches, catalogues, whatever you need, and bring it in. We'll meet back tomorrow with Pierre. Same time."

At five o'clock that afternoon Julia finally made her way out to the grand steps of the Met that spilled onto Fifth Avenue. Her head was spinning and her eyes were sore and she realized that she had not done that much research since college. But it was fun, and exhilarating. Starved from skipping lunch, she walked over to the street vendor and purchased a Coke and a soft pretzel, then sat down wearily on the bottom step to watch the crowds of tourists filter by. As she gobbled down her pretzel—she could only imagine Polly's face if she told her she ate something off the street, carbs no less—she stared at the Stanhope Hotel, which proudly stood directly across Fifth Avenue.

"Mommy! I want a pretzel!"

Julia saw that a small boy was standing next to her, pointing longingly at her doughy salted ring. "Oh, hello," she said.

"Oh, hi Julia!" Hope stood over Julia, scooping up her stray son in her arms. "Sorry about that! Come here, sweetness."

"No problem. Hi there, cutie," Julia said, patting his little brown mop of hair.

"Can you say, 'Hello, Ms. Pearce'?"

Gavin dutifully took her hand and shook it like a tiny gentleman.

"Hello, Mrs. Pearce. Pleased to meet you." Just watching him made his mommy warm with pride and love.

"Pleased to meet you," Julia said, crushed by his adorableness. "Look at these great curls."

"Ugh, I need to get him into Cozy's for a cut. Don't we, Gav?"

"No, it's cute! He looks like a Gerber baby. And by that I mean Rande Gerber and Cindy Crawford."

"Totally," Hope laughed. "Maybe we have time to run there now and get a chop? I hate to be inside any longer, though. God, isn't this a gorgeous day?"

"Amazing. I've spent most of it in the museum, myself. Design research."

"Oh, cool. We were just looking at the Greek vases for Gavin's arts-and-crafts project."

"Wow. Big stuff for a little guy."

"Don't get me started. His school literally studied the solar system at age two."

"Mom! I want a pretzel!"

"Sweetiekins—"

"You can have a piece," Julia said, breaking off a chunk. "Want some?"

"Yeah!" Gavin said, grabbing it with glee.

"Thank you. Sorry," Hope said, shaking her head and sitting down next to Julia on the steps. "So how is work going?"

"Good, I guess . . ." She felt comfortable with Hope and wanted to be more open, but she was one of Lell's best friends. "Lell's given me such a great opportunity. I just . . . sometimes miss the slower pace. But I shouldn't complain. This is huge step up for me."

"Well they're lucky to have you. And trust me, you don't want too slow a pace. I feel like I've accomplished nothing today. Just now, I was the only non-nanny when I picked Gav up at school and I thought, 'Should I be working? If so, what would I do?' " She shook her head and laughed. "Maybe I should start a handbag line or ribbon belt company like other moms."

"You seem like the best mother," said Julia, watching Gavin sitting beside her. "And that means a lot. I bet those nannies work for moms who aren't even doing anything more than facials and stuff," she comforted.

"I guess," said Hope. She really liked Julia. She seemed sweet and definitely had more depth than her pals cared to notice.

"Well we should start meandering home, bunny rabbit," Hope said, picking up Gavin. "Good luck with the designs! I am sure they'll be terrific."

"Thanks, Hope," Julia said, waving. Hope seemed like the true gem of the pristine posse. As she watched Hope stroke her son's hair and walk off holding his little hand, she wondered if she'd ever be so lucky to find a great husband and have babies.

Julia started off into space again, thinking about her future while watching a red double-decker tourist bus drive by with binocular-toting Montanans. She'd become so used to New York that she couldn't remember what it felt like to be a visitor, staying in some hotel and trying to make her way through the busy streets.

Suddenly, something across the street caught Julia's eye. It was the arm of a familiar camel hair coat outside the Stanhope. Looking more closely, she realized it belonged to Lell. Julia rose to yell across the street, but stopped. Taking that arm was a familiar hand. And it was not Lell's husband's hand, but her lover's, Alastair's. Julia stood in shock, her mouth agape, as she watched the two laughing paramours enter the hotel, nuzzling. Yikes. A hotel tryst was major. How could Lell do that to Will? Maybe Julia was naïve but she really thought that "'til death do us part" meant something. And they were still newlyweds! It was sick.

Julia walked over to the garbage can and threw out her soda. She dusted the pretzel crumbs off her coat and turned to head down Fifth Avenue. Standing right in front of her was Will. He stared at her with a sad look in his eyes, and she knew he had seen his wife in the arms of another man. Julia was speechless. Before she could muster up anything to say, Will grabbed Julia by the arm and hailed a taxi. A yellow cab slowed and before she could even think about how to react, Will pushed her in.

"Where do you live?" Will asked urgently, turning to Julia.

"Seventh Street and Second," she told the driver.

Then Will grabbed Julia and pressed his lips to hers, slowly pushing her down so that her head lay on the ripped leather seat. As the taxi glided down Fifth Avenue, Will and Julia kissed passionately, forgetting everything and everyone else in the great big city.

chapter 29

Oscar Curtis was wandering the East Village on an aimless stroll when he was stunned to see Julia walking out of a non-descript building.

"Hey!" he said, crossing the street in a truck-dodging jay-walk. "Julia, what are you doing here?"

Startled, she turned around and caught Oscar's eye as he did a dangerous Frogger sprint. "Oh, Oscar, hi—" she said distractedly. She was in a panicked sweat and seemed out of it, to say the least.

"Did you just work out or something?" he said, examining her dewy complexion.

"What? Um, no—not exactly," she replied.

"You live around here?"

"Yes, yes in there—um listen, Oscar, it's great to see you, but I should bolt. I'm . . . really late, Sorry—bye!"

And with that, she was around the corner and Oscar was left in her hectic wake.

Julia was a wreck. She thought her aorta was most definitely pumping way too much blood into her ventricles and that at any moment she'd pass out from a combo of sheer joy and sheer fear. After a heated two-hour make-out session that was so infused with desperate passion she was literally left bruised as their body-consuming kisses had her bashed against walls, Will had taken off for home plate, only to be rebuffed by a very confused Julia.

"Stop, seriously . . . stop," she protested breathlessly as he fumbled to go the distance.

After he heard her for the third time, Will stopped and they sat, hyperventilating, staring at each other for three minutes. The next move was Will's, reaching not for Julia but for his jacket.

"I . . . should go," he said. And did.

The room was spinning. Two wrongs don't make a fucking right. What the hell was she involved in here? Lell was her boss. And a friend. And even though Lell was clearly banging this jet-set dude from the little black book of yesteryear, that did not mean Julia should be hopping on her man. Her husband.

She felt the need to get out of the apartment, the scene of the crime. In the outside air, she walked with a pace so quick it was as if she were trying to shed her actions on the pavement behind her, but no matter how fast she motored, she couldn't outrun her shame.

Uptown, also wallowing in a sea of guilt, was Hope, who stared into the elated faces of her sons as she pushed them with Charlie on side-by-side swings in Central Park's Seventy-second Street playground. But instead of drowning, she pulled herself up and breathed easy—she was proud that she had not succumbed to her desire to pounce on John; she had a private dinner à deux with him and she knew damn well she'd flip if Charlie had done the same with John's female equivalent. But she was chaste. And thank God—she would not have been able to watch him now, smiling ear to ear as his sons flew back and forth with the spring wind through their hair.

"Higher, Mama, higher!" shouted Chip.

"Are you sure? You'll touch the sky," said Hope, breaking out of her reverie.

"Higher!" squealed Chip with delight.

Hope pushed her boys as high as the circa 1970s metal swings would go, and again returned to her thoughts.

"Guess what?" said Charlie excitedly, who was snapping shut his cell phone after checking voice mails. "I just got a message from that guy we met, John Cavanaugh! He said there was an opening at his firm and they want me to come up for an interview!"

"Oh, great," said Hope, the blood freezing in her veins. Was John doing this to fuck with them? Now that she had held fast to her morals, she just wanted to put the whole thing behind her.

"Strange, isn't it? I sent my résumé to more than nine places and this is the only one that's phoned. Except Panther Capital, which said they loved my résumé but that there were no positions available."

"So go for it," Hope mustered, trying to sound enthusiastic. She prayed Charlie wasn't just getting reeled in as some revenge sport for Hope's denying John a Floridian tryst.

"Well, well, well! Look who's here!" said Polly, who happened upon the Matthews family as she walked alongside Quint and his nanny, who pushed the Silver Cross stroller. "How are you guys?"

"Oh, fine," replied Charlie between pushes of the swing.

"Hey, Poll—sorry I didn't get to call you. Thanks for your letter."

"Anytime," Polly said with a serious face, placing a consoling hand on Hope's shoulder. "But look on the bright side, you get to spend the day with your husband! How nice. You're the only dad here!"

"Well, not for long, hopefully."

"Oh? Any nibbles on the job front?" asked Polly, curious.

"Maybe. We'll see," said Charlie.

"Terrific. I'm sure it'll all work out. But we'll sure miss seeing you around the playground!"

Hope smiled but turned back to face little Chip and Gavin as the pushes of their swing had been getting more and more aggressive. She pushed away her growing annoyance with Polly, she pushed away her anxieties, and pushed away the confusion surrounding Charlie's potential work with John. She wanted him to get the job, sure. But she also knew she had to stay away from John or else she could get sucked in by the tractor beam of his overpowering allure.

chapter 30

Lell was completely in the throes of her love affair with Alastair. She was so consumed that she was almost becoming reckless. Almost. She was too careful not to let anyone know what she didn't want them to know. And what she did know was that Will knew, and that was exactly what she wanted.

Lell was one of the most guarded people in the world. Her image was important to her, and she never wanted anyone to see her feathers ruffled at any given moment. Therefore, even with her best friends—Polly, Hope, and Meredith—she never let her guard down. There was, however, one person with whom Lell was completely candid, and that was Maria de Barca, a Camp Arcadia friend from long ago, who was now a South American socialite and one of the most important women in Venezuela. Perhaps because she lived so far away, or perhaps because she was the most discreet and astute person Lell had ever met, she was the only one who knew the hows and whys of Lell Pelham. More than anyone, including Will.

Fortunately for Lell, Maria came to town often, usually to be fitted for designer clothes, and Lell would spend hours with her at her suite in the Lowell, confessing everything. She was Lell's mentor, guide, and shrink (and would have been her maid-of-honor if Maria didn't think bridal parties were gauche). After telling her the details of her life, Lell would sit back and let Maria analyze her.

"This is the classic Lell Pelham story," said Maria, pouring herself another cup of Earl Grey after Lell concluded the story of her affair with Alastair. "You like—" (when Maria said *like* it was with her Venezuelan accent so it sounded more like *like-a*) "the men who are the rogues. You like the men you can never trust. It is because of Daddy."

"Don't start on that Freudian daddy crap again, Maria,"

said Lell, breaking apart a scone. (Maria was also the only person Lell would eat carbs in front of.)

"But you more than anyone, Lell darling, have the daddy problem. Your mama is never pleased, she is mean to your papa, you in turn try to please your papa, to say sorry for your papa."

"Okay, this is gross."

"Lell, your problem is you never open up to people you might care about. You might really love Will, but you never give him a chance to enter your heart because you are worried he will hurt you. That's why you chose to hurt first, and sleep with others to make him mad and jealous."

"No way," said Lell, about to protest profusely. But then she stopped. Maybe there was a grain of truth there.

"I'm right. You know I'm right."

"I'm not sure. I mean, Alastair knows how to treat a woman. He is just totally my type. And everyone thinks Will just married me for the money."

"Do you?"

Lell paused and thought about it. She knew the gossip. More than that, she saw that Will was more than thrilled to chuck his job the second her dad mentioned setting him up with a hedge fund. He was certainly to the manor born with the use of her private jets and clubs. Was that why she was cheating? Because he probably secretly hated her and married her for the money?

"I guess he did," said Lell, softly. "Or else it certainly sealed the deal."

"Will is—how they say in Jane Austen? A fop," Maria said

loudly. "He likes the life of luxury. He likes the toys and good life. But he likes you, I see it. He doesn't understand you, and you push him away, that's why you have these problems."

"Whatever," said Lell, not really wanting to dissect her life any longer. It made it seem sordid and complicated. "I'm having my fun."

"You be careful, Lell," warned Maria. "You can only push a man so far. Men are all ego, they need to be told they are number one all the time. Will is the same. And he will look for someone to stroke him like a cat."

"Good luck. No one would cross me that way," said Lell confidently. That was one thing she was certain about. Because any girl who tried would be run out of town. If they made it out alive.

chapter 31

"Hi, Julia, I don't know if you remember me."

"Of course, Nina, how are you?" Julia's mind raced. Who was this girl? Publicist? Editor? No! Friend of Lell's who had trunk shows, that's right.

"I'm great," said Nina, strolling into Julia's office and sitting herself on the armchair across from her.

"I'm so sorry, Lell has stepped out for the afternoon. Is there anything I can help you with?" asked Julia.

"I came to see *you*, actually," said Nina, taking out a Chanel compact and reapplying her lipstick.

"Oh, how can I help you?"

"First of all, I want to invite you to my dinner party two weeks from Thursday. It'll be small, but fun. And lots of cute single guys."

"That's so sweet. Sure, I'd love to come."

"Great," said Nina, lackadaisically looking around Julia's office. Her eyes scanned every nook and cranny, and she clearly approved of the decor and all of the subtle touches that Julia had added to make it her own.

Julia was surprised that Nina had asked her to her party. She didn't even know Nina knew who she was. But then again, Julia had been showing up a lot in *WWD* and some of the other mags lately, and there had even been a small item on her in Page Six. It had erroneously referred to her as the Pearce glass heiress, but Lell had told her not to bother correcting it. It seemed kind of fraudulent, but Lell seemed so sure.

"Secondly, I'm kind of here on behalf of someone else," said Nina, whispering.

"Oh, okay."

Nina leaned in. "Do you think your office is bugged?"

"No—" Julia was about to protest, but then she remembered that Lell had that Big Brother camera from which she watched everyone at Pelham's. She wouldn't be surprised if she had a nanny cam lasering in on her as well. "Maybe," Julia said.

"Then let's go somewhere else. Can you leave?"

"Um . . ." Well, it was only five and technically she wasn't supposed to leave before six, but she knew Lell was gone for the day. Socializing with the likes of Nina Waters was part of her job, wasn't it? "Sure."

"Good, let's go to Cipriani for some Bellinis."

Fifteen minutes later Nina and Julia were ensconced at a table in the legendary Fifth Avenue by way of Venice restaurant.

"So, Jules, the thing is, I am very connected in this town, as you probably have heard." She gave Julia a look that said *you better agree.*

"Of course."

"So, anyway, my friends have been watching you. One in particular. And she likes your style. You should be very flattered, because this is someone who doesn't like a lot of things or people, but everyone likes and worships her."

Nina gave Julia another look that said *react appropriately.*

"I'm very flattered."

"So the point is, this girl, and I think you know who I'm talking about, is the American ambassador for her family company, which is based in Europe. And she really has her eye on you. She thinks you're totally underused at Pelham's and you shouldn't take it."

Julia was unsure what to say. PR means tact, so she had to act accordingly. "Oh, well—"

"Anyway, she wants you to come work for her."

"That's very nice, but I—"

"It's tricky, because she and Lell are *dear* friends. But it's obviously a much better situation for you. I mean, I know you don't have to work, being a Pearce and all, but it will be very lucrative and far more glamorous."

She wasn't a friggin' Pearce, should she tell Nina? She was tempted to learn more about the offer, but something kept her from moving forward with the conversation. She didn't know if she could trust Nina. Was Lell setting her up?

"Well, I don't know what to say, except that I'm very happy at Pelham's and Lell is great to work for."

Nina took a sip of her Bellini. "We'll see how long that lasts, what with the Will situation."

Julia felt immediately light-headed and panicked. "What do you mean?" she asked, trying to be casual.

"Oh, come on. Polly told me everything."

Julia's mind was racing. Polly couldn't have known about that romp in the back of her cab. And at her apartment. That was the only time—the first and last. What the hell was Polly saying? She had to compose herself.

"I don't know what you're talking about."

Nina smiled. "Oh, okay, whatever."

"No, seriously, Nina. There is nothing going on between Will Banks and me. I don't know what is up with Polly's imagination, but it's not true."

"Whatever you say," said Nina, clearly not believing her.

"Are you sure no one followed you?" asked Julia, pulling Will into her apartment and shutting the door as quickly as possible.

"Yes, what's the big deal? I knew you'd be happy I called, by the way," said Will, leaning in for a kiss. Julia pushed him away.

"Listen, we have a major problem. I just had drinks with Nina Waters, who said Polly told her that there was something going on between us. I'm freaking! What if Lell finds out? I'm dead, you're dead, I'm out of a job and on the street—"

"Relax, relax," said Will, taking off his coat and plopping himself down on the couch with ease. Julia couldn't help but notice how handsome he looked in his blue-checked button-down and khakis. He smiled at her and ran his hand through his hair.

"How can I relax? I feel like the devil. I am Satan. I kissed you, and you're married and I literally made you break vows and I'm probably going to fry in the bubbling lava of hell! Lell is my friend and *boss* and I'm now like, the white trasher from a Lifetime TV movie who deserves every lousy thing that comes her way."

"Sit down. Come on, you're hardly white trash, first of all," said Will, pulling Julia to his side. He put his arm around her.

"But I'm evil."

"No you're not, don't be crazy, Jules."

"How can you be so calm? We broke commandments together, Will. We're on the fast track to Hades. Do not pass go, head directly to the infernos of the underworld."

Will smiled at Julia. "You're so pretty when you're worked up."

"Barf, Will!" said Julia, jumping up. "I'm serious."

"Okay, okay, seriously. First of all, can you get me a drink?"

Julia went into the kitchen and pulled out a Sam Adams. She took the top off, then went back into the living room and handed it to Will. "I hope beer's okay."

"What about you?"

"I'm not thirsty."

"Come on, you need to relax."

"Fine . . ." She stormed back into the kitchen and got herself a beer. She noticed Will's was almost finished by the time she got back.

"Come here,"

"Will, please—"

"Will you just come here?" said Will, his tone now gruff. Startled, Julia robotically came and sat next to him.

"Listen to me, Julia. No one knows anything, just get that out of your head. Nina Waters and Polly Mecox can sit on their fat asses and gossip about whatever they want, but they are just gossips, and liars, and no one listens to what they say, so don't worry about it."

"But what about Lell?"

Will ran his fingers through his hair, exasperated. "You shouldn't think twice about Lell. Lell is so busy screwing that pathetic Eurotrash faggot, that she doesn't notice anything. And don't forget, *she's* the one who should feel guilty. She's the one who cheated first, who . . ."

Will stopped and Julia looked at him closely. The vein in his temple was pulsing and his eyes were on fire. "She's the one . . ."

Will stopped again and took a deep breath.

"What?" asked Julia softly.

"She never loved me, Jules. Never. She told me that on our honeymoon. She only married me because her parents wanted her to, and she thought I was an appropriate match, or some fucking thing like that. I forget exactly what she said. She's a selfish bitch, Julia. There is only one person Lell cares about and that is Lell. So you shouldn't waste your time caring about her, because she totally couldn't give a shit about you or me."

"Will, I'm sure it's not true . . ."

Will turned and looked at Julia. "Don't defend her, Jules. Because you're just a little cog in some master plan she has. People are disposable to her. You should look out for yourself. Because right now you're a fun game to her, but she'll get rid of you soon. You should watch your back."

Julia was unsure how to react. Lell had always seemed so nice, she couldn't imagine she'd *dispose* of her. But then again, she was banging some British dude, totally cheating on her hubby.

"I don't know."

"Well, I do, Jules. And I need you right now. I know it sounds corny, but I need you." Will, with a totally mournful look, buried his head in Julia's chest. Julia rubbed his head, her fingers sifting through his silky dark hair. How could Lell treat this Adonis like shit? Will was the best thing that would ever happen to her.

Will looked up and into Julia's eyes with such a sad look that she melted. And against every moral fiber in her being, she couldn't resist him. She was going to hell, but heck, the journey there would be amazing.

But after ten minutes of passionate, heated kisses, Will (as any dude would) wanted to go further, and something in Julia clicked. As he rubbed her chest under her sweater and began to fumble for the bra, Julia pushed him off and got up.

"Will, we can't."

"Why?" he said, red-faced and panting from their fevered rolls.

"Not yet. Not until you're like not married."

"Come on, Jules, this is it, we both want it."

"No shit. I mean, yes, of course I do, but look how majorly I've been freaking from just messing around. If I sleep with you, I am FedExed to hell. I couldn't deal." He listened while rubbing her leg. "Please don't do this."

"Okay, okay," he looked up into her eyes. "One day."

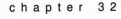

chapter 32

Dearest Auntie Louisa,

Well. I can't say I haven't tried. Your dear Oscar is a lost cause, I am afraid. I know I promised you I'd find your son a suitable wife and get his head "out of the books," so to speak, but the boy is simply not interested. I hate to be the one to break this devastating news to you, but may I simply offer that perhaps he is . . . not so inclined to the fairer sex? Just a thought. I've tried everything—introduced him to several eligible beauties from very fine families, brought him to countless parties and benefits, even hosted him for a weekend at the beach in a house festooned with charmers aplenty. It seems he has little interest for anything outside work. Alas. All

work no play makes Oscar, well, quite a dullard.
Still trying for you . . .
    Yours, Polly

Mrs. Mecox popped her handwritten note into the envelope, penned the Newport address, and dropped it off for her doorman to walk to the corner and mail. Their poor cousin Oscar. What was his issue? I mean, there were plenty of nice girls all around. Polly hadn't wanted to be too shocking with her implications, but maybe he was gay. He didn't have an effeminate aura, per se, but he clearly showed zero amorous penchant for women. Oh well, not her problem! Onto other things.

First and foremost, Polly had to finish planning the trip to see her mother in Scotland. Her stepfather, a prominent politician there, was going to be running for a Parliament seat soon, and she wanted to see her mother and brothers before the race got heated and took up more of their time. After dialing the endless number, speaking to the butler, who treated her as if she were a telemarketer, and then waiting on hold for a full seven minutes, she heard her mother come to the phone.

"Darling, hello."

"Hello, Mother."

"What can I do for you? You know we are quite busy. The boys are simply running raaaaampant! I tell you, these hellions. Be careful there, Charlton!"

"I'm sorry to bother you, Mother—"

"It's all right."

"Um. I just . . . wanted to check in about our visit. For you to see Quint. And have him . . . meet his uncles."

"Right. Well, Ashforth and I thought you and Henny should reside in the Cruxworth cottage. You'll have everything you'll need there."

Polly's heart sank. "Oh . . . okay. I just thought—"

"Thought what, darling? Charlton! Mummy said no!"

"I just thought we could stay with you. In Hill Court."

"Darling, I think the cottage would suit you better. You'll need your space."

"Mother, I want to be . . . in your space. With the boys, Quint's uncles. They've never met him, and—"

"It would simply be faaaar too chaotic, I'm afraid."

"But the manor has over forty rooms."

Her mother inhaled. Polly could hear her mother's silent frustration mounting across oceans of telephone wire.

"Polly, just as I don't burden you by sleeping under your roof, you shouldn't feel entitled to stay here. I always happily check into a hotel when in New York."

"That's because you prefer hotels. It's hardly a favor to us."

"I will not stand for this. We simply have too much going on right now, what with Ashforth's campaign, Charlton entering his new boarding school, and Ashton and Ashby leaving for Eton in a month's time. I have offered you Cruxworth, which is a splendid residence."

"And you're saying take it or leave it."

"You said it, not I," Polly's mother replied in her clipped British accent, then hung up the phone.

Polly was fuming. She felt like her mother's leftovers from a Champagne-submerged wild-teen life she longed to erase by moving across the Atlantic. After having Polly at age seventeen, her race car–driving aristocratic Italian boyfriend was, well, Audi 5000. He denied paternity, but after a few pinpricks to a week-old Polly's infant heel, his blood ties were confirmed and he was indeed the not-so-proud padre. He established a hefty bank account to wash his hands of the whole mess. But her mother's love wasn't enough—it wouldn't be enough for a goldfish. Polly's mother always loved boys and prayed never to have a daughter—too much in-house competition for men. Later on the gods listened—she bore three sons with her husband, who had been a barrister in London. They had courted through the social season, then wed in a lavish five-hundred-guest ceremony as it was her first, and therefore a white, wedding. Polly was absent from the nuptials. Already enrolled at Bement in Massachusetts, a prep school for girls that starts in sixth grade, at age eleven, she knew she was a footnote in her mother's past. Her mother was moving on from the daughter she'd borne at age seventeen and was off with her new illustrious husband to repave her destiny. And now her three sons would probably never know Quint, their nephew, or Polly, their milk-carton sister, for that matter.

The only mother Polly had ever really known was Vanessa Leigh, her dorm mistress, who was more of a fairy godmother who looked after her at Groton, where she attended high school. Sadly, as all her classmates flew the coop for fancy island family getaways in Lyford Cay, Little Dix Bay, or Mill Reef Club, Polly would stay with the Leigh family during her vacations. Many times, even up until the night before Polly's scheduled flights to Scotland, with her suitcases fully packed, Polly's mother would phone and say "it might be best" if she didn't come home to Hill Court on account of a sick Ashton or a colicky Charlton. So the Leigh family became her own. Sort of.

Vanessa's son, Elliot, was a "fac brat" classmate of Polly's and Hope's—he was red-faced and shy, with a bout of teenage acne and constantly averted eyes. Polly and her mean clique of athletic, popular, pretty friends ignored him in the halls, but Hope always stood up for him, saying he seemed kind of sweet and even cute. But Polly still walked by him as if he were invisible. Even though she knew that deep down, come Thanksgiving break, her mother wouldn't send for her and she'd be facing Elliot over a carved turkey once again. She'd gone to Hope's house once, and always had the invitation to return, but something about seeing such a Norman Rockwell happy family celebrating the holiday together made her despondent. She'd rather be in and out, quick dinner then quick escape. Plus, she never wanted to admit that she'd been ditched.

All those packed suitcases waiting by the dorm door, waiting to be loaded into a taxi trunk and sped off to Logan. All those suitcases unpacked into dorm drawers. All those nights as the lonely tenant of an empty hundred-bed house. They say you only can love as much as you were loved yourself. That you run on as many cylinders as you were given by your parents and those who loved you. And as Polly walked by her son's nursery, she lightly touched the little hand-painted baby blue elephant border, afraid that maybe she was running on very few cylinders. And even those, due to years of incessant disappointment, were cased in cold, impenetrable steel.

chapter 33

Douglas was cooking his famous pheasant potpie for Lewis, who had just had a really long day at work. The tiny kitchen was overflowing with bubbling pots and pans, cutting boards, and produce. There was barely enough space for Douglas to squeeze through, let alone create a culinary masterpiece.

"It's four hundred degrees in here," said Lewis, entering the apartment. "What's going on?"

When he turned the corner into the kitchen, he instantly beamed. "Ahhhh, my favorite!" Lewis said, chucking his jacket down and giving Doug a kiss on the cheek. "I couldn't need this more. I'm exhausted. Thanks, sweetie."

"My pleasure. Jules was supposed to come though, I don't know where she is."

"I'm sure she's on the way."

"I hope. I know she's been swamped and all, but . . ."

They heard her key turning in the door. "Hi guys!" A blushing, glowing Julia walked in and attacked both with giant hugs. "Oooh, let's turn this up!" She ran to the radio and pumped the dial up and shimmied into the kitchen.

"Holy shit, girl! You have way too much energy for the end of the day," observed Doug, smiling curiously.

"Next you're going to start singing into a wooden spoon," teased Lewis.

"Oh, you know, good day at work."

Lies. She had been walking through Central Park with Will, on the West Side of course, so as not to be seen, drinking in the pale pink cherry blossoms that fluttered down on them whenever a breeze hit. It was like bathing in petals, blessing their secret stroll from above.

"How's work going, Jules?" said Lewis, grabbing a drink from the fridge. "I haven't seen you in ages."

"It's great. It's so amazing working for Lell. She's just such a great boss."

"Yes, we hear a lot about Lell these days," said Douglas, with the slightest hint of sarcasm. It seemed to him that all Julia could talk about was Lell Pelham and her little coterie of society bitches.

Julia ignored Douglas's tone. "Well, I do work for Lell, so of course I talk about her."

"How do you like her?" asked Lewis.

"She's good to work for. Don't ask me what I think of her personally, because I think she really takes a lot of things for granted in her life"—this was lovesick Julia's attempt to defend Willoughby—"but she's a very good ambassador for the company."

"Jeez, you sound like her PR agent," sneered Douglas.

"Well, I am in a way," sniffed Julia. She was sick of Douglas being jealous. Granted, it could not have been easy that she was now working *upstairs* while Doug toiled downstairs with the customers, but hey, it wasn't her fault, was it?

"I saw Lell Pelham today," said Doug. "She was leaving early for a management conference. Everyone said it was at a spa."

"They do it at Canyon Ranch in the Berkshires," said Julia knowingly. "She said I could go next year. Can you imagine *moi* getting pampered at a spa? That place costs more for a weekend than I make in a month!"

"Tough work," sighed Lewis. "Too bad my business trips aren't like that. I get cold quesadillas from room service at the Atlanta Westin."

"It's so funny," said Doug. "She's going to the mountains so she's all decked out in, like, Patagonia, but it's designer fleece, hilarious."

"Patagucci," laughed Lewis.

"Totally!" said Doug. "I call it Pradagonia!"

"This girl's life sounds insane," said Lewis.

"It's pretty awesome," Julia agreed dreamily. She knew that Alastair would probably be sneaking up to Lenox to "hike" with her. She knew when Lell announced she was leaving to "get away" for a few days and "research," the only hiking going on would be Alastair hiking up her skirt. But Julia didn't care. In fact, she loved it because Lell's actions unbound Julia's moral strictures; if Lell was cheating, her marriage was no longer sacred. And if sweet, doting, gorgeous, kind Will was wounded by her dalliances, why shouldn't she swoop in as his emotional Florence Nightingale? Just thinking of him then, recalling their talk on the park bench, their shared milk shakes in the grass, made her feel charged with a joyful jolt she'd never experienced. She put a hand to her stomach as if to quiet the rambunctious butterflies flapping wildly within.

As a new song started, Julia spun around, lifting Doug's arm up so she could twirl under it. Her ladylike skirt spun out into a fabric flower as she giggled giddily.

"Well, you're looking quite blissed out," Doug said. "Another promotion?"

"No . . . just a nice afternoon with the city as my office. We're doing an architecture-inspired line, so I was at the library researching."

Bullshit. Doug knew her too well.

"Really?" he asked, observing her shy laugh and fresh, crisp, very Lell-like outfit down to her pink-polished toenails. "Are they giving out Ecstasy tablets at the library these days?"

Busted. Julia couldn't lie; it was too much outside her nature. She crumbled, guiltily. "Okay, okay, I'm sorry! I just know what you guys think about cheating. But it's chaste. It's not a real cheat. We've only ever kissed."

"Let me guess," said Doug, shaking his head, "Will Banks?"

Instead of confirming with words, Julia shrugged with a slightly guilty smile. Only an hour before Will had taken a momentarily reluctant Julia in his arms and kissed her deeply under the bursting April blossoms. She collapsed dizzily into his squeeze. They could have been anywhere, they felt so transported by the moment.

"Oh shit," chastised Lewis. "It's none of my business, but that is a bad idea."

"Can you believe this chick? It's called playing with *fuego*."

"Come on, you guys, that's why I didn't tell you," said Julia, her balloon of rapture slowly coming down to earth. "You don't know all the details, so don't be so judgey."

"Fine," sniffed Doug. "Do what you're doing. But everyone gets caught. Look at Gunther Moldberg."

"Who is that?" asked Julia, not that she cared. Sometimes she was just so tired of Douglas's righteous little stories about his friends and acquaintances from Fire Island. It was like enough already.

"His boyfriend, Michael, was something like head of Calvin Klein Home and is the sweetest thing ever and Gunther just screwed all these Provincetown himbos behind his back. One day Michael caught wind and Gunther was out on his ass, alone, broke, and miserable. And then he got hit by a speeding taxi and died on lower Eighth Avenue right in front of Rawhide."

"Douglas! What are you saying?" asked Julia with mounting frustration. "That if I continue seeing Will I'll get mowed down as some kind of retribution from above?"

"You yourself know that it's wrong, Julia. That's why you're so testy."

"Don't start, Douglas."

"I just don't want you to get hurt. Because no matter what, Will is never going to leave his wife or his life. That dude loves those private jets and fancy cars, and he needs Lell to pay the bills. You are naïve if you think he is serious about you. Snap out of it."

"Well excuse me, Douglas, Sorry I'm not perfect or part of the perfect couple. Sorry I'm not you and Lewis!"

"You're so defensive."

That was it. Why did she have to take this? He wasn't her mother. He didn't know all the circumstances. He didn't understand that Will was just as much a victim as Lell was. She grabbed her bag and walked out into the spring night, slamming the door behind her.

Oscar Curtis was sick and tired of takeout. How many friggin' bagged sandwiches could one human consume? Not to mention Chinese delivery overload. Each night when he finally exited the office, he began his quest for his nightly meal. For the last decade, he had been so busy he truly thought of food as fuel and would gladly have accepted, if offered, a pill that would satisfy all his FDA-recommended calorie needs. But then as his company grew and then went public, he really was at the helm of an already flying ship; he had a bustling, competent, devoted staff that he had assembled and trained; he had built a machine that was now coasting on its own. So why the cheesesteak eaten at his keyboard? He knew the answer was because work had eclipsed his life. And now he didn't know what his life held for him outside work. He knew that in the city that never slept there were men his age drinking at bars and going to baseball games and dating girls, but how could he start that now, out of the blue? It wasn't like he could just walk into a bar and start talking to people. Plus, who was he kidding? He loathed most people anyway. They were just too dumb or would inevitably let him down. But what was the use of all his success without someone to splurge on? So little by little his evenings alone turned from a stuffed-down dinner to a careful search for the perfect meal—it was his activity, to fill the void of walking the streets or channel-surfing alone at home.

On this particular spring evening, after taking a circuitous route home from the office, he suddenly got a craving for a great foot-long hot dog, and Second Avenue Deli was nearby. As he approached the pickup counter, he spied Julia sitting alone at a table with her head in her hands. He froze. He was going to grab the dog and bolt, but Julia looked somewhat sad. He felt an urge to cheer her up.

"You're looking less frazzled than when I saw you last," he said, standing above her.

"Oh, Oscar, hi—" she wiped an errant, confused tear from her cheek. Doug and Lewis had hit a nerve. And it wasn't like she could pick up the phone to call Will about it. She didn't even have his cell number. He was at some poker night, anyway. Plus it was all too fragile and charged with fear.

"Are you okay?" Oscar asked. "Would you like company, or are you . . . wanting some space?"

She was annoyed that she had been caught crying. And while she wasn't thrilled to make small talk, she didn't want to be rude. "No, no, please, sit—"

"I was just ordering some dogs, want one?"

"Oh, no thanks."

A waiter walked up, taking a pen out from behind his ear.

"I'll have two hot dogs with everything, please," Oscar asked. "And this young lady will have a piece of hot apple pie with ice cream." The waiter nodded walked away.

"I will?"

"I think it will cure what ails ye."

"Oh really?"

"Really. And I won't even ask what that may be. But it's a

nice night and a girl like you should never be crying into an empty coffee cup."

Julia smiled. "What's a girl like me?"

Oscar suddenly got nervous again. Part of him felt so at ease and natural around her while the other half remained the bumbling idiot he'd been when he first saw her at Pelham's. But he looked at her tearstained cheeks and had to answer her. "Oh, you know," he shrugged, embarrassed.

She looked away. There was an awkward pause for just a moment, and then as the food was placed in front of them, he got another surge of guts. Hell, he had nothing to lose.

"So maybe I lied. I will ask. What is it that ails ye?"

"Oh, silly stuff," she answered.

"Try me."

"Just work stuff . . ." she trailed off, looking out the window. She looked back at his piercing gaze and felt she could trust him. "And maybe I'm just a bit lovesick."

Ouch. Oscar hated to hear someone else had captured her affections. He didn't know what to say, and finally sputtered out, "What dope would put you through that?"

She laughed. "Not a dope. Maybe I'm the dope. It's pretty complicated."

"Oh."

"Whatever," she said, waving her hand. "I'm fine."

"I'm sure." Oscar watched Julia's sad face and suddenly felt emboldened. "But I will say that this guy is a total zero if he isn't dropping everything to be with you."

How sweet. Oscar was very kind and Julia knew from day one he had a truly warm, nice core. But *nice* and a Metrocard will get you a seat on the subway. *Nice* wasn't the thud-inducing magic of Will Banks calling her to meet him in the park. And *nice* certainly didn't keep you warm at night. Okay, maybe warm, but never hot.

"You know what? It's not important," said Julia, trying to regain her composure. "So what are you up to?"

"Not much."

"No date tonight? Speaking of which, how's *your* love life?"

"Mine?" sputtered Oscar. "Well . . . nonexistent."

"Why's that?" asked Julia.

"Well . . . I don't know. I work a lot."

"That's no excuse. Don't you ever go out and date?"

"Not really."

"Why not? You've got to get out there. Isn't there anyone?"

Oscar bristled. "You know, you're beginning to sound a lot like Polly with this bombardment of questions."

Julia was surprised. "I'm sorry. You're like a total catch. I'm just surprised when you show up alone all the time."

"You show up solo at parties."

Julia paused. He was right. She did show up alone. But she never felt that way because Will was usually around. Julia laughed. "I guess I'm the pot calling the kettle black."

Oscar smiled. "Yeah."

"Well look at us. Two nerds with no dates."

"But obviously there is someone, if you're feeling a little . . . lovesick." It made Oscar cringe to say the words.

"Yeah," said Julia, remembering her anguish.

Oscar watched Julia's face fall. "Julia," he began.

"Yes?"

"Just . . . Just make sure this is the right guy. You shouldn't be wasting your time worrying about some loser. Really. You're a special girl."

"Thanks," said Julia, embarrassed.

"No, I mean it," said Oscar seriously. "I haven't quite figured out why you're running around doing this society thing, I mean, I guess it's for work and all, but you seem so different from the crowd that you're hanging with. I guess that's why sometimes I give you a hard time. I mean, you're unusual. You listen to people, you speak your mind, you have a big heart that really truly wants to help people . . ." he trailed off.

Julia blushed. "Thanks, Oscar."

"No, I mean it," he said, raising his voice a little. "You're real, Julia. Don't change."

Julia stared at Oscar in the bright unflattering lights of the diner. She felt very exposed, and yet, it was not a bad feeling. She felt like Oscar understood her, and liked what he saw. His dark eyes penetrated very deeply into her, and she blinked under his intensity. Suddenly she felt a rush of guilt and foolishness over her dalliance with Will. This flirtation was a disaster in the making—the kind of thing she never thought she would ever be involved with, something that she could not justify, and yet, something that she could not resist. If Oscar knew what she was up to, he would surely disapprove. She felt ashamed, as if Oscar were a moral compass sent to guide her on the right path.

His words echoed in her head again and again. It was both a challenge and a warning, the type you'd get from someone who knew you well and wanted the best for you. Oscar was that type. If only she was strong enough to say no to Willoughby Banks. But her heart was not yet ready.

chapter 35

"I know, Polly, I know," said Hope into the phone. She had been on the receiving end of Polly's rebuke for the past ten minutes. She hadn't been able to get a sentence in, except "I'm sorry" and "I know." She did know, and she was sorry, but that wasn't good enough for Polly.

"I just feel like this is a personal attack on me. You know how much this event means to me. I counted on you and Charlie. You're going to completely mess up the seating. Now who am I going to sit next to Henny? He really doesn't like very many people. I don't want to sit him next to Nina Waters. She totally puts the moves on him, that fat cow. I don't understand, Hope. How could you do this to me? Why?"

Polly was really putting Hope in the most awkward position. Was it really so hard to understand that Hope and Charlie had to decline this year's Crusade Against Scoliosis benefit? Tickets were $500 per person, and with Charlie out of a job that was just out of the question. Polly was just pissed because she was on the committee, although Hope knew for sure she had never attended one meeting and thought scoliosis could be caught by drinking bad water in Africa. Couldn't she at least have a *little* sympathy?

"Polly, this isn't about you. Look, it's just not the best time for Charlie and me, and we really have to pick and choose what charities we support."

"Oh, you mean, 'cause of the job thing?" asked Polly.

"Yes. The job thing. I mean, of course we can afford to go to all of these things," said Hope, lying, "but it just seems better to streamline what charities we show up for. You know, Polly, if you're on the committee of too many charities, people get tired of you. When you call they just think you want their money."

Why not turn the tables on Polly? She was being totally inconsiderate, forcing Hope into admitting that she and Charlie were having major financial problems. Let her worry about *her* image.

"You think so?" asked Polly, nervous.

"Well, come on. Don't you? You don't want to be the person always asking people to spend hundreds of dollars to hang with you at some stuffy ball where the guys have to wear monkey suits and the food is terrible."

"You're totally, right, Hope. I certainly don't want to be that person. Yuck!"

"So thanks for being understanding."

"Do you think I should bag, also? I mean, what is scoliosis *anyway*. Do we really care?"

"You can't bag now. Your name is on the invitation."

"Whatever. I'm not going."

Hope shrugged. She wanted to get off the phone. Charlie would be back soon from his meeting with John Cavanaugh, and she was nauseous with worry.

"It's your decision."

"I'm calling them right now. I'll talk to you later," said Polly hastily. "Oh, I made reservations for Friday night at Le Cirque. Lell and Will are coming, and you and Charlie are too. I won't take no for an answer!" said Polly, hanging up.

Le Cirque? That would cost them $300, minimum. And she knew that Henny would again insist on ordering the most expensive wine, and they'd all have to split it. No. She and Charlie would have to decline. She'd say that one of the kids was sick. She hated doing that; she was too superstitious it might come true, but what other choice did she have?

Hope looked at her watch. Two-thirty. The kids would be up from their naps soon, so she didn't have much time. She was drafting an e-mail to her former boss at Frothingham's. She wanted to sound casual, but she also wanted to know if they'd be willing to rehire her on a part-time basis. Basically, she'd only net about five grand total, with the money she'd have to pay her babysitter to watch the kids, but with their savings dwindling, Charlie and Hope were running out of options.

Suddenly, the phone rang.

"Hello?"

"Shall I give him the job?"

Hope froze. It was John Cavanaugh.

"Um, hello—"

"Charlie just left. He's a nice guy. A lucky guy. What shall I do?"

Hope didn't know what to do. All of a sudden, she felt like she was in the middle of a sordid mess. It was as if she had actually done something wrong, and cheated with John. It seemed so sinister that he'd ask her this, and she felt as if she'd betrayed Charlie regardless of the fact that she'd never so much as kissed John.

"I think you should give him the job if you think he's qualified," was all she was able to muster.

"Come on, that seems a little wishy-washy."

"Okay. Then yes, give him the job. Charlie's awesome, and he's so smart and a very hard worker—"

"Now there's a sales pitch."

Hope stopped. What did he want her to say? "What do you want me to say?"

"I'll give him the job. But I want to see you in person before I do."

"John—"

"Just once. Don't worry. Have lunch with me in Greenwich tomorrow. I'll pick you up at the train station. At noon."

Hope's blood raced. Tomorrow? Greenwich? The suburbs were the bastion of evil. But Charlie needed this job. They all needed him to get this job.

"Okay."

"See you there."

chapter 36

One of the most coveted invitations in town was to Maxine and Derek Jenkins's jazz supper, held every May at their immaculately restored Harlem brownstone near Central Park North. They kept the party small, with maybe only seventy-five or so people included, which meant that everyone who was invited accepted and that, coupled with the fact that they were always able to coax a famous hermit or celeb out of seclusion, lent the evening an extra dosage of excitement. The young African-American couple were society darlings: Harvard grad Derek had founded an extremely successful hip-hop label, and Maxine's line of dresses were sold exclusively at Barney's and Jeffrey.

This year Lell, Hope, and Polly all made the cut, and in a nod to Lell's success in her role of Henry Higgins, Julia was also invited. There were a flurry of phone calls among all the girls about what to wear, as well as general speculation regarding who the surprise guest would be.

As soon as Lell entered the turn-of-the-century mansion and greeted her hosts, she and her husband wordlessly parted ways, with Will heading for the bar and Lell seeking out Alastair to drag him off into one of the dark corners of the thirty-room mansion.

"Lell, you look amazing," said Hope, greeting Lell at the entrance to the drawing room.

"You're so sweet. You look amazing yourself."

"Thanks."

"So, it's Salma Hayek," whispered Hope.

"What do you mean?"

"The celeb guest. Salma."

"Oh."

"I guess she met the Jenkinses when she borrowed one of their Frida Kahlo paintings for that movie."

"Great." Lell could care less about celebrities. They were all uneducated idiots to her, and although she'd fake kiss their ass in order to get them to buy Pelham's jewelry, she thought of them as little more than vaudeville morons. Acting seemed so bourgeois to her, like a wind-up monkey of sorts—someone meant to amuse the paying public.

Charlie came up and handed Hope a drink and greeted Lell with a kiss. "Can I get you something, Lell?"

"No thanks," she replied, scanning the room. "I'm going to wait."

Hope and Charlie both knew what Lell was waiting for, and were embarrassed that it was becoming more and more obvious to everyone. They couldn't ignore the gossip, and the fact that Lell had basically been unreachable—although out every night—for the past few months confirmed their suspicions.

"You've been totally MIA lately," said Lell, turning to the Matthews.

"I was thinking the same of you. But we've been around. Just not really doing the charity circuit."

"Right. Gets boring," said Lell, her eyes still dancing through the crowds looking for Alastair. Where the hell was that son of a bitch? He knew she would be there at seven forty-five. She had told him three times.

"I'm going to go say hi to Patrick Wickham," said Charlie. "Excuse me."

Hope looked over in the corner. Patrick Wickham worked for Tiverton Fowler, a company Charlie was interviewing with. She crossed her fingers.

"How have you been?" asked Hope.

"Wonderful," said Lell.

"Are you sure?" asked Hope, concerned.

Lell looked at Hope with pity. Hope was the sweetest person in the world, but sometimes she just didn't get it. She had not said anything to Hope (or to anyone except Maria) about Alastair because she knew that Hope would be horrified—so traumatized that she would probably need therapy to overcome it. Hope and Charlie had such a *Leave It to Beaver* perfect marriage and had been together since they were like fetuses that they could never imagine anything bad happening in their world, let alone *infidelity*. But they had no idea what Lell had to deal with. Will was so in her debt both financially and emotionally that she felt like he was no longer a challenge. She owned him. It was not her fault that she had no choice. She was creative and couldn't lapse into a dull puddle of boredom.

"Don't give me that look, please, Hope. Just please don't."

"Okay, okay. Sorry."

Lell glanced around the room. She saw Julia enter—wearing a stunning Vera Wang gown. In fact, that was the very gown that *she* had wanted to wear, but Vera said it was on hold for someone else. What was that about? Vera was letting her assistant have first dibs? Forget that, she'd call Vera on Monday to let her know what she thought of that. Maxine clasped Julia's hands and was obviously gushing about how happy she was that Julia had come, because Julia was beaming. Lell made a second mental note, this one to remind Julia of her place on Monday. While yes, she wanted her to be a well-regarded representative of Pelham's, she did not want one of her employees to eclipse her. Not to mention the fact that they were in the new issue of *Vogue* on one of the party pictures pages and Julia's picture was slightly larger. Hmph.

"Hello, darling."

Lell turned around. It was Alastair. Lell flushed as he leaned in for a kiss on the cheek.

"Hope, it's been too long. My my, ladies, you both look ravishing," said Alastair, turning on the charm.

"Thanks, Alastair. How have you been?" asked Hope.

"Couldn't be better. I beat Jeremy Stix at backgammon today at the Racquet Club three times in a row. You should have seen the look on his face. Now, what can I get you ladies to drink?"

"Cosmopolitan," said Lell, smiling.

"I'm all set, thanks," said Hope.

Hope watched Lell's glowing face as her eyes followed Alastair to the bar.

"Be careful, Lell," warned Hope.

"Oh please, Hope. You worry about you, and I'll worry about me."

That little bitch, thought Lell. Who did she think she was? Lell took another gulp of her wine.

"Are you okay?" asked Charlie, her dinner partner.

"Of course," said Lell. Of course not. She was looking across the room at Alastair practically fawning over Tinkly Adams, the twenty-two-year-old rifle heiress. Lell knew his MO too well. He was totally flirting with Tinkly. He'd laugh at anything she said, and then put his hand on hers when he was telling a serious story. Disgusting. What did he think he was doing? Lell had been furiously trying to make eye contact with him so she could shoot him a seriously infuriated look, but he had been avoiding her gaze.

"Well, what do you think, Lell?" asked Julia. She was on Charlie's other side.

Lell had no idea what they were talking about. She had not paid one stitch of attention to them or their silly conversation since she sat down. She was so angry that she had been seated at the opposite end of the room from Alastair. Wasn't Maxine supposed to be this genius with seating?

"I don't know," said Lell, dismissing them.

Charlie and Julia exchanged a look that Lell saw, but didn't care about. They had no clue why she was angry. She ignored them, and they went back to their conversation. Will, who was on Lell's other side, noticed his wife was bristling, even though he was in deep conversation with Maxine.

"Excuse me," said Lell, scraping back her chair. She was just going to walk by Alastair on the way to the bathroom and give him a look so that he would cut out this shit. She knew she looked awesome tonight, so he'd better behave.

As Lell took a circuitous route to walk by Alastair, many eyes in the room watched her. Most because she was so stunning and gorgeous, but others because they had heard some whisperings and rumors about what was going on, and they wanted to be witnesses to a potential scandal.

Lell walked by Alastair, but he didn't look up. He was so engrossed with Little Miss Tinkly that he didn't notice her—or he pretended not to notice her. Lell went into the bathroom and locked the door. She splashed water on her face and plotted her next move. Well, two can play that game.

On her way back to her chair, Lell pinched Alastair on the neck. It was very subtle, and if several sets of gossip-loving eyes hadn't been alert to zoom in on Mrs. Banks, it might have gone unnoticed. But Polly, who had perhaps the best view, saw it, and couldn't believe her eyes. Mouth gaping, she turned to look across the room at Hope, who looked worried. Alastair, meanwhile, flinched ever so slightly, but didn't remove his eyes from his latest heiress. He had a new hotel to finance, and he needed some funding pronto. Lell was fun, but she was married now and couldn't be of that much use to him anymore.

Lell went back to her seat and draped her arm around Will, who was still chatting with Maxine. Will was startled, his wife hadn't been affectionate with him in months. But Lell became fully engaged in the conversation, laughing loudly, tousling Will's hair, and making sure everyone saw how "in love" with her husband she was. And almost everyone did see. Julia saw, and took an uncomfortable sip of wine and felt again like Mary Magdalene. Hope watched Lell's sham continue, feeling embarrassed for her friend. Polly saw and felt vindicated. But the person who didn't see was the one it was all aimed at: Alastair. He could not have cared less what Lell Pelham Banks was doing, because he had moved on. It was all about Tinkly Adams for him now. Lell was history.

"Sweetie, what's wrong? You can tell me."

"Nothing—"

"Liar."

Lewis was calling Doug out on his spacey behavior while the pair was eating a beautifully prepared, tasty meal in the lush garden of a Palma restaurant in the West Village. The full moon shone over the rare plant-filled spot nestled in the concrete jungle of Manhattan. The air was warm but breezy and the plates of delicious comfort food before them were indeed comforting. But Doug's thoughts meandered away from paradise to his roommate Julia.

"Okay, Lew-lew. You know me too well. I can never bull-shit you. I just . . . feel lately like I'm kind of losing Jules."

"I know. But sweetie, she couldn't be joined at the hip with us forever. She needed to find her own place in this town. She needs other friends and maybe love. She can't run around with fags all the time."

"It's not just that I see less of her. She's changing. I saw her go by with Lell today and she barely even said hi to me. Then last night she was packing for her weekend in Montauk and I asked when she was leaving, and in all seriousness she looked at me and said, 'Wheels up at eleven-fifteen.' I mean, that's private-jet-speak—could you gag or what?"

"No, she didn't—"

"Yes! That's what I'm saying. I know it's a glam life for her, filled with fabulosity beyond measure, but *wheels up?* That just ain't her. She's getting sucked into their bejeweled Hoover vac of wealth and pomposity."

Lewis looked at Doug and smiled coyly. "Can you blame her?"

"No. I'm fucking jealous."

Lewis and Doug shared a laugh that was full of humor but mixed with the sad tinge of the semi loss of their friend to the scene Doug had always admired from afar. But now that he had seen what that world was doing to her, he didn't really worship the glitz so much anymore. At the end of the day, he had Lewis, who was all he ever needed.

"Lewis, I'm so sorry I have been distracted with this. By them. I guess from the second I got here I always thought there was this dazzling, alluring life I wanted to be a part of. I worked at Pelham's and saw all these beautiful fast-track people. But now I just feel like there's . . . so much darkness out there. At the top of that golden ladder, it's all sham marriages, and the big bucks in their Vuitton wallets are not even a Band-Aid for all that internal bleeding."

"Listen sweetie, many people say, Oh, if I were rich or I were famous, I'd be happy; if I attain x or y, I would be satisfied. But obviously that's not true! You can still be in your penthouse and be lonely and miserable and die with no one by your side. Private jets don't keep you warm at night."

"They do if they have central heating systems."

"You know what I mean."

"I know. Well, that's what I've learned." He looked into Lewis's eyes. "Nothing really matters to me anymore but you."

Lewis touched Doug's hand and smiled. Behind Doug, two guitarists walked into the garden and started playing.

"What's this?" asked Doug, shocked.

"It's for you. Everything tonight is for you. I even hired a full moon."

"Shut up!" Doug smiled in amazement.

The guitarists approached the table, each playing in tandem harmonies that melted together into the summer air.

"Do you remember when we met?" asked Lewis.

"Of course."

"Well you brought me back from the dead. My heart started that night. I brought you here tonight," Lewis stopped as his voice broke. "Because I want to be with you—always. Lewis rose to his feet, then knelt on one bended knee and pulled out a small velvet box.

Doug couldn't help but notice that the box was from Cartier, not Pelham's. Lewis snapped open the box to reveal a perfect thin gold band.

Lewis took his boyfriend's hands in his. "Douglas, you are my whole life and I love you. I want to marry you. Will you be my husband and be with me forever?"

"Yes," said Douglas. He leaned in and kissed Lewis, his best friend, and now more than his "partner." Douglas kissed his fiancé.

"What the fuck is the matter with you? Be a man!" Lell smacked her husband across the face. "You can't get it up? I'm your goddamn wife!"

"Lelly, I—"

"Don't *Lelly* me. What's the problem? A thousand guys in this town would kill to do me."

"And they have."

Pin-drop silence pierced the Bankses' grand master bedroom as the husband and wife stared at each other, both with tempers raging and hearts burning for other people. Other people who were a long way from their gilded penthouse.

Lell paused, looking down. "*Excuse* me?"

"You know what I am talking about. That Brit?"

"It's not true," she denied.

She was such a lousy liar. "Give me a break, Lell, I'm too smart for that bullshit. How many weeks after our honeymoon were you fucking him again?"

"I will not put up with this sort of language!" she snapped, getting a silk charmeuse robe to put over her sexy negligee, which wasn't sexy enough to do the trick that rainy Saturday night.

"Listen," said Will, putting a hand on her shoulder. "I know all about it. And it's okay—"

"It is?" Lell asked, amazed. What a relief, in a way. What

a load off her shoulders after all the sneaking around and cheating. Not that it was such a tough burden; lying was second nature to her.

"It's okay. Because I've found someone, too."

Lell paused as the blood rose to a sizzling simmer in her miles of veins. "*What?*" she said in a tone so laced with ice it was as if she were breathing and spewing pure liquid nitrogen. "*Who* is it?" she asked with venom rising as she grabbed his collar. "You fucking tell me this instant."

What followed would not have registered on the furious zigzags of the Richter scale. A Ming vase was smashed to pieces, a Steuben olive dish hurled only centimeters from Will's head, a painting thrown to the floor, tears, screams, ire, agony, and a door slammed so hard, a piece of the hand-painted faux-marble fell to the floor outside Lell's bathroom.

Julia was sitting by the window, watching the rain fall and listening to the pitter patter on her crappy humming through-the-wall air conditioner. She was plopped in her sweats, another night alone with her salad wondering what Will was doing. She was dizzy and drained but at the same time longed for him to recharge her. He had become like a drug; she was literally on cloud ten with him, and then all quivery and drowning without him. What a crazy situation. The tension of the evening at the Jenkinses' jazz supper had made her heart pound like a timpani; it was getting too over the top, too dangerous. The flirtations and stolen smooches with Will made her soar up into ecstatic strata, then when she saw Lell, *her boss*, running her hand—the hand wearing their wedding ring—through Will's hair, she would plummet back down, but not to earth. To hell.

The phone rang, ratcheting up her pulse even further. And just when she'd thought nothing could bring it more to a sprinting pace, she heard his voice.

"Julia—" Will said. She heard a car honk behind him.

"Will? Where are you?"

"In a phone booth. I need you. There is so much to say. Run away with me."

Julia gulped. What? "Run away! Are you insane? Where?"

"Just . . . away. Away from this town, this city. This *life*. Come away with me. Let's go to an island. I'm getting tickets now. You're it for me, Julia. Tell me you'll come with me."

Julia didn't know what to do. She had to weigh everything quickly in her head. Here she was with an apartment full of stuff, on a random Saturday night, alone, dreaming of the man who was on the line asking her to run away. Wait, what did she have to weigh? *Of course she would*, this is what she wanted! Right? The stars were aligning. Why not take the plunge? This was meant to be. "Okay, yes, I will. I'll go with you."

"It has to be now. Tonight. We'll be on a beach and won't give a damn what people think," Will said breathlessly.

"Okay . . ." Julia answered rapturously.

"Pack your suitcase. For a long time. I'll be there within two hours to pick you up."

"All right, okay, Will!"

"Bye." He hung up.

Julia was so stunned she couldn't even handle the coronary she felt on deck. How utterly romantic! She realized that her life had become something straight out of a romance novel, and although it was absurd, why not play along? The swirling visions of paradise by Will's side, the sun, the freedom, and . . . the consummation of their pent-up, way overheated desires, it just seemed to good to be true. Not normally a horndog, Julia had gotten so lost in her reveries of sex with Will that she often didn't want to wake up. The only thing that pulled her out of bed was the small chance she'd see him that day; that he'd stop by the office and take her in his arms for a quick kiss. Or just happen to be outside in a tinted-windowed town car to pick her up and spend the trip home in traffic and in heaven until he had to turn back around to go collect his wife for some dreary function. And now they'd be free.

In a Tasmanian devil whirlwind, Julia ran amok through the small apartment, grabbing bags and stuffing clothes into them wildly: toiletries, sandals, dresses, camera, sunglasses. Everything was stuffed into three suitcases. After an hour of frenzied, exhilarated packing, she forcefully zipped the bags and lugged them to the front doorway. There they were: her life in luggage.

She ran around throwing herself together—drying her hair, picking out a dress for travel, and putting on her thin gold Pelham's hoop earrings. Finally, after two hours of running around, she exhaled. With a slow, steady breath meant to temper her overworked aortic valve, she sat down.

And waited. And waited. She looked at her watch. It had been four hours since Will had phoned. Now three a.m., she doubted any flights would be taking off. Ever. Had Lell stopped him? Had he changed his mind? Was he in a terrible accident? Julia was nauseous just thinking of all the possibilities. It was too good to be true, she realized. Just a fantasy.

chapter 39

> *Dearest Chauncey,*
>
> *I am devastated, just destroyed. I cannot even begin to tell you how incredibly sorry I am about the sudden loss of Mercedes. I just heard the tragic news and am shattered for you—I know you spent a small fortune on those lady breeders in Minnesota! Mercedes was truly a special dog. You are in my thoughts—Henny and I send our deepest condolences and support for what I am certain is quite a difficult time for you and Bucky.*
>
> *Sincerely yours, Polly*

Oh fuck. Polly was just about to seal the letter to Chauncey Rutherford when she realized something. Her blood pressure rose as she noticed her grave error. It wasn't Chauncey's cocker spaniel *Mercedes* that had been run over by the Hampton Luxury Liner this past weekend in Southampton, it was her Yorkie, *Porsche*! How could she be so stupid? Oh goodness. Polly got up from her desk to retrieve more stationery from the brown and red Mrs. John L. Strong box on the mahogany-stained office shelf. She gasped. It was empty.

After practically lashing venom through the phone wire at the Barney's rep after being told it would be six weeks for her new supply to arrive, Polly hung up. She simply could not deliver something to Chauncey that was not *top of the line* couture stationery. Chauncey, like Polly, had a fabulous eye for printed matter, and always turned cards over to make sure they were engraved. Polly practically got hives when she saw that people—supposedly of taste—used thermography instead of traditional engraving. Chauncey was the same, and Polly simply could not give her anything but the best. She sniffed in disgust! A condolence note written on crappy paper would make her feel even worse—like she was downgraded to the B box of personalized stationery.

As Polly's stress levels were beginning to climb, she had a cartoon lightbulb over her head. What about this e-mail thing everyone does? She knew Chauncey frequently used it—she always whispered about the items on PageSix.com—perhaps instead of using flimsy lower-quality paper, she should use the Internet? Brilliant.

Polly entered Henny's study and looked at his Macintosh as if it were a caged lion. Fear mixed with a yearning to touch it. She reached out and turned it on nervously. Well, there! A little smiley face, that was comforting. She moved the mouse as she'd seen people do, trying to open icons, but the result was a series of clicks that froze the computer. Actually nothing was really wrong with it—she could have just turned it off and started again, but the screen's inaction sent her over the edge. She dialed Hope.

"I am freaking out."

Uh-oh. "Why?" asked Hope.

"The computer just crashed. I don't know what to do. Henny will kill me. Kill me. It's his; he's very territorial about his computer! What should I do! I've killed it!"

"Okay, calm down," instructed Hope, rolling her eyes. Thank God it wasn't something really tragic. "Just call Mac-Menders. It's really not a big deal, they can save anything."

"Oh thank God! Thank heavens!" said Polly, hanging up.

Ahhhh, 411, Polly's best friend. After pressing 1 for the fifty-cent connection, the helpful friends at MacMenders answered, telling her to drop it off.

"Well, I can't go down there! Can't you send someone here?"

"Uh . . . we don't normally do that, ma'am—"

"What kind of a junior varsity operation are you running there? This is New York!"

"Well, I can send a messenger service, but that'll cost a pretty penny."

"Pennies aren't pretty. They're expendable. Arrange for the pickup."

"Yes, ma'am. Let me just get an order form . . ."

chapter 40

Julia was green.

"Come on, sweetie," said Douglas, standing sympathetically in Julia's doorway. "I know it's so hard, but you have to get ready for work. You can't just lie here until he calls you."

"Why not?" she asked blankly. She was in a fog.

"Jules, honey, you can't worry about what happened. We'll find out soon enough. We have to go to work now, you don't want to get in even more trouble."

Julia felt like an anvil had been placed on her chest. After all the hopes, the excitement, the sheer joy of the prospect of Will sweeping her up and away, the crash down had not been pleasant. Or even bearable. She hauled her grief-weary bones out of bed and into her clothes. Douglas gave her a hug and held her hand as they walked to the subway.

When they arrived at Pelham's, no sooner did Julia bid Doug farewell and ascend to the top floor than her dread sank in. She had a pit in her abdomen that was worse than any cramps she'd ever experienced. And it was about to get a hell of a lot worse.

The elevator doors opened, and when Julia stepped out there was an eerie silence. It took only a second to realize that all eyes were on her, including those of two burly security guards—the two, in fact, who had first escorted her to Lell's bridal suite on her wedding day. And this time they were here for quite a different purpose.

"Well, well," said Lell, coming out after the receptionist had quietly buzzed her, alerting her to Julia's presence. "I'm sorry, Julia, but you've been terminated."

"What?" Julia started shaking.

Gene Pelham walked out. "Julia, you messed with the wrong family when you made a play for my son-in-law."

"What? Is that what he told you?" she said, incredulous.

"And now the game's over," said Gene. "Our lawyers have already filed a restraining order. Goodbye."

He turned to his daughter and put a comforting arm around her. "Come on, dear, she's out of our lives now."

The guards tried to take Julia by the arms. "I can see myself out," she protested.

"Sorry, miss. Boss's orders."

In a tearful walk of shame more humiliating than Bud Fox's in *Wall Street*, Julia Pearce was paraded off of the polished premises. Out on the street, she panicked. She didn't have Will's cell number and she needed to call him. She started walking toward his office. Her walk became a jog, then a run, then a sprint. Her feet carried her as if her life depended on it. Certainly her reputation did.

Panting and exhausted both emotionally and physically, she approached the security desk, asking them to call up to Willoughby Banks at Marblehead Ventures. She waited as the phone rang.

"It's voice mail," the guard answered to a sweating Julia. "Should I— Oh! Here he is right now, hello, Mr. Banks!"

Will Banks froze in his steps as Julia spun around to meet his stare. A full five seconds passed before either could speak. Julia couldn't read his expression, but it was markedly different from the last time she had seen him. She could see his shoulders stiffen through his custom-made suit.

"Will, I—" Julia started, her voice breaking. "I just got fired. What did you tell Lell?"

Will paused, keeping his cool. He gripped the handle of his briefcase tighter and took a deep, controlled breath.

"I told my wife that perhaps you had taken my affection toward you too far and misinterpreted—"

"Wait, what?" interrupted Julia.

Will looked over at the guard, whose eyes were bulging and mouth was agape. He quickly looked at his computer, but was clearly taking it all in. Will gently grabbed Julia's elbow and guided her away from the desk.

"I think you misconstrued what I had said to you, as well as my intentions for you. I was merely being nice to you, because you are an employee of Pelham's and directly report to my wife. Any other reason for my acts of kindness toward you were obviously misinterpreted."

He had been rehearsing this little speech, and Julia felt like she was going to hurl. "Are you fucking kidding me? Me? Misinterpreted? How should one translate the words, *Run away with me!*"

"I'm terribly sorry," he said coolly. "If I have misled you or hurt you in any way. I wish you the best, Julia." He walked past her into the elevator and out of her life forever.

chapter 41

Two nights later, at the Erase Cataracts Today ball, there was talk of nothing but that social-climber Julia's unwanted advances on Will Banks.

"What was she *thinking?*" Polly asked her table, which included Hope and Charlie, Lell and Will, and Meredith, who was back in good graces with Polly, and Oscar, who was a human seat-filler.

"That little upstart trash," said Polly. "I never had a good vibe from her. She gave me the creeps. What a loser."

"It's sad, really," replied Lell, her hand on Will's shoulder. "Poor thing. She messed with the wrong people."

Hope looked at Will, who was busy eating his roll, which had just been placed before him by a tails-wearing waiter holding bread tongs. What a lucky distraction, thought Hope, who pitied Julia. It was awful of her to go for Lell's husband, just awful. But if there was one thing Hope knew, even about her dearest friends, it was that there was two sides to every story.

"Is this—Julia? Julia *Pearce*?" asked Oscar, stunned.

"Helloooo? Where have you *been*?" Polly taunted Oscar. "You've been in your office too damn much. Julia Pearce is out of our lives. And out on her ass. She tried to go for Lell's husband!"

Oscar was quiet. Suddenly, the pieces aligned. As he looked at Will with his eyes focused on his bread plate, he knew this was the man who had been putting Julia through all her traumatic ups and downs. That motherfucker, Oscar thought. Now he's going to pass it all off on her and come out clean on the other side.

"I believe there are two sides to every story," Oscar said to the table in Julia's defense. Hope looked up, shocked her thoughts were not just shared by someone else but were being articulated.

"Pardon?" said Lell, squinting her eyes. "What are you insinuating?"

"You tell me."

"Okay, let's not get all crazy here," interrupted Polly, shooting Oscar a look. "Maybe you don't know the whole story. But I assure you, that trailer-trash dork who climbed us is over in this town. History. She's gone the way of the brontosaurus."

"Oh, is that how it works with you people?" asked Oscar.

"Oscar!" Polly said angrily. "*Us* people? That freak slithered into our lives and passed herself off as the glass heiress and turned out to be a nothing from Nowheresville!"

"I don't think so," he responded, sickened by the company at the table.

"Oh, what are you, her little Lancelot? How cute? Does someone have a little crush?"

Now Will looked up from his plate. Oscar shot him a look of death.

"No," he said, standing up. "I'm not her Lancelot. She is her own knight; she has strength and character, something you all know nothing about. And if perhaps she did make a mistake," he said this last part shooting Will a deathly look, "it is only because someone else took advantage of her and exploited her. You all used her as your little plaything, then didn't hesitate to throw her away. I think it's disgusting."

With that, he walked away.

"Well," said Polly, dumbfounded. "Of all the insane things! I believe he is half cracked! What a total loon! What a fool!"

The table remained quiet.

Polly continued. "I don't think I've seen a bigger

brouhaha in all my days! The nerve of that louse storming out of here in that manner!"

She truly did believe nothing could rock their clique's polished, perfect little world more. The fact was, something could. Something very, very bad was brewing and about to hit the holders of calligraphied *Table 27* cards like a hurricane.

"Mr. Henderson Mecox?" a voice boomed.

The table turned to see a detective in a trench coat along with two blue-uniformed NYPD cops.

"Y-yes," Henny replied, as the surrounding tables stopped clanking their dinnerware and started looking over.

"You're under arrest for two counts of child pornography and solicitation. You have the right to remain silent." Henny was lifted from his Pierre Hotel ballroom chair. "Anything you do or say can be used against you in a court of law." His arms were pulled behind his back and his wrists cuffed.

"I didn't do anything!" protested Henny. "You've got the wrong guy!"

"Mr. Mecox, we found several hundred downloaded pictures of underage children in provocative positions and states of undress on your computer. That is a federal offense."

"You can't just go in and get my computer!" protested Henny, shocked.

"No, but when your computer is serviced, the store has an obligation by law to turn the evidence over to the police."

Oh my God, thought Polly. What have I done?

As the officer continued Mirandizing Henny—"You have the right to an attorney—"—Polly let out a shriek, then a sob, then fell dizzily to the floor.

Hope was exhausted. She and Charlie had spent half the night at Polly's comforting her, which really meant keeping her from jumping out the window, and supplying her with sedatives. It was surreal. But it had to be true. Hope couldn't help but feel a little guilty—she was the one after all who had referred Polly to MacMenders. But still, how creepy and sick was it that Henny was a pedophile and a pervert? Perhaps it was all for the best to have him put away. Maybe now he could get help. She had no idea if it was little girls or boys he'd been looking at. And to think, Gavin and Chip had been to Polly's a number of times! Hope shuddered.

She had never had a good vibe about Henny. He was like a man-child, still living as if he were back in boarding school and it was all about drinking as much vodka as possible and referring to old chums by their childhood nicknames. So immature. But what was Polly going to do? Hope was so lucky she had Charlie and that she knew him inside and out. He would never ever be part of a scandal like that. He would never betray her. And yet, she felt horribly guilty for the way she had nearly betrayed him.

"Oh, my Lord, I just heard, just heard!" squealed Franny Corcoran into the phone. "Poor Polly! How will she live? This is so humiliating! I could never show my face in town again."

Hope was not in the mood to field these fake condolence calls. Franny was the town crier, and she just wanted to pump Hope for any additional info so she could spread it around and be the first with the news. Forget that.

"I know, it's terrible. Listen, Franny, I'm so sorry but I'm on the other line. Can I call you later?" lied Hope.

"You better. Because I'm so *concerned*. I want to know what I can do for Polly. Shall I send her a basket from Fauchon? Oh, but she doesn't eat carbs. Hmmmm . . . Let me think about it. What do you get the wife of a pedophile?"

"I'm not sure, but I gotta go. Talk to you later."

Hope hung up the phone. She was at her desk, sipping tea and trying to revive herself so that she could write some cover letters. But her lack of sleep and anxiety was totally blocking her. Frothingham's had not bitten on the part-time work application, much to her frustration and embarrassment. And that coupled with the fact that John Cavanaugh would most definitely never give Charlie the job was enough to put them in dire financial straits. She had no choice but to try to gain employment somewhere.

The front door shut and Charlie entered the apartment. "Good news!" he said, excited.

"What?"

"John Cavanaugh called and he wants me to come in for another meeting. It looks good!" Charlie looked at Hope expectantly. She smiled, but inside she felt nauseous. What was John going to say? Was he going to tell Charlie about their flirtation?

Hope had no idea what John was thinking. She had not gone to Greenwich to meet him. She had stood him up, making it as far as Grand Central Station only to sit on a bench for hours watching the giant clock. She didn't want to play games. She didn't want to have an affair, or do anything that could remotely be construed as leading John on. No. Better to stay away, and if it meant that Charlie didn't get the job, it would be her cross to bear. She'd just have to get back in the workforce and do her part for the family. But there was no way she'd deceive Charlie. She loved him too much.

John had called her cell twice, but she hadn't picked up; she'd only heard his messages. He had not tried contacting her again. But now this. Hope didn't know what he was going to say to Charlie. Would he tell him about their dinner in Florida? Would he make it seem like she led him on? *Had she?* She never actually did anything. But she felt horribly guilty nonetheless. Hope swallowed hard and smiled.

"That's great, honey." And she hoped it would be.

Charlie scooped Hope up and gave her a hug. "This could be it," he whispered.

Yes, thought Hope. This could.

chapter   43

Julia hadn't left the apartment in days, nor the bed, for that matter. She lay there, motionless, save for her finger on the remote changing channels. She was now a full-fledged *View* addict and decided she wanted Elizabeth Hasselbeck's job. Boy, she'd love to sit there and just have fun and dish every day.

But now everyone was dishing about her. It all started with Franny Corcoran, who got wind of the supposed "situation" from Polly, then told every gossip columnist in town. The week before it was a blind item on Page Six: *"WHICH young, beautiful jewelry store heiress discovered one of her dear friends/employee was making a play for her investor husband?"* Then, like clockwork, sure enough on Gawker.com, a flood of e-mails poured in. "I heard it was Julia Pearce, of Simon Pearce Glass Blowers in Quechee, Vermont!" Then another typed in "She *wishes!* She's no heiress! She just let everyone believe she was, but she doesn't have a pot to piss in!" Nice.

And then the *Daily News* item and then the *Gotham* magazine piece. New York was abuzz about this mysterious girl who had managed to infiltrate this tight clique, usurp the limelight, then steal the queen bee's man. All lies. Julia shuddered at her naïveté—she should have listened to the red flag warnings Douglas tried to give her. She should have blown off Will's very first advance. But then what? She only would have been friends with them even longer, and therefore had an even later wake-up call. She just couldn't believe Will had sold her out like that.

"I brought you the paper," Douglas said, walking through the door with a half knock, holding a Starbucks cup and a *New York Times*, which he placed on her bedside table. "The paper with all the news that's fit to print, not that other trash."

"You mean that other trash that *everyone* reads?" she said, sitting up to take sip the coffee.

"That a few people read," he corrected. "Think macro. This will all blow over," he said, putting a hand on her shoulder. "There are bigger things in life. Bigger problems, graver issues. You'll get through this and it will seem a distant, meaningless memory."

"Thanks, Doug. I love you." She hugged her friend.

"You, too."

There she was, no guy, no job, no hope. She was, most of all, ashamed of herself and embarrassed. She thought about Lell and Polly and the rest of the posse, and could imagine them eviscerating her the way she had heard them do to others so many times. She knew she could expect that. But she also thought of some of the other people she had met, and could only imagine what they were thinking. For the most part, she really didn't care, because they would ultimately move on to the next scandal. But for some reason, Oscar Curtis kept coming to mind. In fact, she started thinking a lot about Oscar. He'd as much as warned her. It was as if he'd foreseen the outcome. And maybe he had. He obviously knew this crowd better than she did. At the time he had seemed irritating, but she wished she'd taken his advice. But what made her most ashamed was that he had expected better of her. And he'd always seemed to connect to the real her, not the false Julia that Lell and Polly had labored so hard to project.

Thinking more and more about Oscar made her realize that she had really not been honest with herself. Here was a guy who was totally her type a few months ago, pre–Lell, pre–Will, pre–ascent into high society. He was not flashy, he was not Mr. Life of the Party, but he was introspective and kind. He was the type she would have flipped for in the past, and yet she was so caught up in her glamorous scene, she'd treated him as an afterthought. One day she hoped to make amends. He didn't seem to be the type to say "I told you so." Yes, she actually looked forward to running into him again.

She started flipping through the paper, and with each article she read, she felt more and more emotional. She cried harder than she'd ever wept before. Not just in self-pity, but also in relief. Her experience was not a tragedy, it couldn't hold a candle to the war or families torn apart or hunger or a real, bottomless vat of grief—she would be just fine. In fact, at the end of three hours with the Gray Lady, Julia felt . . . encouraged. She got up, showered, and decided to stop being a whimpering lump and start doing something. Helping people was surely the way to help herself. And since she'd been pressured by Lell to leave Girls, Inc., she hadn't felt the same.

She hopped off the 6 train in Harlem and walked to the after-school center, where she hugged her former fellow helping hands.

"I have no idea where I'm going to work now," she said. "I want to keep designing jewelry, but I have no clue how or when that will happen. One thing I do know is I missed you guys," Julia wiped a tear. "And no matter what I do next, I'm never leaving again."

"Glad to have you back, Jules," said her old department head, Purva. "It wasn't the same without you."

chapter 44

Polly:

While I sympathize with you during this horrid time, you must understand that it is simply impossible for me to drop everything in my life and come and be by your side. You're a big girl, Polly, and you made your own bed, so you should lie in it. Things are in such a tizzy now, with the boys out of school on summer holiday, so it is really for the best if you stop trying to contact me incessantly and learn how to handle your own problems. I think a divorce is the best way. Let's reconnect when things get sorted.

Mummy

Polly ripped up the FedExed letter and hurled it across the room. How dare she? How could her mother abandon her in her darkest most dire time of need? Why had she never ever, ever made any effort to help her or to act as a mother? Polly started sobbing bitter tears. She felt sorry for herself. She was now a social leper, she was married to some sort of pervert, and none of her friends, well, except Hope, were talking to her. It was disgusting and, most of all, unfair! What had she done to deserve this? Nothing!

Polly sorted through the rest of her mail. Nothing good. No invitations, no thank-you notes, no letters of support.

Junk mail. Finally, she noticed a cream-colored envelope, where her name was boldly addressed in blue ink. No return address. Polly used her silver letter opener to slice it open.

> *Dear Polly,*
>
> *I hope you don't think that it's presumptuous that I write you and let you know that I know you are going through a hard time (I guess we all are these days) and I just want to say I'm sorry. I guess we have to take the good days with the bad, and although everything sucks right now, I can only hope that everything will be better soon. You've always been really nice to me, and I appreciated your friendship. I hope you will be well and take care of yourself and give your adorable son a kiss for me.*
>
> *Love, Julia*

Hmph, thought Polly. The nerve! How dare that little trailer tramp equate their situations! Sure, Henny was a pervert, but she could divorce him, whereas Julia was a pariah and a charlatan and there was no getting around that! Polly hurled Julia's letter in the trash, just as there was a knock on the door.

"Come in," said Polly.

Polly's maid opened the door. "Mr. Charlie is here."

"Thank you, send him in."

Polly had asked Charlie over so that he would be present for her first face-to-face with Henny. She was scared of Henny, now that she knew he was a maniac, and did not want to be alone with him in the same room. She quickly got up and looked at herself in the Art Deco mirror. Her eyes were not so red, Charlie would barely notice she had been crying. She fluffed up her hair and smoothed down her collar before there was another knock on the door.

"Hi, Poll, how are you?" asked Charlie, coming in and giving her a kiss.

"Oh, Charlie, so so bad," said Polly, tears in her voice. She arranged herself carefully on the green velvet sofa, and motioned for Charlie to sit down on the fauteuil across from her. "This has been the most horrid time for me."

"I can imagine."

"You're so dear to come. Can I get you something to drink?" Before he responded she buzzed her maid on the little button on the wall. "Gladys, bring in the tea caddy."

"No need to go to any fuss—"

"Charlie, please. You are doing me *such* a favor. And thank Hope for taking Quint tonight. Because I am just terrified, *terrified*, to go through this alone, and certainly don't want Quint around him. I don't know what I'm dealing with, now that I've learned Henny is this monster. And to think I slept next to him for all those years!"

"Well, don't worry, he's still the same Henny. I doubt he'll do anything."

"You never know. I feel like that girl who dated Ted Bundy. She had no idea he was off murdering in the middle of the night. I mean, I had no idea Henny was off looking at kiddie porn at three a.m.! It's so disgusting. Vile. I knew I hated computers for a reason. Everyone said, Oh, you should go on-line, the Internet is amazing, blah, blah, blah, but I was right! The Internet is evil! There's a reason I was a Luddite!"

Charlie laughed as Gladys brought in a tea caddy with sandwiches. She laid everything out on the black lacquer coffee table, then whispered to Polly: "Mister is here."

Polly's hand flew to her throat. "I can't . . ." she said, bursting into hot dramatic tears.

Charlie came over and patted Polly on the back awkwardly. He was not used to consoling crying women, and wished Hope was around to assist.

"Don't worry, Poll. It'll be fine."

"Oh, Charlie, you're such a good decent man. Does Hope know how lucky she is?" she asked, looking up at him.

"Don't worry. Let's get through this."

Polly turned and buried her head in Charlie's shoulder. She knew she could never get Charlie, that he would never betray Hope, but since this was the only opportunity to nestle into the neck of the man on whom she'd harbored a secret crush on for years, she thought she'd seize the opportunity.

"What's this?" asked Henny, entering the library.

Charlie pulled away from Polly and stood up. Polly, meanwhile, shot Henny the most vicious, evil look.

"How's it going?" asked Charlie, stretching out his hand. Henny and Charlie shook hands awkwardly.

"How can you shake his hand?" sneered Polly.

"Shut up, Polly," snapped Henny. "If this hand didn't have to do so much work whacking my cock, I might not be in this jam."

"Guys, guys, let's not start off this way," said Charlie, mediating.

"I want him to sit as far away from me as possible!"

"No problem!"

Henny sat on the other side of the room, while Charlie took a deep breath. This wasn't going to be easy.

"So listen, let's just make this a productive meeting. I know you both have a lot of emotions, but let's just try and settle the pressing issues."

"I get everything. He never sees our son again. He agrees to leave now," said Poll, defiantly.

"Yeah, right."

"Listen, you have no choice. You're going to prison!"

"You couldn't care less about our son. I get him. I'll tell everyone that you have never once fed him or bathed him or been alone with him."

"Neither have you!"

"Well, I'm his father, we're not supposed to do that shit. He's better off with me."

"You just want him to make me look bad!"

"So what?"

"Guys, this is really sad and pathetic," said Charlie, interrupting. "This is your *son* that you're talking about. He's a cute little guy. You both have to grow up and be mature. Figure this out. What's best for Quint? Stop thinking what's best for Polly or Henny."

"Polly doesn't know how to think that way."

"Fuck you, you pedophile perv!"

"You're just like your mother. It's all about you, you don't give a shit about your kid."

"And you like kids too much!"

Charlie sighed. He could tell that this wasn't going to be easy. "Look, let's just try and be productive. Let's hammer something out."

Two hours later, after Charlie had managed to make a temporary arrangement for custody, spousal support, and other pending issues between Polly and Henny, Quint returned home from the Matthewses' with his nanny. Polly heard the door close and Daria clucking at Quint, who was babbling something as she carried him to his nursery.

Polly walked down the hall and listened through the bathroom door. She heard gurgling and water running, and knocked on the door. Daria was giving Quint a bath, and he was bobbing in the water.

"Missus! You came to visit us! Look, Quint."

Quint looked up, and Polly noticed his face totally brighten. Then her baby boy smiled at her. She couldn't believe it. It felt so good.

"Daria, can I have a minute alone?"

"Sure, after I finish the bath, no?"

"Oh, I meant, alone with Quint, not you."

Daria looked surprised. "Of course," she said, rising from her knees. "Do you know how to do this?"

"Of course."

Polly took Daria's place, and held Quint's head as he sat in the bath. She watched Daria linger for a minute, but then gave her a reassuring look that it would be okay. After Daria left, Quint looked at his mother and smiled.

"Hey there, Quinty," said Polly, splashing water on his tummy. He gurgled in delight.

It was at that moment that Polly realized that Henny had been right about one thing: she was acting like her mother. She had totally ignored her son. And he was pretty damn cute. Bathing him wasn't so hard and scary. And then and there, Polly decided to be a better mother. There was no reason to repeat history and the loveless maternal cycle that she had been subjected to. It wasn't fair to Quint. She'd do the opposite: she'd be the best mother in the world.

chapter 45

Hope's nightmarish satan-in-law, Diana Rockenwagner, was talking her ear off about petty bull once again.

"Listen, Hopie," she started with her affected accent. Hope hated that. No one called her Hopie, it was an Indian tribe. "I've been thinking . . ." *Really? That's a first,* thought Hope. "And for Gavin and Chippie's sakes, I really think you should consider moving to the suburbs. Your money would go a lot further there and it's just not fair to the boys. They should really have a yard."

Hope was stunned. Her anger mercury was rising fast and would quickly burst if she didn't take deep breaths to calm herself. "Well, Diana, I'm sorry you think my boys are deprived. They have a lot of love and a hands-on mom, so I'm really not concerned for their well-being." Hope stuck in the hands-on part because she knew her sister-in-law had a full-time live-in nanny who did everything, including the fun stuff, like push the swings and organize the birthday parties.

Diana was too dumb to get the jab. "I just think they need more space! A yard."

"But you don't have a yard."

"We have a thousand-square-foot terrace and a country home," she replied.

Who says country home? What a bitch from hell. Hope could not abide her presence or even her poison voice through the phone. "Thanks for your input, Diana. But we have a yard. It's called Central Park."

"Don't be defensive, Hope. It's just a suggestion. It would really look much better if you had a nice house in Westchester or Connecticut instead of that rental. It just doesn't look right."

Hope, who never truly fumed, was fuming. "So it's not about the boys, it's about how things appear? To whom? To you and your catty competitive cronies? Goodbye, Diana." And with that, she hung up.

Hope stared at the phone for a moment afterward until the sounds of two hands clapping turned her around. It was Charlie.

"Great job, sweetie! What do I always tell you? Tell Diana off if she's being a bitch!"

"You heard that?" she said, getting up to give him a hug. "Sorry. She was just being so evil, telling us to move to the suburbs, meddling in our lives. What's her problem?"

"Her problem," Charlie said, taking his wife in his arms, "is that with all her money and fancy crap, she's miserable. And she's jealous 'cause she knows we're happy."

"I guess . . ."

"But we're no longer poor and happy—"

"What? Did you hear?"

"An hour ago. Greenwich Equity just gave me the offer."

"No way!" Hope was elated. So John Cavanaugh came through. And she didn't have to put out or anything. He was, after all, a nice guy.

"But . . . Panther Capital just called just now. They offered twenty percent more! And it's in the city!"

"Oh my God! That's amazing!"

They hugged tightly and Hope jumped up and down. "I am so proud of you, sweetie."

"I'm proud of you."

"Me? What for?"

"You do everything. You're the best wife, the best mom, and a true friend."

As they leaned in for a kiss, the phone rang.

"Let's just let it go to the machine," said Hope, kissing her husband and pulling him to the bed. As they kissed on the down comforter, the machine picked up and beeped.

"Mrs. Matthews, hello, my name is Lyster Sargent. I'm your Aunt Edna's attorney. I'm terribly sorry to tell you this on your machine, but—"

Hope bolted up and grabbed the phone. "Hello? I'm here."

"Oh, hello. Mrs. Matthews, I'm so sorry to tell you this, but your Aunt Edna has died. My deepest condolences."

"Oh my God," she said. Aunt Edna . . . dead? She was a royal pain in the butt, but still, that was really due to the fact that she had been in very poor health for the last few years of her life. Hope could remember a time when she was actually a fun great-aunt. Hope felt herself get choked up. Charlie sat up and gave her a hug from behind as she reached for a tissue.

"She left a long note, it seems she knew she was on her way out, saying you were the only one who ever truly loved her, sending care packages and photos of your sons."

"She loved the boys so much," Hope sobbed.

"She loved you as well," he said, pausing, then clearing his throat. "And she left you her entire estate."

Hope was stunned. "What?"

"Everything. And she was a good little saver. After estate taxes are settled, you will receive about three million dollars."

Silence.

"What did he say?" asked Charlie, studying his wife's shocked expression.

"Oh my God," she said, shaking. "I can't believe this."

"It's true. I am FedExing her letter to you and I'll be in touch with you next week. Again, sorry for your loss."

Hope hung up the phone. As Charlie stared at her tear-stained face waiting for news, she stared off into space, thinking how very strange life was.

 chapter 46

Julia was leaving for the airport and was frantic because the Tel Aviv car service buzzed from downstairs, five minutes early. And she needed those five minutes desperately. Aside from shoving her clothes haphazardly into a suitcase, knowing full well they'd look like accordions when she later unpacked, Julia threw shoes, a toothbrush, and jacket into her bag. But before running downstairs to the car, she grabbed a pristine Michael Kors hanging bag from the closet.

"Off to Laguardia?" the driver asked, opening the door for her.

"Yes, but I have one stop on the way."

Julia had just one sole leftover from her whirlwind year running with the rich. In her ascent to party-picture princess, she'd won the hearts and threads of many of the city's top designers, who offered her access to their PR closet, since she was getting snapped so often. And Julia happily borrowed the goods; after all, she couldn't afford them.

So into the office of Michael Kors she walked to return the last of the lent gowns. She thanked the press assistant profusely.

"Anytime, Julia, you know that."

"Oh thank you. I don't think I'll be back, though. I'm going a way for a week and then I'll be . . . laying low, so to speak."

"Well, we're here if you need anything," she said, knowing what Julia was talking about. Everyone knew. But she liked Julia, everyone who knew her did. "You were always so nice," she added. "So many of those girls, they come in, demand we messenger and pick up stuff, and it always looks like shit after. They treat this stuff like garbage."

"That's awful," Julia said. "I can't believe people behave that way."

"Anyway, good luck with everything—"

"You too, take care."

As Julia exited and walked toward the elevators, she

turned the corner and came smack face-to-face with Lell, who was walking out of a fitting room. Julia was totally surprised, and she could tell Lell was also, and she was unsure what to do. Would Lell make a scene? Should she acknowledge her? What to say to her former boss–slash–friend turned foe? There should be a textbook for this.

"Hey," said Julia quietly, giving a weird slight wave, which was more like a flick of the wrist. She was nervous.

Lell's face didn't even register that she had seen Julia.

Okay, so she's ignoring me, thought Julia.

Just then, the elevator rang and the doors opened. Julia looked at Lell, who looked at her. Neither made a move. Finally, Julia gulped, and walked into the elevator, just as Lell did.

In the elevator, they stood like stone statues, erect, cold, and mute for two floors. Never have two people paid more attention to the numbers on the wall as they made their descent. Julia was very conscious that they were going down, down, down, as if to hades.

Finally, Lell spoke. "Just so you know, Julia," she hissed her name as if it were Jezebel. "You really shouldn't be here borrowing clothes. I introduced you to these people and you're out of Pelham's and out of our lives."

"I was returning things. Trust me, I don't plan on coming back," Julia answered.

"I sure hope not. 'Cause you're history in this town. You're over. You are a pathetic social-climbing loser, and trust me, my family and I are fully networked in this town. And as long as I live, I will personally see to it that you are nothing here. That you accomplish nothing, that you have access nowhere, and that you see nobody. Of any interest, that is. You're nothing. You're a total zero."

Julia looked at her. At first her face flushed with anger and embarrassment, but then something inside her snapped, and she quickly changed. What a sad case. The girl she once admired for her style and class now seemed graceless and crass. And childish.

"Well, I'm sorry you feel that way, Lell, but I'm not afraid of you. This is New York City. And you can't 'ruin' me, or anyone else. And while you're hurling empty threats my way, I have one for you." Julia moved in closer to Lell, who backed up nervously. "Your precious Daddy put his hand on my thigh and tried to stick his tongue down my throat. You don't see me filing lawsuits or calling Page Six or telling the gossips, as you did. The news you circulated was pure lies. And mine's the truth. So you make one more damning move, and I'll make my own."

The doors opened and Julia walked out, leaving Lell astonished in her wake. Lell wasn't surprised about her father, and she knew from that moment on, she'd better zip it or she could get slammed with a suit that would cost the family millions. Or worse, have their good name dragged through the mud.

Julia checked her bags to Toronto and walked through the long airport hallway. She was off to Doug and Lewis's wedding and would be spending a full week doing prep work with Doug, plus a full spa day and another on a shopping spree. He said she would have been a bridesmaid, but they weren't having attendants at the small, outdoor wedding. Instead, he had sent her a Pablo Neruda poem that they wanted her to read at the ceremony. She had a bit of time to kill before her flight and realized she hadn't even looked over the words she was meant to read. She took out her organizer, pulled out the small piece of paper, opened it, and took a deep breath as she read the second stanza, which particularly moved her:

> *But this, in which there is no I or you.*
> *So intimate that your hand upon my chest is my hand.*
> *So intimate that when I fall asleep it is your eyes that close.*

Julia closed her eyes. The last weeks had been exhausting and they were finally over. As she held the poem in her hand, she thought about her own next chapter and what the new moons ahead would bring. Would she ever be this intimate? Would love come and find her ever again?

"Julia?"

A familiar voice was coming from above, as Julia looked up. Oscar Curtis was standing there.

"Oscar, hi! How are you?"

"Fine, fine, where are you going? Did they run you out of town?"

Julia looked at him carefully. Was he being a jerk or was he just blunt? "Um . . ."

"Sorry, that came out wrong. I just meant, I heard what happened. Don't worry about those girls, they're all lame."

"Yeah, I know."

There was an awkward silence.

"So, where are you going?"

"I'm going to Toronto for a wedding."

"Oh."

Oscar looked at Julia questioningly. She was always a little disconcerted when he did that.

"Yeah, I love weddings. I mean, people bash them so much and bitch about having to go, but I can't get enough," said Julia.

"I guess it depends what kind it is. Showcase or the real deal," he gave her a knowing look.

"Exactly. This'll luckily be the real thing. True love. Very *Princess Bride*. Although," she smiled. "It's actually two princes."

"Oh yeah? How long will you be up in Toronto?"

"Just a week. And you?"

"I'm just coming home from a conference in San Jose. It was a few long ugly days. San Jose's a bummer town. I was slaving the whole time."

"I see. Well at least you have work. I'm jobless at the moment."

"What do you think you'll do next?"

"I'm not sure. My friend Douglas—one of the grooms— and I have talked about starting a jewelry company."

"Oh yeah? I bet you would be a huge success."

"What makes you say that?"

"I don't know. Your style. Your whole . . . way. People would love to buy a little piece of that."

"That's so sweet," Julia said, touched.

"It's not sweet," he corrected with a smile. "It's fact. In fact, I'd bet on it."

"Oh yeah? Do I smell an investor?"

"Maybe," he teased. The loudspeaker announced the boarding call for Toronto. Oscar stood up. "I guess that's you," he said.

Julia was bummed to say goodbye, since his was the first calming face she'd seen in a while. After ripping on "nice" in her own head, Mr. Nice was suddenly a real comfort to behold.

Oscar, meanwhile, ever nervous in her midst, after a lonely week of misery, decided to combat another dark day of working by just being balls out.

"Julia," he said, almost regretting it as soon as the beautiful word came out.

"Yes," she answered, warmed by the sound of her name coming from his ever-nervous lips.

"Have dinner with me next week."

"I'd love that," she said, looking up at him with a smile that melted away all his fears.

"Okay then, that'll be great. I'll call you. Uh, bon voyage."

He waved awkwardly and turned to leave. Julia watched him shuffle away and suddenly felt a pang. For Oscar. All the supposed excitement and electricity with Will left her miserable and wounded. And here was the guy who all along was always kind and soothing, a calm, healing fire instead of a sparking explosion.

"Oscar?" she yelled after him.

He stopped and turned around. "Yeah?"

"Any desire to come to Canada for a few days?"

One Year Later

Hope was returning home from the greatest, most romantic vacation of her life. Surprised by Charlie only hours before their departure, she'd been supplied with tickets, packed bags, a chauffeured car, and a flight to the One and Only Palmilla Resort in Mexico. She didn't know if it was the poolside massages, the delicious food, the oceanfront private cottage, or the sun warming their skin, but she had never experienced better chemistry with her husband, not even when they were dating. It was the recharging of a marriage that was never down, but certainly had reached a natural plateau. And now the passion was spiking again. Little did Hope know, as she unpacked not only her suitcases, but also the boxes from their move to a terrific new apartment, that she brought back something more from Mexico than painted maracas for her boys—who she'd missed terribly. She was pregnant, with a little girl.

After a jury found Henny guilty of purchasing kiddie porn off the Internet, Polly promptly filed for divorce. She took Quint and left town for a while, stopping in Massachusetts to stay with Vanessa Leigh, her old housemother from boarding school. There she reconnected with Vanessa's son, Elliot, her high school "fac brat" classmate who was strangely quiet back then, but now had become an outspoken lawyer. After cathartic talks, long dinners, and nightly strolls through the nearby woods, he one evening revealed that the reason he was so mute back in school was because he was too smitten to speak. Polly kissed him and they hadn't been apart since.

Lell and Will remained married. Part of the arrangement they made the fateful night Lell told him never to see Julia again (when she made it clear he'd be history—no money, no social status, no friends) was that they would try to remain loyal. Alas, Lell already had her eye on a new Italian designer of Pelham's new small leather goods line, and poor, chained Will could do nothing; he believed her threats and didn't want to lose his fund and be not only an outcast, but a poor outcast. So they appeared at functions together nightly, always arm in arm, and continued to get snapped and written up as society's most perfect couple.

And then, there was Julia. How quickly people forget. The girl who was once slaughtered by the gossips and the gossip columnists was now about to be a boldface name again—not as an infamous husband-chaser, but as a successful jewelry designer, with Douglas, for D&J design, a burgeoning start-up company that had already locked up deals with all the Bs: Barney's, Bergdorf's, Bendel's, and Bloomie's, already making their sole investor, Lewis, double his money.

Plus, she was also about to see her name in print in an entirely different way. In the wedding section, as a bride.

Three months earlier, Oscar Curtis had taken her by the hand, after a whirlwind courtship, and asked her, under a canopy of trees in Central Park, to be his wife. She accepted happily and began planning a low-key wedding in the city that loved her, spat her out, and loved her again—a city with no memory, where scars heal, and the pot keeps stirring its magic stew of faces and places. The city she'd yearned for her entire life and that she could now enjoy by the side of the most wonderful, loving, brilliant, loyal man she had ever met.

As the doors from the small Greenwich Village ivy-covered church burst open, guests threw blush petals at Mr. and Mrs. Oscar Curtis. Their hands were clasped tightly and their smiles could not have shone any brighter. And there were no flashbulbs, no fanfare. It wasn't for the press or the masses or even their extended group of friends. It was for them and the few they cherished, the ones who'd love them if Oscar's company had never gone public or if Julia remained a social pariah.

But there was one guest from the past in attendance. Sort of. As Julia and Oscar took their elated first steps as a married couple from the arched church doorway down the stone steps to the carriage awaiting them, two eyes were upon them from across the street. The onlooker to their over-the-stars joy was not throwing petals, but perched in a white Porsche spying their bliss with a leaden heart. And after the couple embraced with a big, euphoric kiss as the small crowd cheered, Willoughby Banks turned the ignition and drove back uptown.

Acknowledgments

Carrie and Jill thank . . .

Stacy Creamer, editor extraordinaire, thank you so majorly much for all your sage advice, great guidance, and killer jacket copy. You are the best fixer-upper, enhancer, and F-word expunger we could ever dream of. Megathanks to our überagents from heaven, Jennifer Joel and the legendary Binky Urban, who rule, as well to our trusted lawyer of half a decade, Steven Beer. A quote unquote shoutout to the west coast ICM posse as well: Stacey Rosenfelt. Also, we could not get the extremely important and world-altering message of this book out to the four corners of the earth without the help of the amazing Joanna Pinsker, who is a goddess. For the people who hosted bashes for *The Right Address*, Mallory and Diana Walker, Chris Boskin, Bob and Marjie Kargman, Arlette Thebault and the Chanel posse, the Club Monaco gals, and of course, our parents: muchas gracias. Lastly, special mercis to: Jennifer Smith, Whitney Riter, Tracy Zupancis, Allison Dickens, and Richard Sinnott, who is a constant source of inspiration.

Carrie thanks . . .

Thank you so much to the friends and family who helped make *The Right Address* such a success. We really appreciate your support, especially those of you who schlepped to readings and book parties—including the huge Boston relative contingent, as well as the gangs in San Francisco, D.C., L.A., N.Y.C., Santa Barbara, and East

Hampton—it didn't go unnoticed. I want to thank my Mom, Kathy Doyle, and Dick, Liz and Alex, Laura and Zayd, Finn and Liam for their love and family-ness. Merci to my Aunt "Christmas" Anne Doyle for helping me with those dreaded summer reading lists, which obviously contributed to my fantastic writing ability. Muchas gracias to Lesbia Huitz and her special family, Emilio, Bryan, Jairo, and Emily, who have become such a part of my family, and without whom this book would still be a paragraph (at least on my part). Okay, maybe even just a sentence. Thanks to Billy D. up in heaven for reminding me that he's still out there by playing that song every time I need to hear it. And lastly, to my boys: my handsome hubby Vas and my two little bunny rabbits, Junior Senior (James) and Junior Junior (Peter). You are the best.

Jill thanks . . .

In a world, city, and neighb where so many people have frenemies, I am so blessed to have real, true, call-at-three a.m. friends. To the gang, you are my big family, like the Amish. Except different. Vanessa Eastman, Jean Stern, Dana Wallach, Lisa Pasquariello, Lauren Duff, and Trip Cullman, I love you so much, and you are my speed-dial core for sage advice, sponty carbs, and infinite cackles. More 2-D hugs, kisses, and heartfelt thanks go out to cheerleaders like: Frances Stein, Teresa Heinz Kerry, Ruth Kopelman, Herzl Franco, Tara Lipton, and Jacqueline Davy. To the fam, Mom, Dad and Will, merci mille fois for making for making me laugh harder than any humans; if one trillionth of your hilarity can come through in this book, I'm elated; you are the greatest pawents and broddow anyone could ever have. And to Harry, thank you my loving L.C. for being the best sounding board, consigliere, and cubsband ever. And thanks to the love nugget Sadie; the only job title better than writer is mom and I thank you for giving me the best promotion of my life.